DOWNFALL

JAY CROWNOVER

Cover design by: Hang Le, www.byhangle.com
Photographed by and Copyright owned by: Wander Aguiar Photography, www.wanderbookclub.com
Editing and Formatting by: Elaine York, Allusion Publishing, www.allusiongraphics.com
Proofreading & Copy Editing by: Bethany Salminen, www. bethanyedits.net

DOWNFALL

Hi, Friends!

I really hope you take a second to read this if you are new to my books and if you are new to me as an author.

Downfall is a book I wrote exclusively for my monthly newsletter throughout 2018 and early 2019. Subscribers were able to read along with me as I wrote my rough draft. It's something fun I started doing a few years ago and plan to keep doing in the future.

This version is expanded, edited, polished, and pretty, so don't worry.

BUT!!!! Yes, big but: if you are new and unfamiliar you may wonder why there isn't a name for the city in which the story is set, or why a handful of pivotal characters don't have names or fully explained backstories and physical attributes.

All that vagueness is on purpose. I am not lazy. I am not forgetful. I wasn't cutting corners. I want this book to stand on its own, no question, in case it is your first book by me. I don't want new readers trying to figure out who characters are and how they fit into this story vs. who they are and where they fall in their origin series.

This book is an island in an ocean of a bigger series; however, you don't need to worry about what you may have missed to read this one... I PROMISE. This one is its own thing. It has its own vibe, feel, pacing, and history.

If you read and do find yourself wondering about The Boss, Boy Genius, The Devil, and his wife, and anyone else who fills out the cast in the city, please check out my internationally bestselling *Welcome to the Point* series here:

https://www.jaycrownover.com/welcometothepoint

Love & Ink
Happy reading,
Jay

Orley

Being out on the streets when the sun went down was not a good idea in any part of this no-good city.

Not that being on the streets during the day was any better, or safer, but something about the daylight seemed to keep the worst of the predators at bay. When it got dark, all bets were off and the shadows took on a life of their own. Anyone foolish enough to be caught out in the dark, distracted and unaware, was considered prey.

I knew all of this, had learned that lesson the hard way the first few days of living in this god-awful neighborhood. But tonight, everything that could go wrong had, which meant I was walking with my head down, clutching the tiny, sleep-limp body of my daughter in my arms, trying not to draw attention to either of us. It was a nearly impossible task. One look at the fear stamped all over my face, the anxiety which kept my posture tight and stiff, or a glance down at Noble's designer sneakers, and it was obvious to anyone looking that neither of us belonged here. Unfortunately, not fitting in made us even more of a target. We stood out like a beacon in the darkness instead of blending into the shadows that seemed to come alive at night.

Noble muttered something groggily into the side of my neck where her head lolled. My almost-four-year-old daughter was a champ. She took the move to this hellhole far better than I did. She was excited by the noise, the traffic, the endless amount of colorful characters littering the sidewalks during the day. I was the one crying into my pillow at night, not her. She could sleep through anything, including me hauling her like she was a sack of potatoes while I sprinted the six blocks from my broken-down car to our tiny apartment. I put a hand on the back of her head, letting her dark curls slide comfortingly through my fingers and prayed the rest of the journey home would be uneventful.

She had no idea I was frantically scanning every alleyway I passed. She had no clue my car was dead as a doornail, abandoned on the side of the road, useless and billowing smoke. It was going to have to stay there. I didn't have the means to get it towed or fixed. Being carless wouldn't be a big deal if my job wasn't all the way across town in the more affluent district of the city. I had to have my car to get to work, but I could get Noble to her babysitter by foot in a pinch. It was a slightly scary six-block walk in the daytime; at night it was downright terrifying.

Not that I'd need to worry about getting either of us anywhere tomorrow. Right after the car malfunctioned, Mrs. Sanchez, the lovely older Hispanic woman who watched Noble for me during the week, informed me that she would no longer be able to watch her. It seemed her husband was tired of coming home from work and finding an extra mouth to feed. What she didn't say was that her husband hadn't ever approved of her babysitting Noble in the first place. Apparently, he never liked her "privilege" and the fact she wasn't a child from the inner city. He didn't like her bright attitude and endless questions. My daughter was very different from the quiet, solemn children from the Sanchez's neighborhood, and that never sat well with the man. But, instead of crumbling into a hysterical ball of emotion at Mrs. Sanchez's door, I thanked her for everything she'd done for Noble up to that point and told her we'd be in touch.

I could see her sympathy for my predicament, but her unwillingness to defy her husband did me no good, especially when she patted my arm and told me, "I'm so sorry, Orley. You know how much I love having Noble here."

The only reason I stopped myself from wilting into a mess of tears and desperation was that I'd already had one breakdown today: my boss at the salon had pulled me aside right before closing and informed me that she had a cousin who needed a job, so she was cutting my hours to accommodate the teenager. Working less than part-time with minimum wage barely kept my kid fed and the lights on in our apartment. Losing a single cent of that moved us into dire straits, but I refused to let my snotty boss see how terrified her words made me. I knew I could get another job, or two, if need be. At least I could have before my car crapped out on the way to pick up Noble tonight.

For the last year, it had been one thing after another. Blow after blow. I couldn't believe I was still standing. And if it weren't for the precious bundle clutched in my arms, there was a solid chance I wouldn't be. There was no way I could stay down when my daughter needed me to get back up after every new hit. I was going to take the damn beating that life seemed determined to foist on me, but I was never, ever going to let Noble see the bruises. It didn't matter what lengths I had to go to, what lies I had to tell, or what part of this dreadful city I had to hide away in.

"Mommy?" Noble's tired voice jolted me out of my thoughts and I realized I'd made it two more blocks on autopilot. That wasn't good. I was supposed to be keeping watch for any number of threats that could jump out at us from any number of places. Reflexively, my fingers tightened on the cylinder of pepper spray that dangled from my keys.

"Go back to sleep, sweetie. We're almost home." I cringed as I said it. The rundown, dingy apartment was never going to feel like home, no matter how well adjusted my kid was.

"I'm hungry. I want cake." She leaned back in my hold, her bright blue eyes that were identical to mine gleamed with mischief. She was such a happy little girl. It was like she was completely immune to the filth that surrounded her every time she stepped outside her very pink bedroom. The sheer innocence of children was nothing short of amazing.

I huffed out a laugh and wrinkled my nose at her. "Are you sure Mrs. Sanchez didn't already give you dessert?" I wondered why Mr. Sanchez had such an issue with the fact that my daughter looked distinctly different than the rest of the kids his wife watched. She sounded different as well, which was something he'd pointed out more than once when I went to pick her up. There was no hiding the fact that Noble had started off life with privileges most of the kids in this neighborhood would never know. It didn't seem to matter that *she* couldn't tell the difference between herself and other kids her age, or that I no longer had the means to give her every little thing under the sun. She was exactly like the rest of the children in this derelict part of the city now. It broke my heart whenever I thought about it. I was supposed to protect her from the things that could harm her, and I'd only managed to do an okay job thus far. It was hard when I was on my own, but better that way.

Noble smiled, that crooked grin lighting up the night, making the places warm inside of me that felt frozen and brittle.

"She gave me a churr-oh." She stumbled a little over the words and drew the 'o' out in a silly way. "But that's not cake."

I guess she had a point.

"I'll see what I can do when we get home." I already knew there was no cake. There was rarely anything sweet. I couldn't afford to indulge, but I did steal her a cookie or cupcake whenever someone at the salon celebrated a birthday or special occasion. I tried to remember if I had anything stashed somewhere I could give her. Right now, her request seemed like the easiest problem to tackle out of all the ones that were piling up.

"Hey." I jolted at the sound of a deep voice way too close. A screech that, at one point, I would have attributed to a cat, but now knew more than likely belonged to a rat, sent a shiver down my spine. I watched a man step out of the shadows shrouding a nearby alley directly in front of me.

I could see the stoop of our building and the bundle of dirty clothes that indicated that Lester, the homeless guy who called the stairs out front home, was already passed out for the night. We were a hundred yards away. So close yet so far.

I should've seen him lurking. I should have been more vigilant. I was just so damn tired and feeling so hopeless. No matter how hard I tried, my best never seemed to be enough.

I took a deep breath and put a protective hand on the back of Noble's head. She complained about me pushing her face back down into the hollow of my neck, but she was a smart girl and easily picked up on the tension that stiffened me from head to toe.

I knew the rules. Keep walking. Don't make eye contact. Don't engage or act afraid.

The first few were easy enough to follow; it was that last rule which was a real bitch. I *was* afraid, and it bled out of me so strongly I was sure the man purposely blocking my way to the apartment could smell it.

I tried to take a step to the side so I could walk around him, but he followed my movement. I went so far as to step off the curb and into the street to evade him, but he followed. I clutched Noble tighter to my chest and forced myself to breathe.

"Move." I wasn't nice, or timid, when I said it. That was one thing I appreciated about this place, maybe the only thing. There was no reason to play nice with everyone, because chances were the other person was out to get you. It was the first time in my life I'd freely spoken my mind whenever and wherever I wanted. It was liberating, but it wasn't getting me anywhere with the man in front of me.

He was several inches taller than me. He had a shaved head and nasty-looking eyes. They were small, narrow, bloodshot, and locked on me like he was envisioning every horrible thing he could possibly do to me. He was the cold, slithering snake, and I was the helpless, fuzzy mouse dropped unwillingly into his cage. Predator and prey. It wasn't a nice feeling at all.

"Pretty little thing, ain't ya?" His tongue darted out to lick his lower lip, and if I hadn't been holding onto Noble, I would have pepper sprayed him then and there. "Not in Oz anymore, are you, babe?"

Nope. I wasn't.

I was in hell and every day it felt like I was running across another devil to battle. It was exhausting, and I never wanted to put my daughter in such a dangerous situation.

"Move." I said it again and gasped as he lifted a hand like he was going to touch my daughter's shiny black ringlets. I took a step backward and glared at him. I could feel Noble starting to shake in my arms. "Get away from us." I narrowed my eyes and returned his glare, aware I didn't look half as intimidating as he did.

He laughed. It was an ugly, dark sound and I heard Noble sniffle against my throat. She wasn't crying yet, but she was close. This man was not putting his hands on my daughter, no matter what.

"I've seen you coming and going. Scared of your own shadow. Turning your nose up at the people you pass on the street. You think you're too good for this city? Too good for the rest of us?" His eyes skated over me and his mouth twisted into a sneer that sent shivers racing across my skin. "Stuck up bitch."

He was so angry, but he didn't even know me. It was confusing and terrifying.

When he took another step closer to us, I squeezed Noble so tight that she squeaked in complaint. He was lifting a gnarled hand again, so I turned, making his heavy palm land on my auburn ponytail instead of my daughter's hair. It was a dumb move, one made on instinct alone, but I was kicking myself as I felt his finger latch onto my hair and yank. He pulled hard enough to bring tears to my eyes, and I stumbled back a step.

I felt his chest bump against my back and bit down on a cry.

"Mommy?" Noble's voice quivered, and I could feel her body shaking against mine.

I tried to shush her, but my throat locked when a pair of rough, abrasive lips hit the side of my neck. He licked a wet trail up the side of my neck and I couldn't bite back a gag.

"You taste expensive, pretty thing. Can't wait to take a bite out of you, and I got a buddy who likes them young. The younger the better." The implied threat was horrifying.

I kicked backward with my foot, aiming for a shin, a knee, anything. The heel of my sneaker glanced off something hard, which earned me another furious yank of my hair.

I opened my mouth to scream. Noble was crying, her tiny hands clutching my clothes and my skin. I wanted to believe that if I was able to make a noise, someone would step in and help. If not for me, then for my daughter. Even in this terrible place, surely strangers wanted to keep children safe. Only I knew that wasn't true, and the more time that passed in this fucked-up situation, the more I realized that we were truly on our own.

I yelped as a hard hand slid over my ass and blinked back helpless tears.

I couldn't let this happen. I had to keep Noble safe.

The panic was rising to an uncontrollable level. I was whimpering and desperately trying to pull free without losing my hold on Noble. My frantic mind considered putting her down and telling her to run, to find somewhere safe to hide while I was mauled by this aggressive stranger on the street. But she wasn't even four yet, and I wasn't convinced anywhere in this city was safe. I thought I knew what it was like to be trapped between a rock and a hard place before, but that wasn't even close to the pressure squeezing my heart right now.

The groping hand was trying to find purchase between me and Noble, looking for a handful of skin. Any more of this and I really was going to throw up. I opened my mouth to scream, to call for help, even if it was useless, but suddenly I was released. I had to focus on not falling forward and crushing my kid between me and the broken sidewalk.

I whirled around, placing Noble on her feet so we could run if we had to. I pushed her protectively behind me, ready to flee or fight. Her small hands latched onto the hem of my shirt and tugged. She was as ready as I was to run for safety.

Only, the scary man who had grabbed me was now dangling from the hands of a guy twice his size and twice as scary. My intimidating rescuer towered over six feet and was built like a damn tank. His short hair was covered by a ratty and worn baseball cap, and his darkly handsome face was set in furious, tight lines. The thug was dangling in his grasp high enough that his toes were barely touching the sidewalk.

"What did I tell you about lurking around my place, Skinner? I don't fucking like it." The guy's voice was a low growl. Intimidating without even trying. "I don't fucking like you."

Out of habit, I reached back and covered Noble's ears with my hands. She wasn't new to foul language, but I didn't need her repeating this stranger's garbage words, which she absolutely would at the most inopportune moment.

My eyes widened as he shook the lurker hard enough to snap his head back and forth comically. The smaller man whimpered and clutched at the hands locked on the front of his dirty coat.

"Let me go, Solo. I was just having some fun. She's a prissy bitch. You've seen her walking around here like her shit don't stink." The pleading was wasted. The larger man was clearly unmoved.

The new arrival's massive arms tensed and flexed as he practically threw the other man on the ground.

I noticed he was dressed in nothing more than a dark t-shirt even though it was chilly outside. The short sleeves showed off more than his impressive build. In the faded street lights, I could hardly make out the designs that were inked over almost every visible inch of skin. That wasn't an uncommon look in this neighborhood. Gang tattoos, prison tattoos, and general outsiders who called these streets home tended to rock some serious ink, but this guy's looked more deliberate and artistic than a simple statement piece.

As soon as my attacker was back on the ground, the bigger guy stepped forward. I reflexively cringed as he lowered his big, booted foot down on the other man's unprotected private parts. A wail of agony shrieked through the air, and I realized belatedly I should be hauling ass for my apartment, not standing around waiting to see how this brutal display of street justice played out.

I clutched Noble's hand in mine and briskly jogged the last few yards to my apartment building. I lifted Noble over the sleeping homeless man and hustled up the five flights of stairs to our floor. The elevator had been broken since before we'd moved in, not that I would dare let either of us get trapped in a small place with anyone from this complex.

I was a panting, quaking mess when I finally slammed the door. I dropped to my knees and pulled my daughter into my arms, covering her tear-streaked face in kisses and whispering soothing words over and over again.

There was no way this could be our new normal.

But it was.

Noble deserved so much better than this.

I sighed, pushing her hair off her precious face. "You know what, sweets?" She blinked big, watery blue eyes at me and shook her head. "I think we both need cake."

She nodded and cuddled close to me.

It wouldn't occur to me until much later that I hadn't bothered to shout a thank you or shown any appreciation at all to my savior. I had no clue if he was any better than the scumbag who had grabbed me, but he had at least kept my daughter safe, so I owed him, even if he was one of countless things in this forever dark place that scared the life out of me.

People didn't help other people in this neighborhood... but he had stopped and helped me, whether his intentions were altruistic or not.

And I owed him... well... at the very least, more than a piece of cake.

Solo

I looked down at the man at my feet who now had a broken nose, two black eyes, and a split lip. His rat-like face was scrunched up in pain and covered in drool and blood.

Skinner was a bully when it came to anyone weaker and smaller than him. He liked to shake down the kids in the neighborhood for money, and I'd warned him on more than one occasion to leave the women and girls alone. He got off on scaring them and sending them running. I was done with him and his bullshit ways.

I didn't like the way he lurked around, and I didn't like that he sold drugs on the corner near my apartment building, because drugs brought around more shady, sketchy people like Skinner. I was done with warnings and threats. He was manhandling the young mother right out in the open. The little girl in her arms was hysterical, and I could hear Skinner laughing at their fear and panic all the way down the block.

I was exhausted. I'd put in a full day of work at the garage. It was a terribly kept secret in the neighborhood that the garage was actually a chop-shop, but that didn't mean the job and the amount of time I spent working on the classic cars, which were my specialty, was any less labor intensive. I'd also spent a couple hours training at the gym around the corner from the garage. I always put in extra work when I had a fight coming up, so I was tired, sore, and in no mood for an altercation with someone like Skinner. I had zero patience for people who didn't listen to me. It was disrespectful, and I made sure no one got away with openly disrespecting me. It was how I stayed the scariest thing on the streets I called home.

Plus, I'd seen the redhead and her kid around the block the last couple of months or so. I was pretty sure she lived in the same building as me, but I kept weird hours and wasn't in the market for new friends or fragile females with baggage. The mother was very young and so out of place on these streets that she practically had a bright red and white bullseye painted on her back.

It was obvious to anyone with eyes that she didn't belong here. She was like a newborn lamb trying to blend in with a pack of wolves. I had no idea what brought her to my city, but it must have been pretty bad because this was the last place anyone wanted to end up. My city was the last resort and the end of the road for most of the people who lived here. The young mother was already scraping the bottom of the barrel; she didn't need to fend off an attack from a loser like Skinner on top of it. I had a feeling she would have fought tooth and nail to keep him away from her kid, and I admired that. This town wasn't my last-ditch effort. For me, it was simply home, because I had a mother who would also fight tooth and nail to make sure nothing bad touched me. I was done with Skinner, and I wanted to make sure he understood that if he ever put his hands on the redhead or her child again, he was going to need machines to keep him alive because I would beat him into a damn coma.

I pointed a finger at the cowering man in front of me and told him flatly, "I warned you about hanging around my block, Skinner. It's like you purposely want to piss me off." I took a step back and crossed my arms over my chest. My shoulders screamed at the move, reminding me that I may have pushed a bit too hard when I was using the bench press tonight. "Do I strike you as the kind of guy who tolerates being ignored?"

The bloody man whimpered and curled his body into a protective ball. "I was just having some fun. That bitch needs to be knocked off her high horse. The kid was just in the way."

My back teeth ground together and my hands curled into fists. "She was trying to get her kid home and she was scared shitless. She clearly knows being out after dark isn't a good idea. You showed her why that's true." I narrowed my eyes and lowered my chin so he wouldn't miss the glare aimed his way under the brim of my hat. "I don't want to see you again, Skinner. If I do," I nudged his leg with the toe of my boot. "I won't have to worry about you being on the corner because you'll be calling the hospital—or the morgue—home. Are we clear?" I pressed the sole of my boot deliberately on the side of his knee. A tiny bit more pressure and his kneecap would slide out of place. It was really hard to hustle poison when you couldn't run from other dealers and whacked-out junkies.

He nodded jerkily, spraying blood and saliva on the sidewalk. I grunted and turned on my heel to walk toward my building, but something made me pause and look back at the man on the ground. "The girl and her kid. They are off limits to everyone else, too. Make sure you let the other rats who scurry around in the shadows know that. Let her come and go in peace so she can take care of that little girl."

Skinner grumbled something under his breath but gave a nod. I turned on my heel and headed toward my building. Lester, the homeless veteran who called the stoop home, rolled over as soon as my boots hit the first step. The man was a war hero and unfortunately an addict. He deserved better than sleeping outside and scrambling for his next hit, but this is where he ended up. At least he had a few residents, like myself, who looked out for him. He blinked rheumy eyes at me and furiously licked at his dry, cracked lips.

"Glad you got home when you did, Solo. That girl is really nice, and her kid is sweet as can be." His raspy voice cracked on every other word, but I was used to his unusual speech patterns.

"Been trying to scare off Skinner for over a month. Should have done a better job of it." I rolled my stiff shoulders and blew out a breath. "Don't know how long someone like that can last out here. She sticks out like a sore thumb. Bound to draw the wrong kind of attention."

Lester cackled, which quickly turned into a wheezing cough. "Sounds like she needs someone to keep an eye on her."

I rolled my eyes under the bill of my hat and hopped to a higher step. "I barely have time to shower, shit, and shave most days. If I get five free minutes, I use them to fight or to fuck. Don't have time to be a hero for some chick I don't know." I didn't even have the time to be a hero for the people I actually cared about most days.

Lester made another gasping, rumbling sound and pointed to the spot where Skinner had left a bloody puddle on the sidewalk. "Found time tonight."

I snorted as I made it to the top of the steps, pulling the front door open. There weren't things like security doors and buzzers in these old buildings. Hell, the elevator hadn't worked in over five years. I blinked when I realized how long I'd been calling this crumbling building home. It wasn't supposed to be that way, I was supposed to get out, but it hadn't worked out. Somewhere along the way, I'd forgotten what life was supposed to be like and had learned to accept how things really were. The unidentifiable smells lingering in the corners and stairwells didn't even faze me anymore. I didn't blink at the peeling paint or the sound of screaming voices that came through the paper-thin walls. I hadn't even noticed that I'd settled into *this* as my reality over time. The thought was as comforting as it was depressing.

When I walked into my dingy little apartment, I immediately started stripping my clothes off. There was blood on my shirt, so I threw it in the trash, knowing I didn't have the time or patience to get a stain out. I tossed my hat and keys on the small table I kept by the front door, so I would remember to grab them on my way out in the morning. I could hear the couple who lived in the unit on the left side of my apartment fighting about something. It was all they ever did. They were either yelling because they were pissed at each other or screaming because they were having vigorous rounds of make-up sex. I was super glad my miniscule bedroom was on the other side of the apartment. Whomever had moved into the vacant apartment on the right side of mine was as quiet as a mouse. I only knew I had a new neighbor was because I could hear the pipes groaning when they took a shower, and occasionally something smelled really good through the vents when they were cooking.

I was glad that there were no sounds of rowdy sex coming from that side of the building. My bed was pushed up against the wall and it had been longer than I cared to admit since there had been anyone but me between the sheets. If I had to listen to someone else getting some while I was in the middle of the world's longest dry spell, it would be nothing short of torture. I wasn't lying when I told Lester I didn't have time for much of anything anymore. Between my job, working out, online classes to get certified as a legit mechanic, and fighting on the weekends in the Pit so I could pay for my mom's care, I was stretched so fucking thin I wondered if you could see my veins and heart beating through my skin. At twenty-five, I knew I should be living it up and having the time of my life, but I wasn't doing either of those things. No, I was barely holding my shit together and it felt like any little thing that went awry had the ability to make me break.

Which was why it was a bad idea to be so curious about the redhead and her kid.

I couldn't stop myself from wondering why someone who so clearly came from somewhere else ended up in my neck of the woods. I was curious about the kid, as well. They looked enough alike with their matching sky-blue eyes and freckles, there was no question the ebony-haired toddler belonged to the tall redhead. There was something about the way she fiercely protected the little girl that screamed motherly concern. She'd been in such a hurry to get away from Skinner that I hadn't managed to catch her name, not that I could blame her for scurrying away. Still, a thank you would have been nice. After all, I did find the time to be her hero, even if it was a one-off occurrence.

I sighed, getting a bottle of water and a slice of cold pizza out of my fridge. I plopped down on the couch, kicked my feet up and fell asleep with my snack in hand before I took the first bite. I could throw down with men twice my size, even those who fought dirty, but there was no battling the exhaustion that pulled me under each and every night.

Orley

I struggled to find answers the next day when my daughter asked why I wasn't going to work like normal, and why she wasn't going to stay with Mrs. Sanchez. I'd disrupted her life so much already, I hated that I was forced to do it all over again. It was my job to provide her with a sense of normalcy and security, and since we'd been on our own, I'd failed spectacularly at both. I was fortunate Noble was such an easygoing child. She made things far easier on me than I deserved. She even stopped asking where Grandma and Grandpa were, which I couldn't be more thankful for. I didn't want to lie to her, to set a precedent of dishonesty, but the truth was even harder to try and figure out when I had to explain it to a toddler.

I kept her occupied most of the morning by playing games and letting her help make breakfast. I set her down in front of my used laptop with an annoying cartoon movie while I called around, trying to find someone to look at my car for a price that didn't make me cringe. Getting it towed to a garage was going to cost more than I was willing to spend, and it was starting to look like I might just have to give the thing to a junkyard and take a few hundred bucks when they scrapped it. I half-heartedly scrolled through job listings on Craigslist and any other site I could think of, but all it did was depress me. The pickings were slim, and anything that seemed promising had hours that wouldn't work for a single parent. I wanted to keep us fed and keep the lights on, but I also wanted to spend time with my daughter. I didn't want to miss a minute of her growing up. It was a treacherous balancing act for me. These formative years were precious, and I refused to give them up.

As usual, I wanted to hit my head against the wall and scream in rage and frustration when I thought back on the recent events that landed me in this awful place. Every day I felt like this new normal was bound to eat us alive. Things hadn't always been this difficult or complicated. There was a time, not too long ago, where I never once worried about the future, never gave a second thought to how I was going to provide for myself and my child. Those days felt more like a dream now that the harshness of my reality was so difficult to escape.

I looked up from my phone and watched as Noble did a little twirl and belted out the wrong words to the song squeaking from the overtaxed speakers on the laptop. She was adorable, and even though I was struggling to find something to be cheerful about, she effortlessly put a smile on my face. She always did. No matter how badly I screwed up, or how hard things were, she was a delight and the one thing in my life I knew I got absolutely right. She was the only reckless choice I didn't regret.

Noble clapped her hands and wiggled her tiny hips with such exaggeration I couldn't hold back a laugh. The sound brought Noble's head around and she smiled at me, bright eyes gleaming. She ran across the space separating us, grabbed one of my hands in hers, and pulled me toward the living room where the movie was still playing.

"Dance with me, Mommy." The words came out in an excited rush, tumbling over one another. She wiggled again, arms swinging and feet stomping on the floor. The walls in this apartment were super thin, and I was sure her impromptu dance party was going to annoy the neighbors, but I had a hard time denying her anything when she looked up at me like I hung the moon and stars. I dreaded the day she realized I was the one who stole all the beauty and ease from her life.

I held her hand as she spun around until she was dizzy. She collapsed in a giggling heap on the floor at my feet. I bent down and dropped a kiss on the top of her head, my heart swelling with love and gratitude. I didn't have much anymore, but I had this little girl, and really, she was more than enough. She was everything.

I rubbed my thumb over her cheek and gave her a genuine smile. "Mommy has to go check on the car." It would be a miracle if it was still there. But on the off-chance it was, I needed to clean it out if I was going to send it off to an early grave. There were things in the car I couldn't afford to replace right now, like Noble's car seat. "Want to go for a little walk with me?" I was going to have to find a replacement for Mrs. Sanchez sooner rather than later. I didn't want Noble out on the streets any more than necessary. Especially not after last night. I needed someone reliable to keep an eye on her for me.

My daughter must have been thinking the same thing because her tiny nose scrunched up and she gave as fierce a scowl as a three-year-old could muster. "Are we going to see the mean man again?"

I sighed and smoothed some of her dark hair back from her cherubic face. "No, honey. I'll make sure we don't see the mean man ever again." It wasn't a promise I was sure I could keep, but I felt the likelihood of running into the thug in broad daylight was slim. And I was hoping the threat from my huge, tattooed savior was enough to keep the creep at bay. I couldn't stay locked up in this apartment forever. I could hardly stand to be imprisoned within these desolate walls as it was. It was like a jail cell. Just the idea of shorter hours at work with nowhere else to be made me antsy.

"Go get your shoes and we'll go. We can stop somewhere along the way and get ice cream." I hadn't managed to scare up a cake for her last night, so even though it was a frivolous expense I couldn't afford, I owed my kid a solid, and I was going to pay up.

She came back with a mismatched pair of tiny Chucks. Instead of making her find two that matched, I let her wear a black one on one foot and a pink one on the other. It was cute and irreverent, just like her. After tossing my hair up into a messy ponytail and shoving my feet into my own battered Chucks, I clutched Noble's hand and headed out the door.

We had only put one foot in the hallway when a door down the hall swung open and an angry woman popped her head out. She had curlers in her hair and a cigarette dangling out of her mouth. She squinted in our direction and gave a nasty sneer.

"You're too loud. Keep it down." Before I could open my mouth and apologize, she slammed the door closed, forcing it to rattle on the hinges and the bang to echo down the hall.

Noble jumped and I shook my head in irritation. Her slamming the door was twice as loud as our dance party had been. I soothed Noble when she started to bounce around nervously and guided her down the steps. I helped her skip over every other one, and by the time we hit the entranceway, my arm was screaming and I'd worked up a sweat. I was going to be gross by the time we trekked to the car and hauled everything back with us. I was tempted to call a cab, but if I did, there definitely would not be enough money for ice cream. I wasn't about to disappoint my kid if I could help it.

We both hopped over Lester who appeared to be sleeping soundly on the front steps, as usual. At first, the homeless man freaked me out and I hated stepping over him like he was nothing more than a discarded piece of garbage on the street. It took a few weeks and several awkward conversations with him to realize that if he was passed out, it was because he got his hands on something nasty, and it was better to leave him be. When he was awake and sober, he was a perfectly lovely man. Unfortunately, those times seemed few and far between.

Noble was making sure not to step on any cracks in the sidewalk. There were so many, it proved to be a daunting task which had her skipping around like a deranged bunny. I was so focused on her antics that I didn't notice the huge figure coming around the corner at a rapid pace. Noble was directly in his path. His long legs ate up the distance at a steady jog, and he had to jump to the side to avoid plowing Noble over. She fell backward onto her butt as the tatted-up man leapt to avoid her.

He had on the same hat he had been wearing the night before, and a pair of mirrored, aviator sunglasses covered his eyes. I could see my shocked reflection staring back at me as he paused, putting his hands on his knees so he could catch his breath. I wasn't sure if he was winded from his run, or from the near-miss with the wide-eyed three-year-old at his feet. He wasn't wearing a shirt, so I could see he was inked from his collarbone all the way down to the waistband of the black, nylon shorts he was wearing. Even his legs had random images and swirls of color decorating the strong lines. A light sheen of sweat covered every inch of his taut, artistic skin, highlighting his well-defined muscles and the lines of strength that made up his impressive build. He wasn't my type. Not at all. In another life, I wouldn't have thought to look twice at a guy who looked like him. Tattoos weren't common in the circles where I used to travel. Now, caught unwillingly in this new life, I was having a hard time looking away.

I helped Noble to her feet, and noticed my daughter was also stunned into a rare silence in the presence of this imposing, impressive man.

He popped out one of his earbuds and pushed to his full height. I wished he weren't wearing the mirrored glasses so I could see the color of his eyes. It was an odd reaction, so I cleared my throat and wiped my free hand nervously down the front of my jeans.

"Uh... Sorry. She's been inside all day and has excess energy to burn." He lifted his chin in acknowledgment and I tried not to swallow my tongue as a single drop of moisture slid down the strong line of his throat. I cleared my throat and squeezed Noble's hand so tightly she squealed and gave me a questioning look. "Umm... thank you for the rescue last night. I should have said something before taking off, but yesterday was quite possibly the second worst day of my life and I wasn't thinking clearly. That guy was very scary; I don't know what I would have done if you hadn't intervened."

He took out the other earbud and wiped his forehead with his forearm. "Don't worry about it. Skinner won't be around anymore, and if he is, just let Lester know and he can pass the info on to me."

I glanced at the homeless man in surprise. I wondered how the stranger knew his name. "I'll do that."

The nearly naked man in front of me stretched his arms over his head and I couldn't look away from the ripple and flex of his clearly defined abs. His body was ridiculous in all the right ways. I'd never seen a man in person who looked like he did. He was like one of those irrationally, unrealistically hot Instagram guys, but one who was standing in front of me in all his muscly, sweaty glory. I knew somewhere in the back of my head he was dangerous, and I shouldn't be so nonchalant about chatting him up, but I figured I owed him the common courtesy I bypassed the night before. One thing I had left was flawless manners.

He cocked his head to the side and asked, "If yesterday was the second worst day, how did you survive the first one?"

That wasn't a day I ever talked about. It was the day that changed everything. The only reason I survived the day was because I *had* to for the little girl clutching my hand and watching the stranger with wide, curious eyes. I blew out a breath and changed the subject as quickly as possible.

"You ever have one of those days where it's one thing after another and it feels like the universe is trying to tell you something? Trying to tell you to give up?" I shrugged before he could answer me. "My car broke down. My babysitter quit. My job cut my hours. The icing on the cake was getting attacked on the way home. Like I said, it was a bad day, but that doesn't excuse me running off without thanking you properly. I owe you more than I can ever repay." I couldn't think about what might have happened if he hadn't shown up. My mind wouldn't allow it.

He dipped his chin again. "No worries. I happened to be in the right place at the right time." He moved to put the earbuds back in and I considered myself dismissed, but before he could block out the sound, the homeless man on the stoop roused himself into a sitting position and pointed a finger at the man looming in front of me.

"Go help the girl with her car, Solo." His finger wavered but his voice was surprisingly clear as he issued the order.

Noble bounded up on her toes and tilted her head to the side. "Solo?" My kid was obsessed with *Star Wars* so there was no way she was going to miss the unusual name.

The man looked down at my daughter, and finally, a grin cracked the stern expression chiseled on his ruggedly handsome face. "Solomon. Solo is my nickname."

Before I could stop her, she stuck out her hand for the big man to shake. I gulped when her tiny hand disappeared in his much larger one. "I'm Noble."

He nodded at her. "That's a pretty name."

His head moved in my direction and I bit back a sigh. "Orley." I tossed out my own name reluctantly. "And don't worry about the car. We'll figure it out. Seriously." I wasn't sure I wanted to spend any more time in his company. He made me feel weird and unsteady. There was a low vibration I could feel humming throughout my body standing this close to him, and I had no time for any kind of distraction.

He didn't bother to hide his sigh or his aggravation. He whipped off his hat and ran his fingers through his hair. "No, just let me run up and change and I'll look at your car. I don't have to work until this afternoon. I'm a mechanic. If I can't get it running, I can get it towed to the garage where I can work for half of what you'd pay someone else." He snorted. "If I don't help you out, Lester will never let me hear the end of it. It's the neighborly thing to do, after all."

Before I could argue, he dashed up the stairs, stopping to say something to the homeless man that I couldn't hear. I wanted to tell him I couldn't afford a mechanic, half-price or not, but he never gave me the chance.

So not only was he a hero, but he also lived in my building. I hated the way that knowledge sent an excited shiver up my spine.

Lester shifted and leaned on the step he was using as a bed. His words didn't sound slurred, and his eyes seemed incredibly focused as he watched me decide if I was going to wait around for the stranger's help or not. "Solo's a good kid. Let him help you out. He's a wiz when it comes to anything with a motor. He'll fix you right up."

Only an idiot would take the word of a homeless junkie at face value when it came to someone else's character, but damn if I didn't want to.

Solo

had a mile-long list of things I was planning on getting done before I had to go to the garage. I'd already been to the gym, put in a few hours sparring, went for a run, and threw in a load of laundry. I still needed to go to the grocery store so there was more than water and old pizza in my fridge, and I wanted to stop by and check on my mom. It had been a few days since I'd had anything resembling free time, and I didn't like to go too long between visits. I was going to take her flowers and see if she wanted to go out for a walk. She didn't get out nearly enough when I wasn't around. But now I was committed to helping the pretty redhead and her adorable kid. I wasn't exaggerating. If I walked away, ignored the fact she was having car trouble, Lester would never let it drop. When he was sober, the man was part pit bull and part guardian angel. I stepped over him at least twice a day and really didn't have the time or patience to deal with the hassle he would give me every opportunity he could.

Plus, it was the right thing to do. The poor girl looked even more lost up close and personal. Those huge baby-blue eyes of hers were completely guileless and entirely too innocent. She didn't belong here; this city would eat her alive. While she was slumming it, it wouldn't kill me to give up a few of my precious free minutes to make sure she could get herself and her kid from point A to B. It was better to keep her off the streets. There was less of a chance she would run across another loser and user like Skinner if she had a working vehicle. I didn't want to give a shit, didn't want to give her a second thought... but I did. And may have even risked a third and fourth thought.

That little girl was adorable and sweet as could be. She was too young to realize how hard and ugly the world could be. She still smiled at strangers, still laughed and played like she didn't have a single care in the world. Her mom was obviously doing everything she could to protect the little girl from this place. It was impressive, and I admired her dedication to her kid. I didn't want the little girl's unchecked delight to be stripped away from her, the way it was so mercilessly stolen from most of the kids who called this city home. I told myself it was an appreciation for the redhead's selflessness and determination that had me rushing to switch over my laundry and hurry through a quick shower so I could once again play her hero. I refused to think about the fact I also appreciated the way she filled out her skin-tight black leggings and the way her hair turned into flames when the sun hit it just so.

Swearing under my breath, I grabbed a handful of tools and jogged back down the stairs. There was a part of me hoping the woman, Orley, had tired of waiting for me and gone on about her day. She didn't seem the type to accept help easily. If she was, I doubted she would be living in the Skylark, one of the city's most rundown apartment complexes, and dodging guys like Skinner once the sun went down. Anyone who had help at hand didn't end up here. And if she had someone to lean on, she wouldn't be so out of sorts over the minor bumps in the road which comprised her 'second worst day ever.' Things like broken-down cars, lost jobs, and unreliable people were par for the course in this part of town. But it sounded like this was the first time the redhead had ever had to deal with the fairly common occurrences that were in no way the end-of-days she made them out to be. I shouldn't judge her. I didn't know her story, but I knew it was a hard one to tell. She was going to get eaten alive by this city if she was ready to throw in the towel every single time these streets showed their teeth.

Lester roused himself into a sitting position and was watching the girls race each other up and down the sidewalk. The little girl was quick, but her mom had long-ass legs. I'd noticed she was on the tall side when she thanked me for the night before. She barely had to tilt her head back at all to look me in the eye, which was a nice change of pace. I was used to contorting into all kinds of uncomfortable positions to make sure all the good stuff lined up whenever I got my hands on a willing woman.

I frowned as I stomped down the steps. I was not looking to screw one of my neighbors. I didn't do clingy and needy. I didn't do time-consuming and permanent.

I only had time for one woman in my life, and she gave birth to me.

At the last second, Orley pretended to trip over something on the sidewalk, letting the little girl sail by her in a flurry of dark curls and infectious giggles. The tiny human paused by the stairs and slapped Lester's hand in a loud high-five. I was waiting for the redhead to scold her for touching a homeless person, but all she did was grin and throw her hands up in mock defeat. The little girl turned to me and I obediently tapped her palm with mine as she celebrated her victory with a whoop.

"I'm fast." She twirled around, and I watched as Orley slyly produced a wet wipe from somewhere and swiped it over the little girl's hands. "Do you wanna race, Solo?"

When she said my name, it sounded like two words, So-Low. It was pretty cute, and I couldn't help but grin at her.

"Maybe later. We gotta look at your car before I have to head to work." I lifted my eyebrows at the redhead and noticed she was chewing on her lower lip and shifting her weight from one sneakered foot to the other. "Can we walk or do we need to drive to where you left it?"

"Ummm," she cocked her head to the side and seemed to waffle. "It's more than a few blocks away."

"So, we should drive." I was working with a clock ticking down in the back of my head.

She practically vibrated in front of me. I could see the way tension coiled around her. The chick was strung so tightly she was going to snap. "Noble's car seat is still in my car. She needs it if she's going to ride in a car." I could tell she didn't want to burden me any further, but she wasn't going to budge when it came to the safety of her child.

"It's fine. We can walk. Hopefully, it's an easy fix and you can just drop me off at my car once I get you up and running." I was in a hurry, but I wasn't unreasonable. For some reason, one I didn't want to examine too closely, I wanted the twitchy, nervous woman to realize she could trust me. That there were good men and women in this rough part of the city. In fact, I was convinced we outnumbered the people who gave it such a bad reputation in the first place.

Orley nodded gratefully and reached for her daughter's hand. They both told Lester goodbye and I overheard the redhead offer to bring him something to eat when they came back home. It was obvious she was struggling, but she still took the time to think of the lonely man so many people overlooked. Lester declined the offer; he always did. I'd stopped asking him if he wanted something years ago. Now I simply ordered two of whatever I was having or made sure I made enough for both of us when I was home to eat. He never refused when I handed him something to eat, but I knew he would never ask for anything outright.

We walked the first few blocks in awkward silence. Even the little girl was quiet, minus the song she was humming under her breath as she swung her mother's hand, skipping over every crack in the sidewalk.

"So, what do you do?" My tools clinked together with every step I took. I'd always been the kind of guy who was better with his hands than sitting at a desk struggling to find interest in a boring textbook. I had a busy mind and an even shorter attention span. The only thing about school I liked was playing different sports and the endless number of cute girls who couldn't get enough of my dick. I barely made it through high school, and by the time graduation rolled around, I was already more interested in figuring out how to make money and survive than I was on getting a degree or pursuing higher education. I was lucky I never fell in with the wrong crowd, because most guys my age with the same prospects ended up in jail, or slinging illegal shit on the streets. My mom made sure I kept my nose clean, even though it was a nearly impossible task. I owed her everything, and I never forgot it.

"Oh, nothing too exciting. I'm a part-time receptionist at a salon. I answer the phone and make appointments." She flashed a wry grin and nervously looked away. "The only reason they hired me was because my mom used to go there forever ago and the owner felt sorry for me when I called and begged her for a job. But now, she has a family member who needs a job so she cut my hours down to nothing." She huffed out a breath and lifted her chin. "I'm not exactly qualified to do much of anything, and it's really hard to find a job that still allows me to spend time with Noble. I want to be there for her as much as possible before she starts school." She waved a hand in front of her and let it fall in defeat. "It's also hard to look for something because I can't leave her alone and now I don't have anyone to watch her, so even if I did get an interview, I'm not sure what I'd do. I guess I'll just show up with my kid and hope they're cool with it." She barked out a laugh which had zero humor in it.

I remembered my mom working two and three jobs when I was little. My dad was never around, so it was always just me and her. Fortunately for her, we'd had a neighbor, an older woman who lived down the hall from us. She watched me after school and on weekends when Mom had to work. She was actually the one who taught me everything I knew about cars. Her husband was a collector before he passed away, and the woman was living comfortably off selling and restoring his collection. She had a mechanic, an older guy named Gus, who was no longer around. But when he was alive, Gus never minded me kicking it in the garage and asking questions while he worked. There was no telling what would have happened to us if Mom hadn't befriended that neighbor back in the day. She had to work, and just like Orley mentioned, it wasn't like you could show up for your shift with your kid in tow.

I grunted and dug out my phone, scrolling through my contacts until I landed on the information I was searching for. "I'm going to give you a number. There's a woman who lives a few floors down from me at the Skylark. Her name is Erica. She works from home and she has a kid, a daughter who's a little bit older than Noble. She sometimes watches a few of the other kids in the building. She's nice and very reliable. She knows the score in the city and will keep your kid safe. I fix her car for her when it acts up, so she owes me a favor. You can give her a call if you want and see if she's willing to help you out with Noble."

Orley stopped walking and looked at me like I'd suddenly grown a second head. "I can't leave her with a stranger."

I sighed and gave my head a little shake. "So, call Erica. Hop over to her apartment for five minutes. Talk to the other moms who live in the building. There are a bunch of them. Carmen, the woman who lives across the hall from me, has lived in the Skylark for years. Both her boys hang with Erica after school when Carmen's at the diner across the street. Go knock on her door. People are only strangers if you refuse to get to know them." I lifted my hand and pulled my sunglasses down to give her a pointed look. "Things will be much easier for you if you learn not everyone here is the enemy. Believe it or not, some of us are here because this is where we want to be." It wasn't always the case, but I couldn't imagine living anywhere else now.

She gave me a look of utter disbelief, but eventually nodded and quietly agreed to take Erica's number from me. Frankly, it wasn't like she had very many options.

Luckily, Noble was done being quiet and the last few blocks she kept up a steady stream of chatter, trying to explain her favorite movie, which I guessed was *Star Wars* if I was interpreting her rambling, slightly skewed words correctly. Apparently, she was a huge fan of Chewie. It explained why she used my name every chance she got.

When we finally got to the block where Orley left the car the night before, I was, once again, covered in sweat and needed another shower. I was acutely aware of the woman next to me. I expected her to complain about the heat and the walk... and the company. But all she did was entertain her daughter and repeatedly thank me for taking the time to look at the car, assuring me over and over again how I didn't have to. She let it slip that she was planning on scrapping the car if I couldn't get it started. She softly told me she didn't have the money to get it fixed or to tow it to a garage. She watched me like she expected me to bolt after the admission, but the truth was, her words made me even more determined to get her car up and running.

When we rounded the corner, I heard Orley suck in a breath and could feel her preparing herself for the worst. It was a good bet the car would be up on cinder blocks, wheels missing, and everything else stripped down to the frame. It was good she had realistic expectations, but I was hoping against hope my city might surprise her.

"Oh my God." She stumbled to a halt next to me and her hand landed on my arm. I was pretty sure she had no clue she was clutching me in her obvious excitement. "I can't believe it's still here."

Her blue eyes were wide and there was no disguising the delight shining from them.

"Looks like your luck might be turning around." I wasn't going to think about how nice it felt to be part of that. "Let's see what we can do to get you back on the road."

I needed space because her light touch felt far better than it should.

There weren't enough hours in the day for my skin to be buzzing and for my dick to be twitching every time she looked at me. There wasn't enough of me to go around as it was. I couldn't afford to lose any of the pieces I had left of myself to her, or to her kid.

5

Orley

I was too pragmatic to believe my luck would suddenly do a total one-eighty. But, when Solo managed to get the car started after only a few minutes of tinkering under the hood, I felt like I could actually breathe for the first time since it had crapped out the day before. If I could get around, then maybe, just maybe, I could find a job. That is, after I figured out what to do with Noble while I was out pounding the pavement. Solo muttered something about corroded battery attachments and loose connections and told me the car needed a tune-up in the worst way. I pretended to listen and promised I would take care of it as soon as possible. It was easy enough to lie to the back of his head. Not as easy when his knowing gaze, which I now knew was a deep, dark brown color, seemed to pick apart every word out of my mouth and judge every move I made. Considering the car was around four-thousand miles past due for an oil change, a tune-up was the least of what the vehicle needed. It was going to be a miracle if it kept running until I could scrounge up the funds to fix it. Fortunately, I was getting good at dealing with one crisis at a time. I was going to run the car into the ground and deal with the blowback of that decision when I had to. For now, Solo had saved the day, and once again I owed him more than a simple thank you.

Sadly, my thanks was literally the only thing I had to give to show my gratitude.

I watched with appreciative eyes as he unfolded his large body from the abyss of the engine. For such a big, broad man, he moved with a fluid grace, indicating he was very much in control of all the strength and brawn rippling enticingly under the cotton of his sweat-dampened t-shirt. I chewed on my lower lip and reminded myself how he wasn't my type. I had no idea what to do with a guy who knew how to fix cars and toss around scary creeps on the street like it was nothing. I had no experience with someone who radiated barely contained power and solved his problems with his fists and fear.

I tried to hide my obvious ogling as he wiped his hands on his jeans in a move that seemed practiced and familiar. He closed the hood with a thunk and turned to look at me with a lifted eyebrow. It was hard to read his expression under the shadow the brim of his hat cast over his face, but I was pretty sure he was once again judging me and finding my basic life skills lacking. If you owned a car, it was your responsibility to take care of it. I knew that, I simply didn't have the money to do so, and didn't need him poking at that particularly sore wound. I got enough daily reminders about how spectacularly I was failing at pretty much everything aside from being a good mom.

Solo snatched off his hat and ran a hand through his short hair. When he sighed, it was deep and long, as if I'd single-handedly added a thousand more pounds to whatever burden he was already carrying. He cracked his neck, which made me jump, and narrowed his dark eyes in my direction.

I was holding Noble close to my chest. The combination of the heat and the walk to the car had proven too much for her. I wouldn't let her wander far from my side, so boredom and exhaustion won out. She fell asleep as soon as Solo started tinkering around with the car. I squeezed her tighter under the weight of his penetrating gaze and purposely buried my nose in her sweet-smelling curls so I didn't have to face his eyes directly. I was used to people looking at me with a mixture of disappointment and disdain, so I couldn't figure out why I wasn't ready to face it from this big, brooding stranger.

"You're not working the rest of the day, right?" He wiped a hand over his grim face and sighed again. "Instead of dropping me at my car, take me to work and I'll give you a tune-up before your car gives up the ghost. I'll catch a ride home with one of the guys."

I shifted Noble's weight and automatically shook my head in the negative. "You don't have to do that. You got it running. That's more than enough. You've already saved me from more than one really terrible situation. I can't repay you for either, but I am so grateful you seem to have a knack for being in the right place at the right time."

He propped a hip on the front end of the car and watched me unwaveringly. "You don't need to repay me. In both instances, it was the right thing to do, and even though most people around here don't adhere to the philosophy of doing right by others, my mom raised me better than that. If you can help out, you should. I can keep your car running for you beyond the two or three weeks it's going to last if you don't let me take it to my garage. Don't turn down help around here when it's offered. It doesn't come by very often."

It was my turn to sigh so heavily I was almost surprised that the whoosh of air didn't blow him over. "It's been my experience that nothing comes without the expectation of reciprocation. I can't repay your kindness, and I doubt there's any scenario in which I am going to be of any help to you. I'm not looking to get myself buried in a debt I can't repay." I didn't know much about the way this dark part of the city operated, but I did have enough common sense to know that digging my hole any deeper was not a good idea. I didn't want to owe anyone anything. This guy already made me uneasy. The last thing I wanted was to feel like I *had* to give in to him.

Solo pushed off the car and gave his head a shake. He put his ball cap back on and rolled his impressively built shoulders. "Trust me, you don't have anything I want. I'm trying to be a nice guy and help a neighbor out. You don't want my help, it's your funeral. You don't want to believe it's possible there are people here who actually have a conscience and give a shit about the people around them, that's on you. I have too much going on in my life to try and change your mind. Favors are not unlimited, no matter where you live, and bad people are not limited to these streets." He gave a grunt as he bent to pick up his tools and gave me a cold look over his shoulder. "My car is in a lot a few blocks over. Since I'm already late, I'll need you to drop me off after all."

His sharp reprimand made me cringe. I felt like a little kid getting scolded by a teacher. A lot of times I forgot just how inexperienced and naïve I really was. I'd had Noble so young, and watched my world implode so recently, it was easy to forget how all those things happened before I was old enough to legally drink.

Freeing a hand from underneath Noble's weight, I blindly reached out, locking my fingers around one of Solo's solid, heavily tattooed forearms. Muscle flexed under my fingertips and I fought not to gasp at the sensation. His skin was so warm. He felt dynamic and unbreakable, nothing like the polished and smooth men I was used to. There was nothing soft here, and suddenly his level of hard made all kinds of sense. Everything in my new life was hard. The choices I had to make. The day-to-day survival. The act I had to keep up in order to fool my daughter.

"You're right. I'd be an idiot not to take you up on the offer to fix my car for me. Thank you for the offer. I'm sorry if I'm being difficult. The last time someone offered to help me, I lost more than you can imagine." I was used to be being pulled close with one hand, while the other stabbed me in the back. It was my own judgment I questioned, more than his intentions. "It's no longer in my nature to take someone doing something nice for me at face value. I see hidden motives behind every good deed. That's my issue, and it isn't fair to cast every new person I encounter into the role of villain." I huffed out a breath and shifted uncomfortably under Noble's weight and his gaze. "I'm stuck here for the foreseeable future. There is no way out for me, but I don't want this for Noble. I want her to thrive and succeed, and go wherever she wants to go in life. I know I need to learn how to live here so she can see it's possible to have a home and be happy wherever you happen to end up." I forced a smile and fluttered my eyelashes at him. That move used to work back in the day to soften whomever I directed the look at, but Solo seemed totally unaffected by the overt flirting. "I will be forever grateful if you can squeeze my car into your schedule today. I promise I will pay you back as soon as I find a new job and get on top of all the other bills I haven't paid over the last few months."

It was easy to see he wanted to argue about me paying him back, but eventually, he relented. He seemed to know it was a sticking point for me. I couldn't take something without at least the illusion of being able to give something back. The arm I was still clutching like a lifeline flexed again and then he shook me loose. Solo inclined his head toward the back door, wordlessly indicating I should put my sleeping child in her car seat so he could get back to his busy day.

After a sleepy Noble was situated, I straightened and blinked in surprise at the sight of the big man already behind the steering wheel of my car. Sure, the stupid thing had been nothing more than a paperweight before he worked his magic under the hood, but it was my paperweight. Shouldn't he at least ask if it was okay for him to drive?

Our eyes met briefly in the rearview mirror and I watched with a mild flare of irritation as his mouth quirked up in a knowing grin. My aggravation was apparently stamped all over my face. He lifted an eyebrow and the grin morphed into a blindly attractive smile. He had straight, pearly-white teeth and a tiny dimple in one of his cheeks. When he relaxed and smiled, his entire face lit up and made him look younger and less intimidating. It was getting harder to remember why I didn't think guys who looked like him did nothing for me, because there was a whole lot of something starting to happen deep down inside of me the longer we stared silently at each other in the mirror.

"The garage where I work isn't exactly open to the public and it isn't all that easy to find. It's sort of a referral-only kind of place, way off the beaten path, even for this city. It's easier if you let me drive there. I can get in no matter what I'm driving. If you drive, I'll have to get out and explain what's going on to my boss once we get there, and then there's a good chance he might not let you through the gate. Get in and let's get going. I swear I'll have you tuned-up and on your way in under an hour. You just have to trust me a little while longer."

Trust wasn't something I had a wealth of anymore. Those reserves had been tapped and drained long ago, but it wasn't as if I had much choice in this particular situation. Solo was the only person in recent memory who hadn't let me down.

I rolled my eyes at him in the mirror and flounced my way into the passenger seat. It was a place I swore I would never be again once I took back control of my life.

Even if I was going nowhere and running into dead end after dead end, I was determined to be the one driving. Except now this enigmatic, complicated stranger had the keys to my car and he was the one deciding where we were headed. A shiver raced up my spine when I realized I was less bothered by that fact than I thought I would be. Instead of bristling, I wanted to acquiesce and let him handle things for the rest of the afternoon. I wanted a brief reprieve from holding the entire universe together with nothing more than grit and determination. It was unnervingly easy to relinquish all the control over to him that I held onto so tightly.

That kind of thinking was going to get me in trouble. I knew what happened when you let someone else call the shots, and it wasn't anything I ever wanted to relive again. I needed to accept the help Solo was offering, and then quickly rebuild all the walls I'd erected around my life since moving to the city. It was too dangerous for me to let anyone else in. The ledge I was clinging to was too narrow as it was, there wasn't room for anyone else in the mess which was my life. He might not have time to hold my hand and show me the way the world worked in this broken city he seemed so fond of, but I sure as hell didn't have a minute to waste on the kind of complication and heartbreak the man sitting next to me was sure to bring wherever he went.

6

Solo

I watched as the massive metal gates wrapped in barbed wire slowly slid open. I actually found the groan and creak of the motion comforting. Once I was behind them, the rest of the world fell away and it was just me and whatever project the Boss handed down for the day. I didn't have to worry about the ever-expanding laundry list of things I had to take care of day in and day out. I didn't have to think about the future or what it was going to look like for me. I didn't have to obsess about my mother or all the different ways I wished things were different for her and if I was doing enough to take care of her. Once those gates slid closed, I knew my role and what was expected of me. It was about the only time while I was awake when I fully managed to switch the hyperactive, overachieving part of my mind completely off. Here, I wasn't spinning my wheels, I was working on the Boss's wheels, and I knew exactly what he expected of me: hard work and perfect execution.

I felt Orley tense up. Good Lord, was she an uptight little thing. I wanted to tell her she was too young to have permanent frown lines etched into her forehead. She was also too pretty for me to take the scowl cemented across her elegant features seriously. It was clear she had a redhead's temper hidden under her outer shell of fear and unease, but her fire was barely a spark in a place that burned with rage and anger on a daily basis. She was going to have to let go of the rigid hold on her emotions if she wanted to compete with the torrent of fury that flooded the place we called home.

I nodded my head at Nestor, one of the guys who stood guard inside the gates. I noticed the way his gaze traveled over the woman in the passenger seat, but he waved me through without question, just like I knew he would. The barbed wire and armed ex-con were good indications that this side of the garage wasn't exactly on the up and up. You wouldn't find minivans needing tires rotated and four-door sedans waiting on an oil change back here. The Boss didn't do those things. The Boss owned the entire block. This was the original garage Gus handed down to the new owner when he passed away. These cars weren't going back to their owners unless they paid an astronomical amount. These cars were collateral. They were snatched in the middle of the night, and either held until debt was paid or stripped down and sent overseas. This part of the garage was the largest working chop-shop on the West Coast. The regular garage was on the other side of the block, and just like I told Orley, the only way you were getting your car through the bay door on this side of the street was by referral. The line between the legal and illegal sides of the Boss's businesses was blurry, at best.

When I first started working here, it was because the Boss knew Gus. I'd stopped by to pay my respects when the old man passed and the new owner immediately saw something familiar when we met. He told me it was easy to spot trouble waiting for me, and if I wasn't careful, bad decisions were going to get away from me. I flatly informed him I was way too busy and had far too much responsibility for any kind of trouble, and he had laughed at me. He informed me trouble would find me even if I wasn't looking for it. I had no interest in putting my hands on stolen cars, no matter how beautiful and luxurious they might be. I wasn't licensed or trained professionally, so he couldn't put me in the front garage, not with the way the law in this town kept their eyes on him. And if I landed in jail, my mom would have no one, which was a risk I wasn't willing to take. When he offered me a job, I politely turned him down, expecting a fist in the face as I did so.

To my surprise, the Boss was completely under-standing, even sympathetic, to my situation. Instead of putting me under the hood of a stolen sports car, he of-fered me a chance to show him what I could do by re-building a thoroughly battered Ford Coupe. Gus loved old rat-rods and hot rods. The property was littered with unfinished projects. It was a treasure trove of untapped potential the Boss couldn't do much with on his own, considering his other obligations. He told me if I could get the Ford up and running within the month, he would let me sell it and split the profit with me sixty-forty. It was an opportunity too good to pass up.

I finished the car and sold it for twice what we were asking for. The following month the boss handed me a rusted, patchworked Chevelle and we repeated the process. That restoration took a little over two months, and once it sold, I had enough money to enroll in some online classes. I wanted to be a legit mechanic. I wanted to know how to fix anything and everything that came my way, from the oldest and simplest cars to the high-end, luxury models. I wanted a job that would never be obsolete. I had to have a way to support myself and my mom no matter how often the world ended up on fire around me. I was still working my way through the junkyard, finding hidden jewels and turning them into custom rides. The Boss let me have free rein; the arrangement put money in both of our pockets and kept my hands clean.

The Boss offered to pay my way through school as long as I agreed to go work for him on the legit side of things when I was done with my classes. I turned him down. I'd been around long enough to know it was never a good idea to end up indebted to the kind of man who built his business on blood and broken bones. I did, however, take him up on his offer to train me to fight when he found out I had a knack for tossing a punch and dodging fists. The money was impossible to pass up and the Boss was a good teacher. A broken nose and a dislocated shoulder were nothing as long as I had money in the bank and a way to take care of my mom.

I pulled Orley's junky car into my reserved bay. I parked it next to the Barracuda I was currently working on and glanced into the back to see if Noble was still asleep. Blurry blue eyes met mine in the mirror and I couldn't fight the smile pulling at my lips. The little girl really was adorable, full of light and life. Her smile was infectious.

"There's an apartment upstairs you can take Noble up to and wait while I give the car a once over. It should only take me an hour or so." I made sure my tone left no room for argument. She didn't need to be wandering around the shop floor. I trusted most of the guys the Boss handpicked to work here with my life, but not with hers. There was something about her wide-eyed innocence and trembling fear that called to every single protective instinct I had.

She delicately cleared her throat and I watched out of the corner of my eye as she fiddled nervously with the ends of her hair. I never really considered myself a fan of redheads. I wasn't opposed to them, but if I had a type, it definitely wasn't the fiery-haired, pale variety. I was drawn to flashy women who went out of their way to grab my attention, not timid females trying to hide from everything and everyone. I tended to go for chicks who knew the score. Girls who were in the same game and didn't complain about it being played dirty or unfair. I liked quick and easy, because it was all I had room for in my life. None of which explained why I was inexplicably drawn to the woman sitting next to me. She was everything I avoided like my life depended on it, and yet here I was, practically forcing my help on her. She obviously would rather crash and burn all on her own.

"Umm... should we be here? The police aren't going to come barging through the door any second with guns drawn, are they?" She shifted in her seat. "There are limits to what I'm willing to expose Noble to, even if it means my car remains dead on the side of the road."

I was going to snap at her for being so condescending, but one look at her face and I realized she wasn't being snide. She was honestly worried about a raid, and I couldn't deny I'd been through more than one since coming to work here. Luckily, because the Boss's big brother was a bigwig in the police department, the unexpected busts had dwindled down over the last few years.

"You'll be fine. We were raided last month and the cops left with nothing. That usually keeps them off the Boss's back for a little while." I tried not to laugh as she gasped and moved her mouth like a beached fish. "I'm kidding. The Boss's brother is on the police force. Usually if anything is going down, we have a lot of advance notice. I'll make sure to smuggle you out the front if anything goes sideways while you're here."

The struggle was apparent on her face. She really needed her car fixed, but she didn't want to be at this garage, or with me. Fortunately, logic and desperation won out and she released her hesitation with a sigh. She threw the door open and moved to get her daughter from the back seat. She was muttering under her breath the entire time, and I was shocked to realize I found her hissy-fit kind of cute. Ruffling her very pretty feathers was fast becoming one of my favorite forms of entertainment.

I flicked my fingers in acknowledgment to the Boss when he stuck his head out of the office to see what was going on. You could have heard a pin drop in the shop as everyone stopped what they were doing to watch the young mother carry her daughter up the stairs and disappear into the apartment that ran along the upper level of the entire building. I elbowed one of the gearheads who let out a loud wolf-whistle, causing Orley's back to stiffen and shoulders to lock. She didn't turn around and the door slammed shut. I glared at the young guy, whom the Boss had recently brought on after finding him trying to break into the legit garage one night.

Crawley rubbed his shoulder and glared at me. "What, dude? She's smoking hot. I don't usually go for moms, but she looks more like a model than a mother."

I punched him in the arm for good measure and pointed a finger at his face. "She might be hot, but she is also a human being who deserves respect. Mom or model, no woman likes being harassed when she's going about her day. Now she's going to have to explain to her little girl why what you did isn't cool and why she isn't obligated to pay attention to any random asshole who hollers at her. Don't be a dick, Crawley."

He continued to glare at me, but was rubbing his shoulder the entire time. I wasn't sure if I got my point across, but he shut his mouth and stepped away from me. Even if he didn't agree with the lesson, I was a lot bigger than him. He knew if I had to use my fists to drive my point home, it wasn't going to go well for him.

Satisfied that Orley and Noble were stashed upstairs and out of harm's way for now, I made my way back to the car I didn't have time to work on and forced the thought of the woman and child as far out of my mind as I could.

The Boss was right. Trouble did find you even when you weren't looking for it. I wished he had warned me it would come in the form of an irresistible redhead and an adorable, blue-eyed little girl.

Orley

After Solo was finished with my car, it was the only thing that ran smoothly in my life. I still had no luck finding another job, and my current job didn't appreciate that I was forced to call in for one of my few measly shifts because I still hadn't found someone to watch Noble. My meager funds were dwindling down to nothing, and on top of it all, the air conditioning unit in our apartment decided to crap out. The super promised he would be by to fix it three days in a row, but had yet to make an appearance. I was on edge. I felt like every time I turned around, I walked into a new brick wall, and when I attempted to get myself straightened out, I ended up tangled in thorns. The heat, combined with too many days spent indoors because it was slightly less blistering than outside—and less dangerous—had Noble acting out.

My normally affable child was currently on her back in the stairwell, refusing to move because it was too hot and she was too tired. She was crying, fat tears rolling down her red cheeks and snot bubbling from her scrunched-up nose as she wailed. From the sounds of it, her little toddler world was ending, and I felt like garbage, because all I wanted to do was cry right along next to her.

We were stuck in an endless loop: I'd tell her I would carry her up the stairs if she didn't want to walk, and Noble would scream back that she was big enough to walk on her own. So far we were lucky and no one else had attempted the stairs in the sweltering heat, but I could hear footsteps coming from above, and I knew I was going to have to haul Noble out of the way instead of letting her tantrum run its course. I was secretly hoping she would cry herself out so I could have a couple moments to feel like my stomach wasn't full of acid and my nerves weren't made of razor wire.

"Honey, you have to stop. I know it's hot and yucky. I know you're bored. I promise I'll take you to the park tomorrow and I'll buy us a whole bunch of fans once I get a new job. I need you to get up and behave yourself." I crouched down so I was hovering over her. I almost recoiled at the obvious anger in those eyes that were a mirror of my own. Not only did my child never show such hot, painful emotion, I had no idea a three-year-old was capable of feeling in such a complex and hurtful way.

"You can't promise if you won't keep it." More tears gathered, but at least she got off her back and sat on the step in front of me. Noble sniffed, long and loud. I fought the urge to cringe as she wiped her hand across her damp face. Since we'd only run down to check the mail cubby in the lobby, I didn't have my purse or anything else on hand to wipe away the mess she'd made of herself. Sighing, I tugged at the bottom of my tank top and bent so I could use one of my last clean items of clothing to clean my daughter's face.

"Of course I can promise. That's what moms do. I promise to give you the world and then work every single day until you have it." I tried to smile at her, but Noble's lashes were spiked together with moisture and her eyes were shiny with unshed tears. "Sometimes promises take mommies a little while to keep, but we always will. You have to be patient. Remember what patient means?"

Noble sighed and kicked her feet, heels bumping against the step as the approaching footsteps got closer. Sweat made my hair stick to my face and neck, and I could feel moisture rolling down my spine, making my clothes clammy and damp.

"I wanted cake. I wanted to play outside. I want to see Mrs. Sanchez and my friends. You promised." She sniffed again and refused to meet my gaze. I was glad she looked away. Noble was way too young to know that her words were like an arrow through my very fragile heart. No mother ever wanted to hear that they let their child down, especially when it came to things that should be so very easy to make happen.

I sighed again and maneuvered so I could scoop Noble up before she was able to launch into another protest loud enough to wake the dead. I squeezed her close and closed my eyes as I inhaled her innocent, but no longer sweet, scent. Ugh. Everything was sweaty and gross, including my precious baby. I had to tamp down the urge to throw myself on the floor and let loose the same way she did.

"I know I promised all those things, and I will do my best to give them to you. It might not be today or tomorrow. But I haven't forgotten. Mommy just needs some more time." And a new job with a big fat paycheck. "How about I call Mrs. Sanchez and see if she has time tomorrow for a visit while Mr. Sanchez is at work?" I sent up a silent prayer that I could convince the woman a few minutes of her time would be worthwhile. She'd always liked Noble and treated her well, but I had no clue if she was willing to go against her husband's wishes. I was willing to bribe her—with what, I didn't know—if that's what it took.

Noble nodded tiredly against my shoulder and I breathed a sigh of relief. I was sure this was only the eye of the storm, but it gave me a window to get my kid back to our apartment so she didn't let the entire apartment complex know what a shitty parent I was.

I'd only made it a few steps before another woman was trotting in my direction. She was holding the hand of a little girl who was probably around eight or nine. The little girl had a swingy, sable bob, bright eyes, and a gap-toothed grin. She was wearing cowboy boots that clomped noisily on every step, but her mother seemed oblivious to the noise. The woman heading toward me was also a brunette but her dark hair was slashed through with pops of pink, purple, and teal. She looked edgier and cooler than I ever would. She had on a pair of glasses that looked both retro and trendy, but her eyes were friendly and curious as she regarded me from behind the lenses. I was getting ready to apologize for blocking the way when Noble suddenly bounced in my arms and pointed at the woman's arm.

"*Star Wars!*" Noble's excited squeal brought a smile to the woman's face as I glanced down at her arm. The sleeve she had tattooed there did indeed depict Noble's favorite movie.

"That's right. It is *Star Wars*." The other woman's daughter giggled as she watched Noble wiggle excitedly in my hold.

"Who's your favorite character?" I could have kissed that gap-toothed face in relief when the other little girl distracted my cranky kid. Noble was more than happy to babble about Chewie and Princess Leia as I focused my attention on the mother.

"Sorry. It's been a day. We'll get out of your way." I offered a wobbly smile and saw a flash of sympathy in her kind eyes.

"No rush. My husband and I are huge *Star Wars* nerds, so Riley is well versed in the Force. She doesn't mind chatting about the movies, especially when someone asks about the tattoo." She cocked her colorful head to the side and gave me a considering look. "Did you move in recently? I thought I knew all the moms in the building. I watch a lot of the kids who live here since I work from home and know just how hard being a working mom can be."

I felt my eyes widen and my teeth snap down on my lower lip. She was the friend Solo mentioned. The one whom he encouraged me to reach out to. The one I'd decided was probably a horrible person without even meeting her, because she lived in this place that I hated. Embarrassment washed over me in hot waves as I shifted uneasily under Noble's animated antics as she mimed the Death Star blowing up.

"I've.. uh... been here a few months. So, kind of new, and we don't go out much. This is Noble and I'm Orley." I offered the weak introduction as the woman continued to watch me.

"Ahhh... You're Solo's broken bird. The building has been talking about you. It's pretty impressive that you got him to give up any of his precious time to help you with your car. That boy is so busy, he's going to run himself into the ground before he's thirty. I'm Erica and this is Riley, by the way." She arched a perfectly groomed eyebrow at me and gave me a faint grin. "Solo mentioned he passed my number along because you needed someone to watch the little Jedi. I was hoping you would call so I could at least give you a list of all the mom-approved places around here you might want to take Noble. It can be scary outside, but, believe it or not, there are some family-friendly options nearby you should have in your arsenal for those days you can't stay inside."

This woman was so nice... and helpful. It was probably clear I'd blown her off and been judgmental, but she was still throwing me a much-needed life raft.

I cleared my throat and put Noble down so she could stand on the step with the other little girl. My daughter had moved on from *Star Wars* to the girl's cute cowboy boots. No doubt as soon as we were back upstairs, she would be demanding a pair of her own. I would end up promising her a pair, one more promise it was going to take me Lord only knew how long to follow through on.

"I would love that list, thank you. Our air conditioner has been on the fritz for three days and Noble is going stir-crazy inside. I apologize for not reaching out sooner. I've been looking for a second job and time has really slipped away from me." It had become a black, chilling void I was terrified I would never escape. I lifted my sweaty hair off the back of my neck and made a face. "I don't want to keep you. I'll give you a call before the end of the week."

She made a hum of agreement and told me, "Let Solo know the super is slacking. If he gives that jerk a call, your unit will be fixed within the hour. The man is useless, but he's terrified of Solomon. I'm in apartment 3F. Just come on down when you have a free afternoon. You can bring Noble by to meet some of the other kids in the building." I nodded and went to move around her, but paused when she put a light hand on my arm. "I would be happy to watch her for you in a pinch if you need to go to an interview or anything. I have a list of references and a whole host of qualifications. Those of us who grew up around here try and take care of each other."

I shook my head and swallowed past a brick in my throat. "I'm not from here though." And I had no intention of asking Solo for another thing. I was not going to be his newest burden to bear. Everyone seemed to know he was already carrying the entire world on his shoulders, and I wasn't about to add another pound to his heavy load.

Erica smiled sadly and patted my arm. "Oh, trust me, I know. Anyone looking at you knows that. But you're here now, so you might as well settle in the best you can with the right people in your corner." She cocked her head and I found myself watching the peacock colors in her hair play hide and seek with the darker strands. "Have you ever waited tables before?"

I balked and tried to keep up with the change of conversation. "Uh... no. I haven't done much of anything other than answer phones." And look pretty. That used to be my number one skill, but I refused to think about that.

"My husband's brother works at this cute little diner right on the outskirts of the city. He just got promoted to a management position after bartending there forever. They tend to hire college-aged kids so they're always looking for help right around graduation. I'll give you Ramon's number." She waited while I dug out my cell phone and could jot down the information she quickly rattled off. "Call him and see if they have any openings. Tell him Erica gave you his information and remind him he owes me a favor." She smiled at me and called for her daughter. Riley hugged Noble and patted her on the shoulder, much like her mother had done to soothe me. "Good luck with everything, Orley. Noble, it was nice to meet you. I'm sure Riley can't wait to show you all her *Star Wars* toys."

They continued down the stairs, my daughter and I both slightly stunned, as we watched them until they were gone. I reached for Noble's hand, wondering how more people in this God-forsaken city had come to my rescue and offered genuine help, than anyone in my affluent, pristine past had? What were the odds?

I took one step back up the stairs when Noble promptly announced, "I want a pair of cowboy boots!"

Well, at least she wasn't asking for a pony. It was the small things.

Solo

practically had to crawl home after my fight on Saturday night. The guy I was up against was new, the size of a house, and obviously had some professional fighting experience. He didn't fight dirty, but he fought hard, and I had a split lip, blackened eyes, ringing ears, and more than a few cracked ribs to show for it. As a rule, I won more than I lost, but last night, it was no contest. I tried to give as good as I got, but once the guy had me on my back and in a submission choke hold, I'd tapped out. I'd done it right before the world started to fade to black. Back in the good old days, there was no such thing as a tap out. You fought until the other guy was dead or unconscious. But the man in charge of the fights was wicked and ruthless enough that most people referred to him as the Devil. He wanted to keep those of us around who earned big cash for him on the regular. So now, he had enforcers on hand to make sure the fight ended if one of the participants knew there was no way to win. I fucking hated being that guy last night, but one more kick to the head or fist to my ribs and I wasn't going to be able to get out of bed for a week. I had too much going on to end up on my back and out of commission for any length of time.

I hated that the only money I'd pocketed was the fee for showing up to get my ass kicked and none of the prize money I could have won. The cash from the fights was the money I used to keep my mom in the best facility in the state. Anything I earned while taking a beating went to her, and everything I earned at the garage kept a roof over my head and my car tricked out. If I came up short during a fight, it meant I was going to have to borrow from my other funds and go without something in my day to day. It happened. It wasn't anything new, but it still made me feel like a loser, even more than having to tap out.

It was really early in the morning when I was slinking into the apartment building. The sun was barely up and the normally busy streets were quiet. Lester was asleep on the bottom step, and my ribs screamed in protest when I had to haul myself over him. Luckily, I had the day off, so I could crash, recharge, then drive out to see my mother before I settled in and worked on any school assignments for the upcoming week. It was about as much of a day off as I ever got, and I was looking forward to the mindlessness of the familiar tasks.

I was reaching for the front door when it suddenly pushed open with enough force to send me back a step. The sudden movement made me clutch my injured side and let out a string of swear words that were loud enough to wake Lester. He blinked an irritated look in my direction. Orley rocked back on her heels and stared at me through sleepy blue eyes.

"Oh. Sorry, I didn't see you." She scooted her way around me, rubbing her eyes and obviously trying to shake herself awake. She looked like a very pretty zombie sleepwalking out of the building.

Sucking in a breath between my teeth and letting it out when the pain in my side was manageable, I roughly asked, "Where are you off to so early?"

She looked at me again and lifted a perfectly arched eyebrow. "I should ask why you're just getting home when the sun is coming up. You go first."

I grunted in response and watched as she suddenly seemed to take notice of the damage to my face. I knew it wasn't pretty, but she gasped and lifted her hands to her mouth like she was face to face with a horror movie monster.

"What happened to you? Are you okay? Who did this to you? Did you call the police?" The questions came rapidly. One of her hands lifted in my direction, almost as if she wanted to soothe the dark spots and lacerations decorating my skin.

I took a step back before she could touch me and lifted my chin defiantly. I was slightly taken aback by her show of concern. I couldn't remember the last time someone had asked if I was okay. I was the one always taking care of everyone else, so my needs tended to be an afterthought. "I'm fine. No need to call the police. This, unfortunately, comes with the territory when I'm at my second job."

She frowned at me and adjusted the purse strap that was digging into her shoulder. "What kind of job gives you black eyes and a busted lip?"

I grunted again and reached for the front door. All I wanted was my bed and eight hours of uninterrupted sleep. "The kind you know nothing about." I flicked a look back over her, noticing she was dressed in form-fitting black pants and a white button-down shirt. It wasn't an outfit that was appropriate for the heat. "You finally get a job?"

She nodded and nervously reached up to play with her hair. "Your friend Erica hooked me up with her brother. He gave me a job at the diner he manages. I'm still training, and right now they have me working breakfast shifts. It's not so bad. I'm home in the afternoon and still get to spend most of the day with Noble." She blushed and had the good grace to look regretful. "Erica is watching her for me while I work. She's great with Noble, and Noble loves Riley. I should have reached out sooner when you gave me her number." She sounded contrite but I was in too bad of a mood to appreciate it.

She should have, but this chick was stubborn to a fault. "I'm glad you found something." I would dig my own eyes out with a spoon before admitting to anyone I'd been worried about her. She seemed so stressed, and I knew desperation was a very dangerous thing in a place where others were just waiting for an opening to take advantage of you. Luckily, I knew Ramon and the rest of the crew who ran the diner. They were all good people and kept a close eye on the young women who worked there. My Boss's woman worked there when she was putting herself through college, so he also kept his ear to the ground for any rumbling of trouble when it came to the diner. It was about the safest, most legitimate job Orley could get in the city.

"Go put a frozen bag of peas on your eyes, and get some sleep. You look like you could use it." Orley flashed a grin at me and I felt the impact low in my gut. It was like taking another punch, and this one almost doubled me over. "Hey, if you need anything, I'm in 5B. Let me know. I owe you for getting my car back on the road. I'd be screwed if I couldn't get to the diner each morning."

I blinked at her but tried to keep my features under control. She was the quiet neighbor on the other side of my apartment. She was my actual neighbor, not just someone in the building I would pass on occasion. She'd also given me her apartment number. I was too tired and too sore to think about why entrusting me with that knowledge sent something much more pleasant than the pain I was feeling shoot along my nerves.

"I'll be fine. This isn't anything new. Do you need me to walk you to your car?" Shit. Why did I offer that? I was barely staying upright as it was.

She shook her head and fiddled with her purse strap some more. "I'm fine. I found a spot pretty close. Thank you for offering though." Her eyes flitted over my face. "Seriously, Solo, take care of yourself."

She turned and walked down the steps, stopping to hand Lester something that looked like a muffin. They exchanged quiet words, and even though I was dead on my feet, I couldn't make myself go inside until I saw her shiny hair disappear into her little car.

Muttering over how much of an idiot I was, I once again tried to walk into the building, but Lester's raspy voice stopped me.

"Those girls have been without air conditioning for over a week. I think that's one of the main reasons she caved and let her little girl go and play with Riley. They had to get out of the apartment before they died of heat exhaustion." The old man kept one eye on me as he picked apart the muffin in his hand. "She called that bastard of a super no less than twenty times and the useless bag of bones has yet to show."

I tried to lift an eyebrow at him, but the motion hurt too much. "Why are you telling me this, old man?"

Lester snorted and pointed the muffin in my direction. "You know why I'm tellin' you. Don't play dumb with me, boy."

Swearing again I jerked the door open and gave the older man a nod. "Can I at least get some sleep before I call that asshole? In case you can't tell, I was not the victor tonight. Got my ass handed to me, old man."

Lester chuckled. "A loss is good for you every now and again. Keeps the ego in check and reminds you that you don't, in fact, rule the fucking world. Help the girl out after you get some sleep. She was right; you do look like shit."

I trudged up to my apartment, body aching, face throbbing. It was early enough that the fighting couple on the other side of the wall were blissfully quiet for once. I immediately rummaged through my freezer in search of something frozen to slap over my eyes and across my lower lip. No peas, but there was a bag of tater-tots which looked like they'd been in there since the day I moved in. There was also a bottle of vodka that looked nice and frosty. I grabbed both, and meandered into my living room. I plopped on the couch, setting an alarm on my phone for a more reasonable time so I could call the super about Orley's AC. The guy was a scumbag of the highest order. I hated having to deal with him, but he would get his ass over to the building if I pushed hard enough. We'd gone round and round enough times that he knew not to push me.

I also needed to call my mother and make sure she was up for a visit before I drove all the way out there. If she was having a bad day, it wouldn't do either of us any good for me to try and see her. I used to think some quality time together would be enough to keep her episodes at bay, but I'd had enough bad experiences, and watched mom break down enough times to know that simply wasn't the case any longer. I knew I was still her favorite person in the entire world, but I wasn't what she needed to keep her stable and safe.

I rolled the bottle of vodka across my forehead before unscrewing the cap and taking a long swig. The alcohol burned on the way down, but the cool liquid did wonders for my throbbing lip. I plopped the tater-tots across my eyes. It was a long day in a series of never-ending long days. They were all starting to blend together.

It made me extremely uncomfortable when I realized the few days that stood out the most were colored with fiery red hair and a splash of gleaming blue eyes. Sighing, I closed my eyes and willed sleep to take me so I didn't have to think about the way my ribs ached, or the way simply passing by my prissy neighbor made my dick hard.

Orley

I was out of breath by the time I dashed up the stairs and skidded to a halt in front of my apartment door. I had a whole new respect for people who worked in food service. I also regretted not paying closer attention to what percentage I tipped in the past. My feet were killing me, my arms were sore, I'd had to tap into a well of patience I usually only reserved for dealing with my three-year-old, and I constantly smelled like any variety of fried foods. All of the aches and pains aside, I liked the job, and I was making enough money to keep my lights on and to finally make good on the piece of cake I owed my kid... times ten. I also worked with some pretty awesome people. Ramon was a riot. He was loud, flirty, and totally over the top. But he was a good manager and he kept a close eye on all the young staff who worked under him, especially the girls. I'd heard a rumor that at one point, a couple of the girls who worked at the diner long before me had run into some trouble. Ramon apparently took on a huge heap of guilt that the incidents happened right under his nose, so now he is extra vigilant. He was also incredibly understanding when I told him I had to leave my shift early this afternoon because the landlord finally agreed to fix my air conditioner. Only, he told me he was going to be at my place at noon, and if I wasn't there to let him in, he couldn't guarantee the next time he'd be around.

He complained during the phone call about the extra locks I'd added to the door as soon as Noble and I moved in, saying it went against fire code. I was secretly glad the creep couldn't just waltz into my apartment unannounced with his master key. My paranoia and obsession with keeping Noble safe had its perks.

I gasped to catch my breath as the older man standing outside my door glowered at me. I glanced down at my phone and noticed it was five till noon, so I was technically early and in no way deserved the dirty looks he was firing my way. I tried to hide a shiver at the thought of letting him into my apartment, and the two of us being alone in the space together, but ultimately my desire for working AC and a non-cranky child won out over my apprehension.

"Sorry to keep you waiting. I had to get off work and find a place to park." I bit back the complaint that he'd taken his damn time showing up to take care of the problem. I'd been waiting on him for over a week.

The man grunted and lifted his chin in the direction of the door, muttering something about stubborn women. He stood too close to me when I went through the process of unlocking the extra locks, and I could feel his breath on the back of my neck. He was a pudgy man, around my height, with a pronounced balding spot and mean eyes. He made me uncomfortable when I looked at the apartment, and when I'd reluctantly agreed to take it. When I'd signed the lease, I clearly remembered him asking if I was going to live alone. I might be naïve, but I was never stupid. I told him I was going to live with my daughter, and that her father would be over regularly to visit. A total lie, but I suddenly wondered if that was why it had taken him so long to make an appearance. Maybe he thought there was a man in my life who was perfectly capable of handling something like a wonky AC.

The apartment felt like the seventh circle of hell after being closed up all day. I tugged at the collar of my button-up and watched as the landlord stomped over to the wall unit. He banged on it with the side of his fist and played with the dials on the front of it. I'd done both those things several times over the last few days, so I wasn't surprised when his Neanderthal tinkering didn't work. When he started swearing, I was super glad Noble was still with Erica. She didn't need to witness a grown man melting down because he couldn't make something work.

He looked at me over his shoulder, eyes narrowed and mouth pulled into a tight line. I stayed by the tiny kitchen area where I tossed my purse on the counter and curled my fingers tighter around my phone. I wasn't sure how fast I could call for help if I needed to, or who would show up, but I felt better having the device in my hand.

"I had all the units checked before summer. Did you mess with it? Are you sure your kid didn't fuck with it?" He huffed and lumbered over to the wall where the thermostat was.

I bristled at the insinuation the malfunction was because of operator error. "I'm positive she was nowhere near the AC. First of all, she can't reach it, second of all, I don't let her play with things like that." I crossed my arms over my chest and glared at his back. "If the entire building had central air conditioning, you wouldn't have to worry about keeping individual ones in each apartment running."

The man snorted and played with the thermostat. "Consider yourself lucky you found a place that has air conditioning at all. Central heat and air don't happen in places like this. Hell, I'm lucky if some junky doesn't swipe my copper pipes for the plumbing to hock for cash every day."

I didn't say anything. I *was* lucky I found this place, but I was even luckier that no one from my old life had found it. Granted, who would ever think to look for me here? It was exactly why I'd taken the apartment in the first place. Even if this jerk couldn't get the AC working, I was staying put. I figured I could stock up on fans if it came down to it.

"It looks like there's a loose wire so the blower isn't working to circulate air." The thermostat came off the wall and the distinct smell of burning plastic wafted from the hole.

I gritted my back teeth, wondering how close we'd come to having the entire place burn down around us.

The landlord played with the wires, still grumbling under his breath, but by the time he screwed the thermostat back into the wall a trickle of cool air was making its way out of the wall unit. It was by no means a refreshing blast of cold, but it was enough to keep the apartment bearable. I wanted to ask about the wiring. I figured I should get some kind of discount for willingly living in a death-trap, but as the older man moved closer to where I was leaning on the chipped laminate countertop, those thoughts fled. I didn't like the predatory gleam in his eyes, or the way he openly leered at me.

"Your baby daddy isn't around today?" He wiped his hands on the thighs of his jeans and lifted a thin eyebrow at me.

I cleared my throat and stood up straighter. I needed to get my hands on a taser or remember to keep my pepper spray out, if I was going to keep having run-ins with men who gave me the creeps. "He could be here any minute. He went to pick up our daughter." I wasn't a great liar naturally, but when I needed to, I could sound convincing.

"But he isn't here right now, is he?" When he took another step into my personal space my blood pressure skyrocketed and a quiver of alarm zipped up and down my spine. Out of the corner of my eye I noticed the door to the hallway was still open and I already knew the walls were paper thin. If I screamed bloody murder, someone was bound to hear me. The question was, would anyone care? Or was a woman in distress so common around here that everyone would simply go about their business like nothing happened?

I flinched when one of his fat hands lifted toward my face and touched a loose strand of hair. I jerked my head away and pushed him away with a hand on the center of his barrel chest. "Stop it. You don't get to put your hands on me."

He snorted and caught my arm when I tried to move away from him. "If you were nicer to me, it wouldn't have taken me so long to come and fix your AC. You might want to remember that just in case something breaks in the future. I have the power to make living here very uncomfortable for you and your daughter."

I bristled at the threat and struggled to pull my arm free. His fingers tightened painfully around my wrist and he pulled until I was pressed up against his sweaty chest. His ugly eyes stayed locked on mine as his other hand reached around and landed on my ass.

I yelped and fought to get free, but the super just laughed and smirked at me. "If you're really, really nice to me... maybe we can work out something so your rent isn't quite as much each month."

I shoved at him and tried to knee him between the legs, but he was ready for the move and used my forward momentum to wrap his arm tightly around me. I was trapped against him, and I could feel his arousal pressing against me. It made me gag. I opened my mouth to scream the whole building down, but immediately a heavy hand was slapped over my lips. I gagged again and continued to struggle as the man ran the tip of his nose over my cheek bone.

"You're so soft and pretty. I don't even care that you have a kid. You're still extremely sexy. We never see many like you around here. By the time they land here, they're all so jaded. They know better than to let a man like me into their apartment when they're alone. But you know nothing, and that makes you irresistible."

Of course, an asshole like him would be turned on by vulnerability and ignorance. He was no better than the thug who tried to assault me the night my car broke down. Around every single corner there seemed to be someone waiting to remind me that I would never be safe, no matter where I tried to hide.

I felt the tip of his tongue slide along the outside shell of my ear and I redoubled my efforts to escape. I swung my hands at his head, catching him with the one still wrapped around my phone. There was a solid *thunk* as my fist connected with his temple, but he didn't let me go. Instead, his hands tightened where he held me, and he barked out, "Bitch!"

His mouth moved to my neck and I felt the burn of tears in my eyes. I threw myself backward, sending my purse flying off the counter. It hit the kitchen floor with a thump, making a racket. I was suddenly very happy that I hauled half a toy store around with me most places in case I needed to keep Noble entertained. One of her toys rolled out and started buzzing and beeping as it skidded across the kitchen floor.

The noise was enough to distract the landlord. He loosened his hold enough that I finally managed to connect a knee to his nuts, forcing him to let go completely as he doubled over with a grunt. As soon as I was able, I bolted for the door like the apartment was on fire.

I shouldn't be surprised that I nearly bounced off Solo's chest the minute I cleared the doorway. He seemed to have an uncanny knack for showing up right when I needed him the most. His hand wrapped around my upper arms to steady me as I started shaking apart in his gentle hold.

"What's wrong?" His deep voice was still raspy with sleep and his black eyes and cut lip looked even worse than they had this morning. Even looking like the battered loser of an epic fight, he was still a sight for sore eyes.

I opened my mouth to tell him what happened, but instead of words coming out, a broken sob tore free and the next thing I knew I was being cradled against his massive chest as I cried so deeply it hurt my entire body.

Strong arms wrapped around me and over the top of my head I heard him growl, "What the fuck, Carl?"

The older man replied, "I forgot you lived on this floor, Solomon."

I heard Solo grunt as he gave me a soft squeeze. "I live next door, you idiot. I heard the commotion through the walls. What did you do to her? If you touched her, I'm going to break every single bone in your body." The super sputtered as Solo went on. "Then I'm going to wait until they all heal and break them again. I warned you months ago about harassing the female tenants. All you had to do was your damn job, Carl, and we wouldn't have an issue. How hard is keeping your hands to yourself? I don't know why people think I'm the type of guy who enjoys repeating himself."

"I own this building, Solo. Not you." It was all bluster, and I could hear the fear in the older man's voice.

The man holding me set me gently to the side, and after asking where my daughter was, he gestured to the apartment next to mine, and quietly ordered, "Go in there and wait for me."

I nodded, feeling numb and completely off-balance. I was a few steps down the hallway when I heard Solo tell the other man, "You own the building, but I'm the one who keeps the junkies and the drug dealers away from it. I'm the one who keeps the crime to a minimum. You get to charge more and keep this place one step above a tenement because I live here, so don't for one second think I don't know which one of us has the power. You can't threaten me, Carl, and we both know you're scared to death of me."

A moment later there was the sound of flesh on flesh, and a moan of pain. Part of me wanted to turn and watch Solo put the aggressive, handsy man in his place while he taught him some much-needed manners. But a bigger part of me wanted to find someplace quiet and safe so I could pull myself back together. It was becoming habit to let Solo take care of everything that seemed broken in my life. It was a bad habit I needed to shake, but right now, it felt too good having someone there to make sure I was all right. It was so nice to have someone to lean on for a change.

Especially when that someone was big, strong, and not afraid of anything. There was some level of comfort in knowing he wasn't likely to topple over, no matter how heavy the weight of my baggage.

Solo

This wasn't the first time I'd been forced to set Carl straight about using his position to manipulate the female tenants. He'd tried to pull the same garbage with both Carmen and Erica; they informed me of his ploy when I first moved in. There was also a different, very cute redhead who used to live down the hall that he used to constantly creep on. Luckily, Carmen and Erica could take care of themselves, and the redhead had an older brother who wouldn't put up with any of Carl's shit. An older brother who just happened to be my Boss's childhood friend. The redhead had hooked up with my Boss long before I went to work for him, and on occasion, he still griped about the shithole apartment where he'd found her. By the time I got to the landlord, he should have known to keep his hands to himself and that he wasn't going to get away with harassing every pretty girl who rented from him. Apparently, Orley's obvious lack of awareness and general softness had been too tempting for him to ignore.

I wrapped my fist in the front of his shirt and slammed him into the wall near Orley's front door. His balding head hit the drywall with a satisfying thud, and I grinned when I saw the small hole the impact created. My sore ribs were furious at the sudden movement, but it was so worth the sting of pain. I was still tired, but the rush of adrenaline pushing through my veins was better than a cup of coffee to bring me fully awake. I was still passed out on the couch when I heard the weird sounds coming from Orley's apartment, so it took me a few minutes longer than it should have to go investigate. I didn't think she was supposed to be home from work until later in the afternoon, and it never occurred to me Carl would haul his incompetent ass out on a Sunday to fix her AC, even after I bitched at him for a solid ten minutes when I called.

"Couldn't resist, could you, Carl? You just had to go and put your hands on the new girl." I slammed him into the wall again and curled my lip in disgust. The motion pulled at the cut bisecting my lower lip and added fuel to the fire of rage flickering under my skin.

The older man sneered at me and wrapped his hand around my wrist, trying to pry my hand free. I narrowed my eyes at him and shifted my weight, pushing him more fully against the wall as I closed my free hand around his throat. I felt him swallow and watched as beads of sweat popped up across his forehead as I started to slowly squeeze.

"She invited me in. We were alone. She should know the score if she's going to live here." The words were barely audible as he struggled to breathe.

"She should, but she doesn't, and you can see it from a mile away. You wanted to take advantage of her." I applied even more pressure and leaned so close that I knew the other man had to feel like he was being squashed like the bug he was. "I don't like that. I like the idea of you touching her, scaring her, even less." I released his shirt and buried my fist into his soft middle. I felt his grunt against my palm and grinned as I punched him again. He made a gagging sound behind my hand and his eyes started to water as I squeezed his throat even harder. The skin around my hold was starting redden and Carl was frantically clawing my fingers as he struggled for any scrap of air.

"I'm sick and tired of men like you giving the rest of us a bad name."

I let go of Carl's throat and took a step back as he bent over, gasping and choking to find his breath. While he was folded in half, I put a hand on the back of his head, pushing downward as my knee came up in a swift motion. It was a dirty move, but one I had no qualms about using on a bastard like Carl. There was a sickening crunch as the cartilage in his nose collapsed under the force of the blow. Blood immediately started to flow, decorating the floor between us a shiny crimson.

"Hands off, Carl. That applies to everyone who lives here and any woman unlucky enough to cross your path. I wasn't kidding about breaking every bone in your body, but more than that, if you don't get your head out of your ass, I'll move, and we both know that's about the worst thing I could do to you. It will be open season on this place as soon as I'm gone, and you'll lose all the reliable rent money you've gotten so used to collecting month to month." I crossed my arms over my chest and stared the man down as he straightened up, wiping his bloody face with the sleeve of his shirt.

"You're going to regret this, Solomon." The threat was weak and Carl's voice was shaky so I rolled my eyes. "You've gotten too comfortable. You forget that no one stays safe in this place for very long."

I didn't know if he was talking about the apartment complex or the city. It didn't matter. There was very little that scared me anymore, and Carl wasn't even a blip on my radar. "Doubtful. Do your job. That's it." I looked toward my apartment, wanting to check on Orley. Dealing with a crying woman was not in my wheelhouse, but for some reason, I was anxious to make sure she was okay. I was fully expecting her to pack her bags and run after her encounter with Carl. It was too close to her run-in with Skinner. I was sure she was feeling like the city was just as dangerous as she kept trying to convince me it was. I kept trying to prove to her that the people here weren't all bad, that only the streets could be dangerous, but now that evil had crossed her threshold, I'd be hard-pressed to get her to believe in what I was saying. Every time I made some headway, an idiot like my landlord pushed my proof back twenty steps.

I did know something that might entice her to stick around a little bit longer. I pointed a finger at Carl's shattered nose. "I think you need to knock off rent this month for Orley. It's the least you can do." I knew she was struggling financially. Having a month free would give her some room to breathe.

Carl wiggled his way along the wall until there was some distance between us. He had a hand cupped over his nose and his eyes were shooting flames of hatred in my direction. "Can't do that. The snotty bitch paid for the full year in advance. Figured she had a rich baby daddy fronting her the cash so he had a place to stash her from the wife. Why else would a classy piece of ass like that be slumming it here?"

That was a damn good question. She didn't have enough money to fix her car. She was waiting tables at a diner to pay her bills. She clearly wanted to be anywhere but in the city, so why was she here, and where had the money come from to pay for the apartment for an entire year? Not that the rent for a year was a windfall of money, but it was more than most of us had lying around. She was full of confusing contradictions, and it really got under my skin that I was curious about her. She was the last person I would expect to catch my attention, but here I was, wondering who Orley really was.

Carl made his escape while I was distracted by my thoughts. Once he was out of sight, I headed back to my apartment. Orley shut the door behind her when she ran for safety, so I found myself knocking on my own damn door so I didn't spook her before entering. Once I was inside, the smell of coffee assaulted my nose, so I followed the scent toward the tiny kitchen. I found Orley sitting on the old linoleum floor, knees pulled to her chest, back against the refrigerator. Next to her on the floor was one of the few knives I owned. It was dull as dirt, and rusted at the tip, but her hand hovered over it like it was a precious treasure that could save her from all the world's evils if she just believed hard enough.

I called her name as softly as I could. I didn't want to scare her. My heart jolted in my chest when she flinched and reached for the inadequate weapon. It took a full minute for the haze of panic in her eyes to clear. I watched her chest rise and fall as she tried to catch her breath. Instead of trying to get her up, I sat on the floor in front of her, cringing when I realized it had been a hot minute since I'd bothered to clean it.

"He's gone. He won't be back. If you need something from him from here on out, let me know and I'll deal with him. I'm sorry you keep running up against the worst the city has to offer." I kept my voice light and reassuring.

Orley blinked those huge blue eyes at me and I felt a tiny bit of my soul slip away. I could have sworn they were darker and cloudier than when we first met. The life she was living was changing her, turning her into someone who had shadows in her sky-blue eyes. It happened so fast and I felt terrible I wasn't able to stop it.

Orley made a sniffing sound and used the back of her hand to wipe away a stray tear that rolled down her pale cheek. "You've saved me twice. Three times if you count getting my car up and running."

"Just in the right place at the right time." It was my mantra where she was concerned. It sucked she needed saving in the first place, but I still maintained I was not her hero by choice.

"I don't even know your last name. Or that you lived next door. I don't have any idea what would have happened to me if you hadn't come along when you did, and you're a virtual stranger." She laughed, but it was a sad, painful sound. "What kind of person does that make me? Ungrateful? Rude? Selfish? Thankless? What kind of example am I setting for my daughter?"

I wasn't following her train of thought. I couldn't figure out why she would be upset about something as inconsequential as my last name after what she'd been through with Carl. I tilted my head to the side and told her, "Sanders. My last name is Sanders."

She let out a hiccupy little sigh as her head fell back against the fridge. "Solomon Sanders. Sounds very distinguished."

I laughed. "That's me. Distinguished down to the bone."

Slowly, she slid the knife across the floor in my direction. "Well, Solomon Sanders, I know I haven't been very good at showing my appreciation, but I am really glad you have a knack for showing up exactly when I need you the most. No one would believe me if I told them they need to come to the heart of this dirty, terrifying city to find an actual hero."

I grabbed the knife and climbed to my feet. "I'm not anyone's savior, Orley. Don't get that confused."

She sighed again and pushed herself up off the floor. "I'm not confused. I'm incredibly lucky." She sounded like she felt anything but lucky. "I want to do something nice for you. I have limited options, but if you want to come next door for dinner one night, Noble and I would love to have you." She waved a hand around my kitchen. "I may have noticed you don't keep much of anything edible on hand when I was looking for the coffee."

Guiltily, I glanced at the abandoned bag of tater tots on the couch. "I'm on the go a lot. I usually just grab something I can eat on the run. Plus, I can't cook." My mom was a great cook, though, or she had been at one point. I couldn't remember the last time I'd had a home-cooked meal. "Do you cook?" She was so young, it was hard to picture her slaving over a hot stove on the regular.

Orley nodded. "Sure. I mostly throw stuff together geared to the palate of a toddler, but I'm sure I can figure out something adult appropriate for one night. I really owe you more than I can ever repay. Being a good neighbor is the least I can do."

I did a mental rundown of my week trying to find a hole where I could fit her in. Not for the first time a wave of exhaustion washed over me when I realized how every hour of my days were packed. It shouldn't be nearly impossible to eke out a night for something as easy as dinner. Finally deciding I was just going to have to skip a training session or get up even earlier to work on school work, I told Orley I would be over on Wednesday night.

She nodded at me and took a step forward. I went to move out of the way so she could get out of the small space without feeling crowded, but she caught me completely off guard when she walked right up to me and wrapped her arms around my waist. I felt her soft breath against the base of my throat and her soft hair brush against the bottom of my chin. I reflexively put an arm around her shoulders and returned her embrace. If she tilted her head back just a little, there wasn't enough self-control in the world for me to keep my mouth off of hers. I would kiss the shit out of her, even though I knew it was the last thing she needed.

"I've never had anyone like you in my life, Solo. You terrify me." She hugged me hard enough I had to bite my tongue to keep the yelp of pain from my jacked-up ribs at bay.

"That street goes both ways, Orley. I've never met anyone like you either." I never thought I would to be honest.

She let me go and took a deep breath. She was halfway across the room when I realized something. "Hey, what about you? You never told me your last name."

She stopped by the door, her back to me. For a minute I thought she didn't hear me, but then she pulled the door open and called softly, "I'll see you on Wednesday night."

She slipped out the door without another word, leaving me with one more piece of a puzzle I was determined to put together. Figuring out my pretty neighbor was going to have to wait. I still needed to shower and drive out to see my mom. My obligations were never-ending and usually I liked being busy enough I didn't have to think about much of anything. Lately, I found myself resenting every minute that took my attention away from the mysterious redhead I couldn't stop thinking about.

11

Orley

Dinner.

It was something I managed every single night now that I had a more predictable schedule. I would sit with Noble and catch up on the day. She had a million stories to tell now that she was spending time with other kids again and had found a new idol in Riley. Adding Solo into the mix shouldn't have been a huge deal, it was just a friendly meal between neighbors, literally the least I could do, but for some reason, knowing he was going to be in my space, within the walls of my tattered sanctuary, turned me into a scattered mess of a human.

I was sticking with something simple and cheap. I planned on making something I knew both a toddler and a big guy like Solo would eat: spaghetti and meatballs. But somehow, I managed to scorch the sauce, burn half of the meatballs, and drop most of the noodles on the floor before I got them into the boiling water. My itty-bitty kitchen looked like a warzone, and I was fairly certain I'd somehow managed to get red sauce on the ceiling.

Noble thought the disaster was hilarious. She made picking up the noodles off the floor a game, making even more of a mess as they cracked and splintered into too many pieces to count. When I told her Solo was coming over to join us for dinner, her little face lit up and her blue eyes glimmered with obvious delight. My daughter was much more comfortable showing how much she liked our handsome neighbor than I was. She asked about the dark-haired man on a regular basis, wanting to know when she would see him again and asking if he would finally take her up on her challenge to race up and down the block. She'd caught sight of him jogging in the mornings a couple of times and was obsessed with the idea of being faster than him.

Ready to throw in the towel and order pizza or call the whole thing off, I took a second to breathe, put my hands on the counter next to the stove, and valiantly tried to pull my shit together. I helped Noble clean up the mess on the floor, and realized I could save most of the sauce if I changed pots and tossed in the remaining, non-burned meatballs. I boiled the noodles that didn't end up on the floor and let out a sigh of relief when it all came together at the last minute. I even splurged and bought stuff to make garlic bread, which I was pulling out of the oven when there was a knock on the door.

Noble let out a shriek of delight and bolted through the living room before I could stop her. Her little feet pounded on the floor as she ran for the door full-out, barely stopping as she reached for the knob.

"Hey! What did I tell you about answering the door without an adult in the room?" I dropped the hot pan in my hands on the counter and rounded the corner of the long breakfast bar in a rush. The door jerked open, bouncing against the chain at the top. Through the small space, I could see Solo's surprised expression. He was missing the well-worn baseball hat I'd grown accustomed to covering his dark hair, so there wasn't the usual shadow hiding his intriguing dark gaze.

The corner of his mouth kicked up in a slight grin as he looked down at the little girl bouncing up and down on her toes in front of him. "I think you're supposed to ask who it is before you pull the door open, little one."

Noble smiled up at him as she continued to tug on the door. "I'm not supposed to open the door at all. I got too excited. Mommy is mad."

I heard Solo chuckle. "I think you should listen to her so she doesn't get mad."

Noble's bottom lip stuck out in an exaggerated way as she moved away from the door in a huff. She turned her bright gaze up toward mine and offered a reluctant apology. "Sorry I answered the door without you, Mommy."

I reached over her head to slide the chain free and pulled her back with the other. "It's not safe to open the door without knowing who is on the other side. That's an important lesson for you to learn. If you don't get dessert tonight for not listening, then next time you'll remember to wait for me when someone is at the door."

I lifted my eyebrows at Solo, tilting my head toward the interior of the apartment so he would walk through the door. Noble proceeded to throw a fit at the threat of no dessert. So far this was turning out to be the opposite of the simple dinner I'd planned.

I tried to calm my daughter down and pointed Solo in the direction of the kitchenette. "There's stuff in the fridge if you want to get yourself a drink. I don't have anything fun. I think orange juice is probably the hardest thing I keep stocked."

He nodded in understanding and gave me a little wink. "It smells pretty good in here."

Noble stopped wailing about getting dessert long enough to rat me out. "Mommy made a mess. I had to help clean it up."

I sighed and rolled my eyes at the back of my daughter's head. "That was supposed to be our secret."

Solo laughed, and I tried not to stare at the way the expression turned his face from harshly handsome to outright breathtaking. He didn't smile or laugh nearly enough. I was suddenly thankful for his serious nature. There was a solid chance I would have tried to climb him like a tree if he was flashing that deadly grin in my direction all the time. I lost all sense of reason and reserve when I was around him.

"It wasn't much of a secret. These walls are as thick as tissue paper. I heard something fall and smelled something burning through the vents. I honestly expected pizza, which I would've been okay with. I know you've been working a lot. You didn't have to go to any extra trouble for me." He gave Noble the same wink he offered me and the way she giggled sent my heart tumbling. It felt like it had been years since she'd had the freedom to be the carefree, lighthearted little girl she'd been before I'd bolted with her in the middle of the night. If I hadn't wanted to kiss him for any variety of reasons before, I wanted to lay one on him right now for the ability he had to make my kid laugh.

"Mommy fixed it. She always fixes everything." Noble grabbed Solo's much bigger, tattooed hand and proceeded to tug him toward the living room so she could show off her variety of toys and whatever new dance moves Riley had been teaching her.

He went without complaint and I felt like I was caught in a trance watching my daughter giggle and prance around the huge, tattooed man in my living room. Noble had never been around a good man before. Her father wanted nothing to do with her. We were both foolish teenagers taking risks we shouldn't have and tried to prove a useless point when she was conceived. He was acting out, desperately trying to win approval for something. I was caught in a downward spiral, constantly searching for attention and any kind of reaction from my father. When I found out I was pregnant, Noble's father couldn't bail fast enough. She was not part of his plan at all. In fact, she was the opposite of whatever it was he was trying to accomplish. He shoved money at me, demanding I get rid of the 'mistake.' When I refused, he convinced his family to send him away to a fancy boarding school in Europe before the truth came out. It didn't take a genius to figure out my baby and I would be better off without him.

Then there was my father.

The man never had time for me, never acted like I existed. He looked through me like I was made of glass. I was used to his indifference. I lived my life being invisible in his house no matter how much I acted out or silently screamed for approval. I had no idea how to react when Noble came along and my father started showing an unexplained, intense interest in her. All the love and affection I'd been starved of as a child, my father heaped upon my curly-haired baby. He treated her like a princess, called her his 'precious little doll,' and finally acted like the father I'd dreamed of having myself. I didn't know his actions were a purposeful attack on both me and my mother, that he had ulterior motives I would never have been able to see coming. I didn't know he was using my child as a pawn to drive my mother over the edge of the mental cliff to which she'd been precariously clinging. I was so in the dark about things that when the truth came to light, it was blinding. I was so happy he'd finally come around, I hadn't even questioned his actions until it was almost too late.

Then there was Mr. Sanchez. Sure, he wasn't as bad as the rest, but he was still a man in my daughter's life who judged her and found her lacking simply because she wasn't from the same place he was. It seemed so unfair to decide a child was unworthy of acceptance when they weren't in control of their circumstances. Sure, Noble had come from a lot when we first showed up, but now she had next to nothing and it totally sucked that her former babysitter's husband was cruel and prejudiced enough to take even more away from her.

But not Solo.

Nope. Solomon Sanders, with all his tough guy attitude and dangerous swagger, sat down on my living room floor and played with my daughter like she was the single best thing in his entire day. He smiled with her, laughed at her silly antics, and promised her they would have a foot race when the weather cooled down. He played with whatever doll she handed him, no matter how frilly, and he didn't blink an eye when Noble eventually crawled into his lap and started tracing the colorful tattoos that snaked up and down his strong arms. He patiently described what each image was and why he'd permanently etched them into his skin. Noble was extremely proud of herself when she recognized MOM in a scrolling banner suspended between the beaks of two birds on his bicep.

"You got an owie." I glanced over from where I was setting the last of our dinner on the breakfast bar and watched as Noble patted Solo's cheek and lifted her tiny fingers to touch the ugly bruise around his eye. The swelling had gone down, and most of the blue and purple had lightened. Now there was a yellowish tinge to the injury which almost got lost as it blended with his naturally bronze complexion.

I was so glad he didn't wear his hat. When Noble used his broad shoulders for leverage so she could touch her lips to the slightly discolored area, Solo's dark eyes melted like sweet chocolate candy. It did something to my insides watching such a big, strong guy go soft over the innocent, childish affection. Clearly Solo hadn't let enough people in his life take care of his owies for him. Suddenly, I found myself blinking back tears and clearing my throat which was clogged with a rush of emotion.

"We can eat if you're ready." I waved a hand at the food on the breakfast bar. "We'll have to sit on the couch and eat on the coffee table." I didn't trust the shaky, dining room table that came with the apartment. I'd already picked up dinner off the floor once tonight.

Wordlessly Solo climbed to his feet, Noble hanging from around his neck like a little monkey. She squealed and demanded I look how high off the ground she was. I smiled, a real one. The first genuine one that'd crossed my face in a very long time. I'd almost forgotten how it felt to relax enough to enjoy such a simple moment.

I handed out plates and helped Noble find a place where she was least likely to make a mess. She blinked those big baby blues of hers at me and asked if she finished all her dinner if I would reconsider dessert. I told her we would see after she was done eating. Solo jumped in and told her their race would be called off if she didn't take my rules seriously.

Noble nodded solemnly and then launched into a story about how Riley and a couple of the other kids Erica watched during the day were trying to teach her how to play soccer. It was the babbling, rambling nonsense of an almost-four-year-old, but it was lovely compared to the threats from the landlord and the arguments from the apartment on the other side of the wall.

Thinking about the thin walls, I cocked my head and looked at Solo through narrowed eyes. "You heard me drop everything in the kitchen earlier? Do we bother you coming and going?" Noble wasn't exactly quiet, and when I had enough money to buy the cowboy boots she coveted, she was going to be even louder.

Solo shook his head as he slurped at a saucy noodle. "Naw. No way you guys could be as loud as the couple on the other side of me. For a long time, I wondered if anyone had actually moved in when I heard this apartment was rented. I'm so busy, when I crash, I tend to be dead to the world." Something flashed in his gaze and I realized it was an apology. He still wasn't over the fact that he'd shown up after that creepy landlord had me cornered.

I tried to indicate none of it had been his fault with my eyes. That wasn't a conversation we were going to have in front of my kid. I changed the subject after taking a bite of the buttery garlic bread.

"So, you've lived in the city your entire life? You've never wanted to go anywhere else?" The sauce on the pasta had just the right amount of bite, and the little chunks of meatball were juicy and savory in all the best ways. Not bad for what started out as an utter disaster.

Solo's jet-black eyebrows arched as he lifted a shoulder and let it fall. "My mom is here. My job is here. My friends are here."

I lifted an eyebrow in return. "So, your future is here?"

He sighed and looked away. "When I was younger, I always imagined I'd leave. I had those dreams, the ones where I left and magically went off and found fame and fortune somewhere else. I was going to buy my mom a mansion on a hill somewhere far away from the city and make sure she never had to work another day of her life. Things didn't really work out that way, but do they ever? When you grow up, you get different dreams, make different goals for yourself, and so far, I've been able to do everything I set out to do, even if it's in a place I always thought I would leave behind."

"You no longer want to buy your mom a mansion on a hill?" I thought I was being funny, but I saw his expression change, shutters came down in his eyes, and the way his big body stiffened gave me pause. Clearly, I'd unwittingly walked into a very touchy subject for him.

"My mother was shot in the head during a carjacking when I was a teenager. She was at her weekend job, one she picked up for some extra cash. She always had at least two, if not three jobs when I was growing up. She made sure I never went without and I didn't realize how much she sacrificed for me until it was my turn to take care of her."

I gasped and looked over at Noble. The conversation had taken a turn not exactly appropriate for a child, and luckily, she was focused on her food and humming a song under her breath.

I cleared my throat and lowered my voice so only Solo could hear me. "I'm so sorry. That's all horrible and I hate you went through it when you were just a child. That must have been so hard."

He shrugged. "She survived. I still have my mom, and that's all that matters. After therapy and rehab she was able to leave the hospital. I brought her here for the first year, but realized pretty quickly she needed more care than I could provide. The bullet damaged her brain, so she has violent mood swings, and often forgets where she is and who the people around her are. She tried to set the apartment on fire once while I was at work, and she came after me with a knife one night when I was late getting home from a date. It was better for her to be in a facility that could monitor and take care of her needs twenty-four hours a day. I visit her as often as I can."

I pushed the end of my ponytail over my shoulder and looked at him from under my lashes. It made my heart soften when I realized he was a caretaker through and through. "So now you work a lot of jobs and push yourself to the limit so you can take care of her the way she always took care of you. That's very sweet, and honestly, admirable. You're a good man, Solo." I was an idiot for thinking he wasn't my type because he looked so different from the polished, boring men I was used to. His loyalty and dedication to the woman who gave him all she had was commendable and explained why he was so good at looking out for everyone else, even when he claimed he was no hero.

"I'll take care of you, Mommy. Don't be sad." Both Solo and I jerked our attention back to our smallest dinner companion. I hated myself a little for almost forgetting Noble was there. Solo's presence was too distracting. Once again, I realized how quickly I could get in over my head with this man.

"Thank you, baby. I appreciate that. But let's hope you don't have to worry about taking care of anyone for a very long time." I pointed at the last few bites of food on her plate and told her to finish up.

Solo cocked his head to the side and asked, "What about you? How did you end up here? That's bound to be an interesting story. They always are."

He had no idea. I was opening my mouth to give him the short, sanitized version when Noble piped up with the last thing I wanted him to know. "We ran away from home. It's a secret 'cause Grandpa's not nice."

I jumped to my feet, taking the empty plates in front of everyone with me. I told Noble to hold on a second and I would get her a small scoop of chocolate ice cream for dessert. Solo shook his head and gave me a questioning look when I asked him if he wanted any. Once my daughter was settled with her treat in front of my laptop watching *Adventure Time,* I walked Solo to the door. I wasn't kicking him out exactly, but I was definitely trying to get him gone before he could ask any questions I couldn't—or wouldn't—answer.

Once he was in the hallway, he reached up above my head and put his hands on the top of the door frame. The move stretched his tall body and made all his muscles flex and ripple enticingly. He was so much bigger than me, but for some reason, I wasn't afraid of him in the least. I wanted to reach out and touch him. He was far too tempting for my peace of mind.

"I figured you were on the run from something. Figured it was your baby daddy. I'm right next door if you want to talk about it, Orley."

I shook my head and nervously tugged on my lower lip. "The less you know, the better. No one is going to come looking for us here, and that's all that matters. Thanks for being so great with Noble. She adores you and there haven't been very many examples of good men in her life to warrant her affection. Another thing I owe you I'll never be able to repay."

Something dangerous flashed in his dark eyes and his head lowered a fraction closer to mine. "I've been thinking about that a lot lately."

"About what?" I could feel the heat coming off of him and smell the spicy, fresh scent of his skin.

"A way for you to repay me. You have something I want."

I snorted and tilted my head back so I could meet the darkness swirling in his unreadable gaze. "My recipe for spaghetti and meat sauce?"

His lips quirked and his head shook slightly. "No. I want a kiss, just a taste. I know it's stupid and I've been trying to talk myself out of it for weeks. I can't shake the curiosity. I keep wondering if kissing you is going to feel forbidden because you don't belong in my world, or if it's going to feel like coming home. Something about you and that kid of yours always manages to get terrifyingly close to my heart, Orley. I'm still trying to figure out how you worked your way in so easily."

I walked right through the door he opened the minute he saved me from the scary drug dealer. He protected me and Noble when no one else in our lives had ever bothered. I couldn't see any of the bright red warning signs after that. I was choosing to ignore the ones lit up in front of me right now, as well.

Putting a hand on his shoulder, I lifted up on my toes just a little so my mouth was level with his. I liked the way his strength and bulk seemed to completely surround me. It was like standing behind an intricately decorated shield of protection, except this line of defense came with a heartbeat and a soul.

When my lips touched his, I wasn't sure what to expect. When I imagined this moment as I laid alone in my bed in the dark, it was rough, brutal. I was quickly overwhelmed and afraid of how easily I would give into his every want and whim. Reality was light years different. Solo kissed with slow, thorough precision. Moving carefully, as if he sensed I was ready to bolt.

Not away from him, but from the rush of feelings he unlocked inside of me. His lips moved across mine with steady intent, coaxing small responses until my mouth opened on a gasp. One of his hands left the ledge above my head and landed on the side of my neck. His warm palm encircled the soft skin, and I could feel my pulse fluttering against his sure hold. His thumb skimmed the line of my jaw, applying just enough pressure to tilt my head back so he could seduce me with the slide of his tongue and the bite of his teeth from another angle.

The kiss scrambled my brain and turned my knees weak. I could hear my heart thundering in my ears and feel the rest of my body reacting to his gentle touch. I was caught completely under his spell, malleable in his hands. I'd never felt this way with anyone before. Not that my previous partners had been mature or considerate enough to take the time to worry about how their touch affected me. My reactions seemed to be the only thing Solo was thinking about. When I moaned softly against his mouth, he made sure to repeat whatever he'd just done to draw the sound out of me again. When I shifted closer, he focused on giving me more of whatever it was that lured me in. It was a dance, and I was blindly following his lead. He had way better moves and far more rhythm than I did.

His tongue twisted around mine and then slicked across the curve of my lower lip. It was still tingling from where I tugged on it when I was nervous. I felt him trying to kiss the owie away, just like Noble had done to him. The gesture was so sweet, so thoughtful, I practically fell into his chest as I surged closer, throwing my arms around his neck in a virtual chokehold. I rested my forehead against the hollow at the base of his tattooed throat and momentarily wondered if ending up in the city was the best or worst thing to ever happen to me.

"Mommy!" Noble's shrill voice broke us apart and left me blinking up at him like an owl. "I want more ice cream."

I took a second to catch my breath and lifted shaking fingers to my lips. "Of course she does." And for once, I could actually accommodate her. It was nice to be able to indulge my kid every once in a while and not worry that ice cream meant my cell phone was getting turned off.

Solo chuckled and fell back a step. He reached out a hand and tugged on the fiery ends of my hair. "You taste sweet and expensive, like really good brandy. The kind you savor all night long."

I barked out a little laugh. "You taste like the best bad idea." And a whole lot of fun, but he didn't need to know that.

"Thanks for dinner. One day you're going to trust me enough to tell me what your monsters look like." He turned to walk back to his apartment and I couldn't tear my eyes away from his retreating figure.

I heaved a sigh and quietly shut my front door. I knew enough about the man next door to understand they would become his monsters, too, as soon as he understood the lengths they would go to in order to keep me and Noble quiet. He already had enough to deal with without taking up my battles as well. It had nothing to do with trust and everything to do with the way my heart couldn't tell which way was up when I was around him.

I wanted to keep him safe almost as much as I wanted to believe he could keep me and Noble from harm.

It was all a convoluted, dangerous mess, but for the first time since I'd crash landed in the city I refused to call home, I couldn't imagine being anywhere else.

Solo

Sleep was elusive the night after I kissed my luscious neighbor. I knew it was a bad idea, knew the fallout would most likely destroy me, but I couldn't resist. It was like someone handed me the keys to a luxury car I could never afford and offered me a test drive. There was no way I was ever going to turn down a chance to see just how fast the high-performance vehicle could go, how well it responded, how sweet it handled when I had my hands on it. In my normal day to day, girls like Orley were not placed in my path. They typically went out of their way to avoid guys like me. But every time I turned around, I seemed to be running toward the uptight redhead and catching her as she fell right into my arms. I was done fighting the curious attraction I couldn't seem to shake.

I could still taste her on my tongue. A lot sweet, a little smoky, and all tentative excitement. She kissed me back like she was afraid of what would happen if she let go of all the rigid control she valiantly tried to cling to whenever we were together. I wasn't the one who scared her; she was terrified of herself and the way she reacted to me. Knowing I got to her on such a deep, inescapable level did more than make my dick painfully hard. It touched something deep inside of me: a primitive, raw place I didn't even know I had. One that swelled with pride and pounded with the need to protect and claim. I'd always avoided any kind of commitment in the past, knowing I didn't have enough left over at the end of the day to give to someone else, but there was something about Orley and her adorable little girl. I couldn't help but want to find a way to fit them into my crowded life.

Temperatures in the city were still stifling. It was unbearably hot, so I went to bed naked, not that I normally bothered to put anything on before crashing. Modesty was silly when you lived alone. During the night I kicked off the covers and woke from a restless dream with my hand wrapped around my hard, aching cock. I couldn't remember dream I'd been caught up in, but I remembered red hair and bewildered blue eyes. For someone who had a child and obviously had some shit they were dealing with in their life, Orley was shockingly innocent in her reactions. It was almost as if she'd gone straight from first kiss to motherhood without pausing at all the spots along the way that showed newly sexually active teens how much fun and trouble they could get into with their bodies as they figured out what they liked. She was innocent and untried in a way that was completely addictive and totally alluring. It was impossible to walk away from the challenge of showing her just how good things could be between two people who had the kind of scorching chemistry we did.

I squeezed my dick as I felt pleasure coil around the base of my spine. I kicked at the tangled covers and let images of long, fiery hair and pale, smooth skin dance behind my eyelids. I felt my heart rate speed up and sucked in a breath as a slick layer of sweat beaded on my chest and trickled down the side of my neck. I remembered the way Orley's lips felt pressed so softly against mine, so soft and supple. I got lost in the phantom touch of her hands sliding across my shoulders and chest. I dived into the fantasy of how hot and slick she would feel wrapped around me. My palm skimmed over the wet head of my dick, slipping through the moisture pooled at the slit, the warmth a poor substitute for the woman I couldn't stop thinking about.

I tightened my hold, a grunt escaping as my orgasm slowly spiraled outward, electrifying my limbs and shooting bolts of pleasure through my blood. I swore as lazy satisfaction tugged at every inch of my body. It was a good orgasm. One that would've been better shared between the dampened skin of the girl next door, but I wasn't going to complain about the sudden release of tension or the sleepy passion that still sizzled in my veins. Grunting, I pushed out of the bed, intent on making my way to the bathroom to clean up so I could grab a few more hours of sleep. I stopped not even a step away from the bed when I heard a quiet moan filter through the wall.

My eyes widened in shock and my cock tried to rally like a champ when another quiet, delicate sound of pleasure made its way through the annoyingly thin barrier. I couldn't tell if Orley was still asleep or not, and I briefly wondered if my own unchecked sounds had triggered hers. It was sexy as hell, and way more fun than listening to the crazy couple on the other side fight and fuck. There was another light gasp, followed by a sweet moan, and finally a long breathy sigh I could practically feel touching my damp skin.

I wanted to be close enough to taste the noises Orley was making as she dreamed of me while she was sleeping. I didn't even stop to question that whomever was giving her pleasure in the middle of the night was me. I knew it without her saying my name. Those sounds, that pleasure, the girl... they were all mine, even if she didn't fully understand it yet.

When I got back from the bathroom, everything was quiet and still once again. I tried to fall back asleep knowing I had a full day of work, a training session at the gym, and a solid two to three hours of coursework to complete later in the day, but rest was elusive. Instead, I stared up at the dark ceiling imagining what I'd done to Orley in her dreams to draw those sounds out of her. I was anxiously awaiting the day when I would get to put my hands on her and try to make her whisper them against my skin. The possibilities she inspired were endless.

The next day at work dragged. I usually loved joking around with the guys and learning whatever I could from the Boss. I liked being up to my elbows in grease and rusty old engine parts. Today, I couldn't seem to put anything back together the way it was supposed to go and I'd knocked my head on the elevated hood three times. When I saw the Boss coming my way out of the corner of my eye, I figured he was going to chew my ass for the less-than-stellar work I was cranking out today, but he surprised me when he asked me to come with him back into his office. The man was hard to read. His eyes were darker than mine. He'd had a lifetime to call this city home, and he fought to keep it from burning to the ground and keep the people he loved safe. It had hardened him in a way I never hoped to be. I didn't want to be stone, unbreakable and cold, but I appreciated those qualities in the man I looked up to more than anyone else.

The older man flicked his fingers in the direction of my face and lifted a black eyebrow. The star tattooed near his eye twitched and I tried not to cringe when he asked, "Why did you lose your last fight?" I was, for all intents and purposes, his protégé. When I lost, when I failed, it was a reflection on him. I never wanted this man to regret giving me a chance to make a better life for myself and provide the means to take care of my mother.

I lifted a hand and fingered the healing bruise. "Guy was better than me, I guess. It doesn't happen often, but it does happen."

The Boss opened the small fridge he had tucked away in a corner and offered me a bottle of water. "It doesn't happen. Because no one is better than you, kid. Not even me."

I cranked the lid off the bottle and swallowed down the cool liquid. I told myself not to blush at the praise. "You're the best."

The Boss snorted and propped a hip on his desk. "I was, but then you came along. I wouldn't waste my time on anyone who wasn't the best. Not when it comes to cars, and not when it comes to a fight. You wanna know what I think?"

I did, but I also kind of already knew what he was going to say. The man didn't pull any punches and his honesty was brutal most days.

"You've got too much going on, kid. All those distractions and responsibilities are going to get you killed if you aren't careful. This place, your mom, the fights, and on top of all of that, there's the pretty redhead you brought into my shop. You're drowning."

I crushed the empty water bottle in my hand and jerked my eyes away from his penetrating dark gaze. "I've got it all under control."

It was the first time I'd ever lied to him and I felt like shit the minute the words left my mouth.

He sighed, reached out, and clapped a strong, rough hand on my shoulder. "We never have control of anything in this city. You're smart enough to realize the truth of that. I think you're also smart enough to recognize when someone comes along who needs you more than the things you already decided were the most important things in your life. If you get hurt because you're spread so goddamn thin, who's going to watch out for the people who need you most?"

I bristled at the implication I was failing in any way. "This was a one off. You know I win more than I lose."

"All it takes is one bad fight, kid, and then it's not only you who ends up losing." He sounded like he knew that first hand. I hated that he was speaking from experience. I tended to think of him as indestructible. I didn't like the reminder he was a fallible human just like me.

I sighed and rubbed a hand across the back of my neck. "I don't really have a place where I can cut ties right now. Everything I'm mixed up with is kind of impossible to walk away from."

The Boss nodded and crossed his arms over his massive chest. "I remember that hamster wheel. Running and running but the view never changing. Which is the only reason I'm about to put this offer on the table." He tilted his chin up and narrowed his eyes at me. "Our mutual friend was approached by some rich assholes with too much money and a thirst for blood. They want him to set up a private fight. One of their guys against one of ours. It's a private event, closed to the usual scavengers. It's going to be a blood sport for bored billionaires. The payout if you win would be enough to keep your mom comfortable in that facility for the next couple of years. You could finish school, get a legit job working on cars, and stop running yourself into the ground." He shrugged. "You know how things work. If you agree, you go in on your own. No rules. No regulations. No escape if it goes wrong, and the bastard in charge still takes a cut."

My breath whooshed out in a rush and I felt slightly lightheaded. That was a lot of money. It would be a huge weight off my shoulders if I could secure enough funding to keep my mother in the private facility long enough to finish the certification I needed.

"Sounds like there should be a catch." Nothing in my life was ever that easy.

The Boss nodded slightly, dark eyes narrowing. "The man in charge didn't get a good feel from the men who approached him. He mentioned the whole thing felt off. He's a piece of shit, but no one in this place has better instincts or can read a room the way the Devil can. If he doesn't trust these guys, then I don't either. But I have seen the way you're struggling, so I couldn't tell him no on your behalf. Typically, I trust you to keep yourself safe no matter what the situation may be."

Surprisingly, I wanted to say no. I remembered Noble's precious kiss on my black eye, telling me she would make my owie all better. I didn't want her worried about my battered face and broken body. She was too young to already be taking care of the adults around her.

Sadly, the truth of the situation was simple, I couldn't afford to say no. It didn't matter how many reservations I, or anyone else, had about the situation. "Tell the Devil I'll do it. I promise to go in with my eyes open and to be extra cautious."

The Boss sighed, because he knew what my answer was going to be. "I'm going to tell that idiot if he lets you die on his watch we're going to have a major problem. I don't like this, kid, but I'm not surprised at the way it's playing out. You be careful, you hear me?"

I nodded and turned toward the door. I stopped in surprise when my phone started ringing from my back pocket. The thing was quiet during the day while I was working, so I had a moment of panic that something had happened to my mother. I didn't recognize the number as I slid my finger across the screen to answer the call.

"Hello?" I sounded far harsher than I meant to.

"Solo?" I stopped with my hand on the door to the interior of the garage at the sound of Orley's voice.

"Yeah, it's me. What's up?" I didn't ask how she got my number, figuring if she'd gone to the trouble of tracking it down, whatever she needed must be pretty important.

"I need to ask a huge favor." She sounded nervous and a little like she wanted to throw up, which made me chuckle.

"Shoot."

She sighed and I heard a thump like she was banging her forehead on something hard. "I'm supposed to pick up Noble from Erica's in an hour. She's got something going on tonight and needs all the kids gone by three thirty. My boss just asked me to pick up a private party. The gratuity on the bill would be enough to keep the lights on this month so I hate to say no. Is there any way I can convince you to watch my kid for an hour or so? Don't feel like you have to say yes, but I had to ask."

I froze for a second and then felt a smile spreading across my face. Last night I told her she was going to learn to trust me with her monsters; instead, she was trusting me with her heart, the most precious thing in her life. It meant so much more. I wondered if Orley even knew how significant this small moment was between the two of us.

"Gotta check with the Boss, but I'm sure I can skip out of here a little bit early." I had no idea what I was supposed to do with a toddler, but Noble seemed like she was easy enough to entertain. She liked to run around and burn out all of her childish energy, so maybe I'd take her outside and give her that race she was always angling for. If all else failed, I figured we could sit down and watch *Star Wars* together. I hadn't seen the originals in a very long time.

"I'm so sorry. I know I'm always asking you for stuff but I just don't trust anyone else to keep an eye on her." she sighed again. "I honestly don't know what I'd do without you."

I glanced over my shoulder and noticed the Boss was watching me with a knowing grin stamped across his hard face. He lifted his chin and pointed at the door. "Beat it. Not like you're getting anything done in here today as it is." I nodded and turned back to the door, only to stop short when his deep voice quietly reminded me, "Keep in mind what you're fighting for in the future whenever you step inside that circle. It'll keep you sharp and more on your game than any amount of training you've ever gotten."

A shiver slid down my spine as I slipped out the door, assuring Orley we would be okay and that I wouldn't let anything happen to her daughter while she was in my care... or ever, if I had my way.

Orley

The party turned out to be a big group of restaurant campers. After dessert, coffee, and paying the bill, they stuck around for at least an extra hour. I was beyond late when I scrambled home to get Noble from Solo. I'd called him twice to let him know I was held up. Each time he assured me my kid was still breathing and they were fine. He even promised to get her fed when it became clear I wasn't going to get out of the restaurant until after the sun went down. He didn't sound annoyed at having a toddler around, even though he was the busiest man I'd ever met. He didn't seem bothered by the fact I kept asking for more from him every time we turned around. He came across as completely unfazed that I trusted him enough to watch the most precious thing in the world to me, even though we hardly knew each other. After that kiss in the hallway, our dynamic had shifted. I wasn't sure how to define what we were doing, or who Solo was to me, but I knew he was much more than a friendly neighbor.

Fortunately, the party compensated me well for the extra time spent waiting for them to leave. The tip they left meant I could get Noble her cake and cookies for weeks, and I wouldn't have to worry about running out of gas any time soon. It was such a relief to finally feel like I was starting to get my head above water. I was finally starting to make things work out, even if it was in an impossible place, and for the first time in a long time I didn't feel like a failure. I didn't feel like I was letting my daughter down.

I practically ran up the stairs and down the hallway to Solo's apartment. I was going to pound on the door and free him from his babysitting responsibility when I realized it was far later than expected and well after dinner time. There was a good chance Noble had fallen asleep, regardless of how entertaining her company was. Not wanting to wake her if she was down for the night, I tapped lightly on the door and tried in vain to fix my disheveled appearance.

I wrinkled my nose at a mysterious white smear on my black pants and groaned when I saw some kind of sauce stain decorating the front of my shirt. Before I could swipe at either, the door swung open and was filled with a shirtless Solo. I blinked at the expanse of toned, tattooed skin in front of me and had to force myself to remember to breathe. He had his baseball hat on, a low-slung pair of black athletic shorts... and not much else. The sight of him made my mouth go dry and had me forgetting the reason I was at his door in the first place.

"You smell like French fries." There was humor laced through his deep voice, but the reminder I was an actual mess slammed the brakes on the surge of lust rising from my belly.

I blinked and shrugged a shoulder in an effort to appear nonchalant. "Hazard of the job. I didn't want to wake Noble up if she was sleeping. It's pretty close to her bedtime. I'm so sorry I'm so late. It was chaos." Seriously. It was starting to get to the point where I couldn't remember what it was like not to have anyone in my corner to rely on. I was starting to forget that hollow, empty feeling of always being alone.

"We had fun. Noble is a riot and she's easy to entertain. We had chicken nuggets for dinner and she watched cartoons while I hammered out a couple of assignments on the computer. She passed out about an hour ago, so I moved her from the couch to my bed. I think I wore her out. I took her to the park so she could swing, and then we went to my old high school so I could race her around the track. I let her win, but don't tell her that. The school has a program for kids who don't have a great place to go after class, so I took Noble to one of the art rooms and let her play around with finger paints for a while. We made a mess, but she had a good time." He chuckled and crossed his arms over his bare chest, making his tattooed skin flex and firm in an enticing way. I couldn't pull my gaze away if I wanted to. Not that I did. He was beautiful. He was his own kind of art. "A couple of my old teachers congratulated me on becoming a father. I think I broke their hearts when I told them she wasn't mine."

A pang struck the center of my chest at the thought of Noble being his. If she were his, that would mean I was his as well. No matter how different we were, I couldn't deny something inside of me adored the idea of being claimed by someone as good, as protective, as strong, and as sure as Solo.

"Well, let me grab her and we'll both get out of your hair for the rest of the night. I'm sure you're busy." He always was. "How about another dinner to repay you?" And maybe another kiss? But I would never be confident enough to throw such an offer out there.

One of his dark eyebrows shot upward and his unreadable gaze skated over my thoroughly disheveled form. "How about you go take a shower and relax for five minutes. You can come collect your kid when you don't smell like a fast food restaurant. And I'm not interested in repayment. What I want from you is honesty. If you want to give me something, come back with the truth. I want to know how you managed to pay for a full year's worth of rent when you could barely afford your phone bill a few weeks ago."

My first instinct was to shove past him, grab my kid, and shut the door on what he was asking of me. The truth was the one thing I didn't think I could give to anyone. Not if I wanted to stay alive and keep my kid out of the hands of monsters. But the weight of everything I was holding onto had started to take its toll, and I was exhausted from carrying it all alone. Maybe if I handed some of it off to someone strong enough to shoulder it, I would stop feeling like I was being crushed.

Slowly, I nodded in agreement. "Fine. Let me go shower and I'll be back over in a few minutes."

Solo grinned in satisfaction at his win. "Did you eat at work? If not, I can probably find something and have it ready for you by the time you come back."

Dear Lord, could he get any better? When was the last time I'd had anyone not only offer me five minutes to myself, but also care for me in the most basic of ways? Swallowing the sudden lump in my throat, I croaked out, "I ate between shifts. I'm good. I'll be right back." I bolted for my own apartment before I threw myself at him and begged him to keep me and never let me go.

I thoroughly enjoyed my shower. Well, as much as I could in the cramped space with terrible water pressure. Usually I was so preoccupied worrying about Noble, I rushed through the few minutes a day I was alone with my thoughts. Not tonight. Tonight, she was safe and sound under the watchful of eye of someone who would burn the world to ash if anyone or anything tried to harm her. If I was certain of one thing about Solo, it was that.

I took my time washing my hair. I shaved my legs and any other part of me which needed to be groomed. I used a liberal amount of body wash and scrubbed myself down until every single part of me felt spotless and smooth. It was a simple luxury, but one I'd missed out on for far too long.

When I got out of the shower, I threw on a stretchy black tank and a pair of yoga pants, figuring I was headed right to bed as soon as I collected my kid and finished the heart to heart with Solo. Plus, he'd already seen me covered in restaurant castoffs looking like something the cat dragged in. At least I smelled like orange blossoms now and not fries.

I tapped on the door again and was immediately ushered inside. The apartment was dim, Solo had a beer in his hand and offered to grab me one from the fridge. Figuring I might need the liquid courage, I accepted as I made my way to the massive couch which filled his living room. His laptop was open on the coffee table and *SpongeBob Squarepants* was playing without the sound on his huge, flat screen TV. The sight made me smile and I realized how lucky Noble and I were to end up in this really bad place inhabited by some really great people. Maybe it was true. Once you hit rock bottom, the only way to go was up.

I took the cold beer and clasped it between my hands. Solo situated himself next to me on the couch, one arm thrown over the back as he turned sideways so he was looking directly at me. Part of me wanted to ask him to put a shirt on so I could get through the little I could tell him without distraction, but a way bigger part of me was enjoying the view too much to say anything.

I looked down at the drink in my hand, then up at the man sitting across from me. "It's weird that I'm old enough to be someone's mother, but not old enough to drink this beer legally." I sighed. "Most of the time I feel like I skipped right over being a teenager."

Solo nodded and took a swig of his drink. "Most of us who grew up in the city feel that way. We never really got a chance to experience being young and carefree. We're born on the defense and ready to fight."

I sighed and leaned my head back against the cushion of the couch. "Oh, I had it pretty good when I was growing up. Both my parents come from money so

I didn't really want for anything." Aside from basic love and affection. I'd been spoiled and bratty enough not to care too much about the absence of either of those things until I realized I was going to be the one responsible for providing them for a new, fragile life. "I had a really nice car, a gift from my mother for my sixteenth birthday. When I had to leave where I used to live, I sold it. I used the cash from the sale to make sure Noble and I would have a roof over our heads for a year. I figured shelter was the most pressing need I had to cover."

I could see a million questions shooting through his dark eyes, but the only one he asked was, "What kind of car did you sell?"

Considering he was a car guy, it shouldn't have surprised me, but it did. "Uh, a Jaguar F-TYPE." It was a far cry from the beater I was driving now.

His eyes widened and he nearly choked on a mouthful of beer. "That's a sixty-thousand-dollar car, Orley. I've never even seen one in person. A year's worth of rent in this dump is barely thirteen thousand. Why are you living like a pauper?"

I sucked in a breath through my teeth and squeezed the chilly bottle between my palms. "I didn't sell it for what it was worth. I took the best cash offer I got. I paid for this apartment for a year, set some emergency money aside, and the rest..." I sighed and closed my eyes. "I paid off Noble's father. I knew he was going to be the weak link, the only tie that would keep me tethered to our old life. I bribed him to sign away his parental rights, and since he's gallivanting around Europe, acting like he doesn't care about a damn thing, he took the money and ran." I didn't regret getting him out of the way in the slightest, even if keeping some of the money would have made things easier for me and Noble along the way. My daughter was mine and mine alone. No one was ever going to have any kind of claim on her. I was never going to lose her. "That's where the money came from. That's how I could afford a year's worth of rent."

I stared at him silently, waiting for the much harder questions. The ones I didn't know if I was ever going to be able to answer. He regarded me thoughtfully while we finished our drinks in a tense silence.

When he reached out and took the empty bottle from my hand, my breath caught and I could feel my heart pound against my ribs. When he leaned in close, I caught a hint of something minty clinging to his skin, and could immediately feel the heat radiating off his bare skin. My eyes locked on the tattoo inked across the base of his throat. I wanted to press forward and put my mouth on it. Sucking in a shaky breath, I reluctantly lifted my gaze up to his.

I went still as a statue when one of his hands reached out and hooked a strand of damp hair which had escaped my messy ponytail.

"I have questions. You know I do. However, I can see you aren't ready to answer them." I nodded slowly as his warm palm settled against my cheek. We both inhaled a noisy breath and started to involuntarily move closer to one another. "I can also see that you didn't bother to put a bra on after your shower. Guess which of those things I can't stop thinking about?"

I shivered when he used his thumb to trace the line of my cheekbone. I lowered my lashes and told him, "Trying to have a conversation with you while you're half-dressed wasn't nearly as easy as I made it look either."

He chuckled and I was suddenly surrounded by his heat as he pressed close enough to touch his lips against my temple. "Good, my plan worked. I like that I can distract you, that I can take you out of your own head where all those secrets live, for a little while." His hand lowered to my jaw and his fingers brushed lightly over my lips. "I like that I can see how quickly you react to my touch and how you aren't hiding from me."

The thin cotton of my tank clearly showed the outline of my tightened nipples and couldn't hide the flush steadily crawling up my chest. Maybe I'd dressed so carelessly on purpose. It was possible I wanted to distract him from the questions as much as he wanted to distract me from the things I was running from. I had to admit I loved the dark heat in his eyes when he looked at me and the impatient vibration in his touch. His mouth was a millimeter away from mine. All it would take was the slightest move of my head to press my lips against his for a second time. I waited breathlessly for Solo to close the infinitesimal distance, and realized after a moment he wasn't going to do it. If I wanted something more, wanted him, I was going to have to take it. I was going to have to be the one who moved toward him... so I did.

Solo

I wasn't sure Orley was ready to come to me.

Sure, she had started to rely on me, to lean on me, but she still didn't trust me with the secrets from her past. I wanted to be bothered by her continued evasion and secrecy, but it was hard to feel anything but affection because she trusted me with her kid, and now, apparently, her body.

When she closed the slight distance between us, I expected her lips on mine. I waited for her to kiss me so I couldn't give into the curiosity that hounded me every single time she looked at me with those innocent blue eyes. She had so many hidden layers, so many facets to her, it shouldn't come as a surprise that at her core, she was as hard as a diamond and just as precious. I watched with hooded eyes as she shifted closer, lips grazing mine in a feather-light caress. They skipped over the sharp breath which escaped and ghosted over my chin. My fingers tightened on her jaw and my free hand caught in the wet silk of her long ponytail. When her warm breath hit the base of my throat, my pulse started to hammer so hard I was sure she could hear the rumble of my heart inside my chest. Her soft lips touched the very spot where her breath had just caressed the base of my throat and slowly, achingly she kissed her way up the ink decorating my neck. Her teeth paused to nip at my Adam's apple and her tongue flicked delicately along the curved line of my jaw.

I heard my breath change to something harsh and rapid as her fingers reached out to trace the wet pattern she left on my skin. Her eyes were wide and guileless when she lifted her head and met my questioning gaze.

"I've never been around anyone like you, Solomon. Never known anyone who looks like you, who acts like you. You're so brave and badass. You're also brilliant and effortlessly caring. So many contradictions. So many surprises. I'm not sure I know what to do with you." It was on the tip of my tongue to tell her she knew more about me than she thought, but the words were stolen away when she shifted again, practically climbing in my lap as she wrapped one arm around my shoulders and used her other hand to trace the outline of my lips. "I know what I want to do with you, though. I've been thinking about it since the first time I saw you jogging with your shirt off when you offered to fix my car."

"Tell me..." I remembered how lost and alone she looked that day. How afraid of everything she seemed. That young woman was nowhere to be found at the moment. The woman in my lap was confident, sure, and bold. I liked both of them. I was pulled toward the timid, single mother by a need to protect and shelter her. I was entranced by the subtle seductress, the Orley who knew what she wanted and wasn't afraid to call the shots.

The hand she wasn't using to clutch the back of my neck dropped to my shoulder and slowly started to slide across my pecs. "I want to put my mouth on each and every single one of these tattoos. I want to know if your skin tastes different, better than boring, plain skin."

She paused in her gentle exploration when she reached the spot on my chest where my heart was racing behind my ribs. Her dark eyebrows lifted a fraction and her lips parted on a sigh. I reached up and caught her wrist, feeling her pulse race in time with mine under her velvety skin. "There are a lot of them and that's a lot of territory to cover. That task might take a while."

Her eyes flashed at the challenge, blue bleeding into something bright and hot. The tip of her tongue shot out and slicked across the curve of her lower lip, leaving a shiny, wet trail I wanted to follow so badly I could taste it.

"Guess I should get started as soon as possible, then." Her voice was breathy and low. I liked the way it sounded. There was no fear, no hesitation.

"Sounds like a plan." I grinned at her and didn't complain when she snatched the hat off my head and tossed it in the general direction of my coffee table.

Once the bill was out of her way, Orley leaned fully into me, chest to chest, softness against unyielding hardness, and sealed her mouth over mine. There was no gratitude or apology in this kiss. No, it was all exploding heat and unabashed passion. It was wet and messy. Lips slid against lips and teeth clashed with unchecked eagerness. Breath mingled and was stolen, only to be given back as the kiss deepened.

Her hand tugged at my short hair and her legs shifted with impatience where they straddled the outside of mine. Since I didn't have a shirt on and her tank top was as thin as paper, I could clearly make out the way her nipples tightened and pressed into me. We both shivered when she moved and the peaks dragged across my skin. It was nice to know she was as out of her mind as I was. Sometimes I felt like I was chasing after her with no hope of catching her. She was running so fast, one eye always looking behind her, but not tonight. Tonight, the only thing she was looking at was me, and she was trying to get closer to me with every second that passed.

My hands curled instinctively in the light fabric keeping her skin from touching mine. I wanted to hold on to her, to this moment, but I wanted to feel her skin against mine even more. I had to believe this thing between us wasn't fleeting, that it was fate. Orley and Noble were put in my path for a reason. I wasn't sure if it was to test me, or to show her there could be good in bad places, but whatever the reason, I wasn't about to squander it. My mother hadn't raised a fool.

Her black tank top joined my hat in a discarded heap. I whispered her name when the soft swell of her breasts pushed against my chest. The tips felt like velvet points as they dragged across my skin.

She pulled her mouth away from mine when my hands climbed up her sides, gliding over her ribs, tracing the outer curve of her breast, until my finger found her puckered nipple. It beaded even tighter under my touch and her eyes went out of focus. Her hips shifted on my lap, and suddenly all her warm and wet places were hovering directly over the hardness my nylon shorts were doing a shit job of containing. It was incredibly intimate and slightly overwhelming. I wasn't new to the rise of desire and pulse of impatient want. But I had no clue how to handle the surge of possession and thrum of rightness that rushed through my blood in Orley's presence. When I was with other girls, when I gave up any of my valuable time to fuck around, it was because I had an itch that needed to be scratched. With Orley, I felt like if I couldn't get closer, if I didn't get to have all of her, I would die. She felt vital and so much more important than anyone who had come before her.

Her lips landed on the side of my neck, tongue darting out and licking along the outline of one of my many tattoos. She hummed lightly against my skin and my dick throbbed so hard it hurt. She must have felt my response because her hips rotated and pressed downward. The sensation had my eyes threatening to roll back in my head. I palmed each breast in my hands and tilted my head to the side to give her more access to my neck.

"Do I taste different?" Even though she was the one who stood out in this dark and dreary place, she was a breath of fresh air when I'd learned long ago to blend in.

Her head lifted but moved so her lips were near my ear. "Better. You taste better." Her tongue traced the shell of my ear and her lips lightly tugged on the lobe, which made me grunt in response.

I put my hands on her narrow waist and pulled until she was hovering on her knees while perched over me. It was my turn to get a taste. I wanted to know how all the different parts of her felt on my tongue. I wanted to savor all her different flavors and find out if she liked it when I used my teeth, or if she was all about the precise flick of my tongue on her most sensitive places.

While she toyed around with my ear and dragged her fingers across my scalp, I sucked one of her nipples into my mouth and assaulted the erect bud with my tongue and teeth. I heard her gasp and felt her nails bite into my skin with more force. Her head dropped backward and the end of her ponytail tickled the inside of my thighs. It tickled, but also made my balls ache, and I wanted to feel the silky strands brushing against my cock. I wanted to know how her mouth felt wrapped around the hard length, and how deep I could go before her pretty eyes glazed over and started to water. I wanted to push her, to tempt and to tease. I wanted to play with her, to lay every sexual trick I knew down on her and show her I was as serious as a heart attack. I was far more wrapped up in Orley than I had ever been with anyone else, and I didn't even know her last name.

I released the nipple I was torturing with a wet pop and moved to the other. They were a pretty color of raspberry, flushed and begging for attention. She had a hot pink flush crawling up her neck and staining her cheeks. She looked a little wild and a lot wanton. She looked like she belonged exactly where she was, a heartbeat away from riding my dick until we were both breathless and lost to oblivion.

I carefully worked just the tips of my fingers under the elastic waistband of her low-riding black pants. I wasn't sure how far she wanted to go, how much of herself she was ready to give. I hadn't moved this slow or with this much careful deliberation since I was a teenager trying to convince the first girl I ever had a crush on to give it up to me one night while her parents were out of town. I wanted to be respectful of Orley's boundaries that I might not be able to see through the fog of lust clouding my vision. She didn't make a sound or protest when my palms dipped below the fabric and skimmed beneath her bellybutton. Her abs contracted and quivered. Her legs trembled against the outside of mine. I heard my name, part question, part plea from somewhere above my head, but she didn't pull back or tell me to stop, so I kept up the glacial pace across her skin in search of her heat and softness.

I used the edge of my teeth on her pert nipple to distract her as the tips of my fingers hit unbelievably soft skin and the proof of her desire. She was slippery and delicate as glass under my questing touch. But once again she proved there was more to her than my misguided first impressions. As I spread her slick folds and went in search of the hot, fluttering opening to her body, one hand tightened in my hair and the other reached out to clasp my jaw. Her fingers bit into my skin as she pulled me off the nipple I was devouring and looked directly into my eyes.

"Solo." Her eyes practically burned into mine. "I'm not going to break. I had a baby. There is no way anything you do down there is going to hurt me or scare me. If you're going to touch me, I want to feel it. I want to remember it." She dropped her head and gave me a hard, quick kiss. "Touch me."

Who was I to argue with any of that?

I spread my fingers to open her up and went in. She let out a strangled moan and set her lips back on mine. I fucked her writhing body with my fingers, while she fucked my mouth with her clever, quick tongue. I loved the way she convulsed and pulsed around my moving digits. I liked how her body swayed closer. I loved that she got wetter and wetter. I nearly lost it when she practically purred the minute I stroked a soaked finger across her excited little clit.

"Oh my God." Her words slipped out and landed on my lips. "Do that again." Her demand was sexy as hell and so was the desperation behind it. When I grinned, she sank her teeth into the curve of my lower lip. I repeated the motion and felt the heat surrounding me pulse as her entire body quivered. If she wanted me to touch her, then I would. I would leave my fingerprints all over her private places, and she would be feeling me all through tomorrow.

I turned my hand forward, curling my fingers just a bit, looking, seeking that hot button inside of her that was bound to make her forget her own name and instead scream out mine. I used my thumb to repeatedly circle her clit, watching her without blinking as she rode my hand and lost herself in the onslaught of sensation.

When she was right on the brink of flying apart, her teeth sank into her lower lip and her eyes slammed closed. She was beautiful in her surrender. Probably the most beautiful thing I'd ever seen. She soaked my hand and my dick twitched with anticipation. I wanted her warmth and her wetness surrounding every inch of the flesh begging to be freed.

Her chest was rising and falling as she tried to catch her breath. It took a long minute before she could pry her eyes back open. When she finally lifted her long lashes, she watched in silence as I brought my shiny, slippery fingers to my mouth and licked them clean. She opened her mouth on a silent gasp and was reaching for the waistband of my shorts with shaky fingers when a sleepy little voice from the back of the apartment suddenly made us both freeze.

"I need to potty. Where's my mommy? I want my mommy." Noble sounded sleepy and confused, but I could hear her moving around in my room.

Orley moved like lightning, shoving off of me and scrambling back into her shirt as she called out, "I'm here, sweetheart." She cleared her throat and gave me an apologetic look while mouthing 'I'm sorry.'

I groaned and cast a dirty look at my painfully erect cock. The situation was not ideal, but it was understandable. Her kid was always going to come first and there was nothing that should ever change that.

"Are you ready to put on your pjs and to go to sleep in your own bed?" Orley came back into the room carrying the beautiful little girl. Noble rubbed a fist against her eyes and yawned. "Tell Solo thank you for taking you to do so many fun things today."

Noble yawned again and flashed me that smile I couldn't get enough of. "Thank you. You're really fun and your bed is comfy." At least, I think that's what she was trying to say. I was still figuring out three-year-old speak.

I shifted so I could use my hands to cover the tent in my lap. I was looking at Orley, not her daughter, when I muttered, "Anytime."

Orley dropped a kiss onto the black curls. "I owe you one."

I hoped to God she wasn't talking about another thank you dinner because my dick would never forgive me. I winked at her as she walked past me to the door.

"You do, and I can't wait to collect." And maybe, just maybe, I'd know her last name by then.

Orley

I slept like the dead.

Boneless. Weightless. Without nightmares or the constant buzz of worry and stress that kept my mind restless and my body tense. I slept so hard and so deep, I was disoriented when I woke the next morning. I'd almost managed to forget where I was and why I was here. There was no arguing Solo was working with some pretty powerful sexual skills. He was light years ahead of me in terms of experience and intimacy. He was so confident and sure of himself. I envied his comfort in his own skin. My skin had never felt like it fit just right. However, in the last couple of weeks, it stopped feeling like it was too tight all the time. There was room to move inside of it, space to figure out how to wear it with the same self-assuredness everyone in this city seemed to have.

Reluctantly crawling out of bed, I checked on Noble. She was still sleeping and we had some time before I had to get her up and ready for her day at Erica's, so I let her be and decided to try and make a real breakfast for once. We usually rushed out the door after a bowl of cereal or a piece of fruit in hand. Luckily, Erica always asked if my kid needed to eat in the morning. She was a godsend, and I cringed when I realized that during all my time spent in my affluent neighborhood behind iron gates, I'd never met anyone as kind or as genuine as her. The people behind those gates always claimed they were for protection, to keep the bad people out. Now that I'd lived on the other side of them for a little while, I was starting to realize that wasn't the case at all. The gates were there to keep the bad people inside, hidden so the rest of the world couldn't see the terrible things they were doing. They used those gates to keep their secrets safe. The people who could spot liars, cheats, and criminals from a mile away were kept at bay. Believe it or not, I was finally starting to feel like it was much safer on the other side of the fence. At least on this side, no one tried to cover up the fact they were out to hurt you. It was far easier to protect yourself from a threat you knew was coming.

I dug pancake mix out of the cabinet, pulled bacon and eggs out of the fridge, and got to work. Noble woke up when she smelled the bacon cooking, so I got her out of bed and let her try to draw shapes with the pancake batter in the skillet. I was giggling over a very misshapen heart when she looked up at me and asked all wide eyed and innocent if we could have breakfast with Solo. Refusing was automatic, defensive, and rushed. But I bit off the no on the tip of my tongue and slowly nodded at my kid. It seemed like my roughly charming neighbor had also worked his way into my daughter's affections.

I made sure the kitchen wouldn't catch on fire and took Noble's hand so we could walk the short distance to Solo's apartment. I let her knock, the sound not terribly loud considering her tiny fist. It took so long for him to come to the door, we were getting ready to turn around and head back to our own place when he finally pulled it open.

It didn't look like he'd had the same peaceful slumber I'd enjoyed. There were dark circles under his eyes, he looked pale under his naturally tanned complexion, and his dark eyes were even more fathomless than normal. He had on the same athletic shorts as he did the night before, but today he'd added a tight, black t-shirt. He still made casual clothes look just as good as an expensive suit from any designer brand.

I put a hand on Noble's curls and offered a lopsided smile. "Did we wake you up?"

He dragged a tattooed hand down his face and blinked his eyes a couple times. I noticed they were bloodshot and tired.

"No... Yes... I must have dozed off." He shook his head and forced a weak grin when he caught sight of Noble looking up at him with huge, curious eyes. "It was a long night. I got a call not long after you guys left that my mom was having a bad episode. I drove out to spend some time with her. Didn't get back until a couple hours ago."

"Oh." I flinched at having woken him up from his obviously much-needed nap. "I'm so sorry we bothered you. I had a couple extra minutes this morning so we cooked breakfast. Noble wanted to see if you would like to join us. I should've just texted so I didn't wake you up." I felt terrible. He was always going out of his way to help us out, and it seemed like all we did was steal the precious few moments he had to himself.

He shook his head again as he let out a jaw-popping yawn. "You don't ever bother me. Give me a few minutes to wake up, promise me a gallon of coffee, and I'll be right over." He reached out and bopped Noble on the end of her nose, which had her wrinkle it in response. "I never turn down a meal made by a pretty girl."

Noble giggled in response and obediently followed along when I guided her back to our apartment. I put coffee on and settled her in her regular spot with her misshapen pancakes in front of her. I dropped a kiss on the top of her head and was walking back to the kitchen to make my own plate when she asked quietly, "What's wrong with Solo's mommy?"

That was a hard question to answer for someone so young. It didn't feel right trying to explain the kind of violence Solo and his mother had faced to a child. I didn't want to scare her, but I didn't want her to have a rosy view of the world forever, either. She needed to know how horrible humans could be to one another, but she didn't need to know today just how horrible they could truly be.

"If he wants us to know, he'll tell us, okay? Don't ask him about it. That's not polite."

Out of the corner of my eye I saw her pout and stab her pancake with a little more force than necessary. She was worried about the big, tattooed man next door. It was cute, but also a little bit concerning. I didn't want

Noble to get overly attached to Solo. Yes, we were finally settling into this new life, in this new place. But I didn't know if or when we might have to run again. I couldn't afford to let her think of this place as home and these people as family when we might have to leave it all behind in the blink of an eye.

There was a rap on the door so I poured a mug of coffee and went to let in the man who rocked my world a few hours ago so he could eat heart-shaped pancakes.

He looked better, more aware, as he took the mug from me with a smile and a wink. His eyes were still red and there were still shadows under them, but he hid his exhaustion well. He smelled clean, and his hair was damp underneath the ever-present ball cap. He stepped close and brushed a coffee-scented kiss across my cheek. "Thanks."

I cleared my throat and stepped back so he could enter the apartment. "Anytime. Come eat. Noble made the pancakes." I gave him a pointed look so he knew not to make fun of the wonky design.

His grin widened and he looked over to where Noble was watching him expectantly. "Hearts. Very cute."

She threw up her hands in delight and smiled a syrupy, sweet smile. I could almost see it steal a piece of his heart. Only distracted for a moment, she turned back to her food, dismissing both of us.

Solo piled his plate high and I watched him as unobtrusively as I could, asking under my breath, "Are you really okay? Can you take the morning off and catch a nap? Your boss seems pretty cool."

He grunted around a piece of bacon and shook his head. "My boss is the best. He saved my life." I could tell by his somber expression and tone that he meant every word he said. "I refuse to let him down after everything he's done for me. Besides, I have to leave work early. I have a... thing... tonight."

He shifted uneasily in front of me as I narrowed my eyes at him. "A thing?"

He grunted again. "Yeah, a thing."

I sighed and poured my own cup of coffee. "A thing that will lead to more black eyes and busted lips?" I hated that he fought for money. Hated the idea of him being hurt and hurting others. It didn't fit with my vision of the strong, brave man who was always there when I needed him.

A grin quirked at the corner of his mouth. "If I do it right, it's the other guy who should have black eyes and busted lips." He cleared his throat. "This is a special event. Something private. I couldn't turn down the money."

I was about to ask for more details when Noble suddenly jumped up and ran into her room. She quickly returned with a piece of paper scribbled with a drawing that actually looked much more like a heart than the pancakes had. Noble wrapped an arm around Solo's knees and thrust the drawing in the direction of his hands. Their size difference was adorable. She was small and he was so big, but he was so infinitely gentle when he reached down to take the picture from her, sticky fingerprints and all.

"What's this, kiddo?"

Noble gave him a serious look as she continued to hug his legs. "For your mommy. So she feels better."

Solo reached out to put his coffee on the counter. He put his free hand on Noble's head the same way I often did. I saw his throat work for a second as he stroked her soft curls. "Thank you, Noble. She'll love it."

"Where is she?" Noble asked the question innocently, but I could see the answer wasn't a simple one. His eyes narrowed a fraction and the expression on his face tightened.

Solo shifted his gaze to mine and it was his turn to clear his throat before he could answer. "My mom lives in a really nice house right outside of the city. She's got a lot of doctors and nurses who take care of her, because I can't do it myself. But sometimes she has a bad day and I'm the only one who can help her out. She's the best mom in the whole world... Next to your mommy, of course." He gently pried Noble off his legs and solemnly promised, "I'll take your picture to her next time I go visit."

Appeased, Noble bounded back to the living room and her breakfast.

It was quiet in the kitchen as I waited for him to tell me, or not. Either way, he looked like he needed a hug so I put my coffee down and moved toward him. My arms went around his lean waist and I rested my head on his chest. His heartbeat was a steady rhythm under my ear, but I could feel tension throughout every strong line of his body.

"She worked three jobs to keep me off the streets. She was gone a lot, but we always managed, just me and her. I'm not kidding when I say she was an amazing mother. I was wild, but she always kept me from going too far. I had a chance to make it out of this city because of her. It was all she wanted. A better life for me." His sigh ruffled my hair as he lowered his chin to rest on the top of my head.

"My mom grew up in the city; she navigated it for years without incident. She was going to give up the car without question the night she was attacked." He sighed again and I felt a slight tremor work though his big frame. "But she didn't want to give up my stupid backpack in the backseat. I left it there when I borrowed the car. She was all about keeping my grades up so

I could get into a good college. She didn't want me to fall behind. She took a bullet to the head for my future."

"Oh my God!" The gasp ripped out of me and my arms tightened reflexively around him.

"She was lucky she didn't die, even if some days it doesn't feel that way." He shook his head. "It was bad, so bad at first. I was just a kid who lost the one person who actually cared about me. I dropped out of school, found a couple jobs and did what I could to get her into a better place. My boss found me when I was at the end of my rope, buried in debt and contemplating a long list of really bad options when it came to what I could do for her. He gave me the opportunity to help my mom, and to earn enough money to support both of us. It's not easy, but it's the only option I have. Like I said, he saved my life."

"I'm so sorry, Solo." His arms wrapped around my shoulders when my voice cracked, and he pulled me close.

"She's got great staff taking care of her, but some nights she gets scared, she remembers, or she forgets. She always calms down when she sees me. I talk to her. I read to her. We listen to music. I promise her I'm doing all right and tell her I'm going to make her proud." I felt a kiss land on the top of my head. "Last night I talked about you and Noble. She smiled the whole time." He squeezed me again, this time hard enough to make me squeak. "Maybe, if you ever tell me your last name, I can take you to meet her. You can't get in unless I put your full name on the visitor's log."

It was my turn to quiver slightly against him. He wasn't asking for much. After all, we were far from strangers at this point. But when I opened my mouth, nothing came out and I could feel his disappointment, so I held him tighter. I wasn't sure I was ever going to let go, which meant figuring out how to share my past with him... while protecting him from it at the same time.

Good thing I'd slept well last night, because it was really starting to get exhausting being me.

Solo

Normally when I had a fight, it was easy enough to slip into a quiet headspace; the only thing I was focused on was keeping my face from getting smashed in and my limbs from being torn off my body one by one. I usually put in earbuds, blasted something loud and aggressive, and warmed up with laser-sharp focus. It was no secret that I won more than I lost for a lot of reasons. My unwavering focus and intensity toward the task at hand was at the top of the list.

But today, my mind was all over the place. I was anxious and twitchy. There was an uneasy tingle all along the back of my neck I couldn't shake. I kept lifting my hand and rubbing at the spot, but the more I became aware of the prickly sensation, the more it buzzed and popped under my skin.

It was an odd sensation to be in the Pit when it was practically empty. I was used to the old warehouse being full of eager gamblers and wild fight enthusiasts calling for blood and broken bones. When people were cheering and screaming my name, it was easy to forget I was doing something barbaric for a paycheck. It felt almost like being an entertainer, like I was putting on a show instead of beating someone to a pulp when the locals were around to root for their favorites. With the massive, open space empty except for the men dressed in the one-of-a-kind, tailored suits I would never be able to afford, this fight felt much more like what they really were... gory, gruesome, blood sport for the entertainment of men who would never know what it was like to have to fight for anything in their overly coiffed, pampered lives. People like them loved to watch because they were used to the violence. For them, these fights were the equivalent of watching the two meanest dogs in the junkyard go at each other. For the men paying for today's private bout, it was something different. It was more like taking the strongest, most ruthless representative from their clan and putting him up against whomever was tough and capable enough to protect the reputation of the city.

If I lost today, it wasn't just getting my ass kicked. No, my entire town would look like we couldn't stand toe to toe with those rich fuckers from the gated neighborhoods up in the hills. There was an added layer of pressure I was trying to keep from getting to me as the man wearing the most expensive suit in the room slowly made his way to where I was hovering in the entrance of the locker room.

If my boss was the person I respected most in this city, then the man now standing in front of me was the only one I admittedly feared. Something happened to the air when the man we simply referred to as the Devil got close. It was almost like the molecules in the very air shifted and changed. Like they moved out of the way to give the man, and the dark, charismatic energy he radiated, enough space. There was a weird change in temperature whenever he was in my orbit. I knew it was all in my head; the man couldn't really carry hellfire with him, but there was no denying I always found myself taking a preventative step back when his unusual gold eyes landed on me. Anyone watching would think I was being a wuss. The man was several inches shorter than me, incredibly lean, and dressed like he was going to a board meeting. He looked like an executive, not a fighter. Outwardly, there wasn't much that would identify him as the biggest threat in the room, but the second those gold eyes settled on you, there was zero doubt to anyone who had any sense that this man was lethal. Those eyes weren't human. They were otherworldly, and so was the man. I'd seen him strip down and fight more than once. He *never* lost. Never.

Boss was wrong when he said I was the best, because the Devil was better than the best. He was untouchable, unstoppable, and when he wasn't hiding in his designer suits, he was both ripped and shredded like a soldier, and if possible, even more heavily tattooed than I was. His ability to hide in plain sight was terrifying. So was the absolutely cold way he sized me up and told me, "Something is off. From the start I didn't like the hard sell these guys gave me, and I didn't like the way they insisted the fighter going against their guy had to be you. Told your boss to talk you out of it, but figured you wouldn't walk because of the money."

I nodded slowly, looking over his shoulder to where the other men dressed like they were going to the opera were standing. I hadn't seen the other fighter yet, so I was even more anxious about the odds being in my favor.

"The Boss tried to tell me to walk. I couldn't. The money will pay for my mom's care for several years." I dipped my chin down and took a calming breath. "Have you seen who they brought in to put me up against?" I hated feeling clueless before a fight. I hated the lack of control. Not knowing killed me. I was someone who had every minute of every day planned out. Unknowns were scary and stressed me the fuck out, which was part of the reason Orley and Noble were taking up all my free time. I didn't want them to be unknown. I wanted to know them as well as I knew myself. I wanted to be able to predict what they wanted, what they needed from me. I wanted to be someone who was reliable and involved.

The man in the suit lifted a hand with an intricate tattoo spread across the back of it to rub his mouth. Rumor had it the tattoo represented his wife, who was also his business partner, but I'd never had the balls to ask. I'd met the stunning redhead he married once or twice. The thing I remembered most about her, aside from the fact she was a knockout, was the fact that the woman was nearly as intimidating as her man. It figured she would be a badass, one who proudly wore a diamond mined from the pits of hell, since she had to stand shoulder to shoulder with the man who checked the criminals and miscreants in my city. He was ruthless and cruel. She was calculating and cunning. They were a deadly match and infamous in all the right ways.

"Kid, you've fought for me for years. You could ask for help. I know your boss would give it without question." A black eyebrow lifted in my direction. "I would also be willing to float you a loan. My conditions for repayment would probably piss off your boss, though."

I cleared my throat. I refused to be indebted to men who could destroy me. My mom needed me too much for me to get into bed with the actual bad guys—even if they were the best of the bad in these parts.

I forced a weak grin and shook out my taped-up hands. "I appreciate it. But taking care of my mom is something I have to do on my own. She took care of me without help; I owe her the same."

"That's a lifelong commitment. Why not make it easier on yourself?" The slightly accented voice didn't sound angry, just honestly confused as to why I insisted on doing things the hard way.

"I don't want to owe anyone anything." I heard Orley's voice in the back of my mind telling me the same thing. When you didn't owe anyone, it was a lot easier to walk away. The more she leaned on me, the more she relied on me, the more she felt she *owed* me, the harder it would be for her to rabbit out of town in the middle of the night if things went wrong. I understood where she was coming from a little bit better now. I never wanted to be under the thumb of anyone, even the men I both admired and feared the most.

Surprisingly, the man in front of me seemed to understand without further explanation. He clapped a hand on my shoulder and gave a squeeze. "Better not to owe anyone. But be smart enough to know when to ask for help if you need it." He gave me a little shake, reminding me of the coiled strength hidden beneath those pinstripes. "Still have a bad feeling about these guys. They didn't bring their fighter in early to check the space out or get a look at you. Something's up. I don't trust anyone with enough money to make setting up a private fight worth my while. That being said, you know I can't get involved. I'm just the middle man."

He kept his expression bland, but we both knew if he let me die my boss would go off the rails, and if those two went at it, there would be a war on the streets no one would be able to stop. Mortals would suffer as gods fought and rained down destruction. I'd like to avoid both dying and setting two formidable men against one another, if at all possible. So, I just grunted my response and found my mouth guard to pop in.

No longer able to talk, I followed the dark-haired man who pulled all the strings in the city into the crudely painted circle in the middle of the cement floor. There were old bloodstains deeply imbedded in the concrete. I'd been responsible for some and others were left from my own injuries. It was a familiar place, one I knew like the back of my hand, but the three men smirking at me from the other side of the circle suddenly made it feel foreign and strange. I was used to the opponent looking at me with confidence and challenge. It was weird to see that same look on the faces of middle-aged men who clearly had never thrown a punch. What did they know that I didn't?

Since my mouth was filled with the plastic guard, my companion was the one who had to address the others in the room.

148

"You gentlemen are paying for this circus. Are we standing around the rest of the night, or did you find a fighter you think can take on our boy?"

His voice was always so smooth, that accent making it sound lyrical and exotic, but his stance and the fire in his odd eyes let the opposition know he was in charge, regardless of who was putting up the money.

The oldest of the other men stepped forward, and for a split second I thought he looked vaguely familiar. He was dressed as fancy as the man in the pinstripe suit, but it was obvious with one look that he went out of his way to flaunt his wealth. The diamond tie tack was ridiculous in this part of the city, so were his big ass rings and the designer watch on his wrist. If he walked out the door unescorted, all of those things would be ruthlessly stripped from him in seconds.

"We're ready when you are. I can't tell you how excited I've been for this fight since you agreed to set it up. You think you're quite impressive, don't you, young man?" He asked the question with a sneer, so I didn't bother to grunt or nod in response.

We stared at each other silently, some kind of wordless battle waging. I had no idea what this dude had against me, but it was becoming obvious the reason he wanted me in this warehouse was to teach me some kind of lesson. All the unease and anxiety started to claw at my bones and tear at me for not listening when I knew something wasn't right.

Suddenly, the man waved his hand. There was a commotion behind him and the sound of echoing footsteps as someone prowled through the empty warehouse.

"I went to great lengths to find an opponent for you. Someone special. Someone totally unique." There was a nasty gleam in his eyes I didn't like at all. He clearly thought he had the upper hand here, and his self-assuredness was obnoxious.

"What the fuck is the meaning of this?" Suddenly the dark-haired man standing next to me stiffened and started to vibrate with barely suppressed rage. That weird heat he emanated started to grow. I watched dispassionately as the older man stumbled back a step in surprise. "A woman? You want the kid to fight a woman? You know this setup is a total knockout or until the other opponent stops breathing, correct? You expect him to KO a female?"

The older man clapped his hands together and pulled the young woman next to his side. She shot him a baleful look before letting her gaze land on me.

She was tiny. Way shorter than Orley and probably only a hundred pounds soaking wet. Her hands were taped similar to mine, and she squared her shoulders after giving me a long once over. We were so unevenly matched it was a joke. One uppercut or kick to the chest and she would break like a doll.

The older man shrugged, eyes glittering with glee. "Any fighter we picked. Those are the rules. We want him to fight her, and if he doesn't, we automatically win."

I spit out my mouth guard and growled, "Fine. You win. I'm out of here." There was no way in hell I was laying a hand on that girl.

I was turning around to walk back to the locker room when the man who set this up grabbed my forearm in an iron grip. "Not so fast, kid. You don't get to just forfeit and walk away. You win, you get the money. You lose..."

I frowned, realizing I should have asked for more precise details before agreeing to this mess. "I lose and they get back the money they paid. I know the drill. I wouldn't have agreed to the fight if I couldn't afford to lose."

The dark head shook in the negative and the old man let out a scoffing laugh. "No, kid, their terms are different. Your boss should've laid it all out for you, but he's convinced you're unbeatable." Normally, I was, but this was not a twist I was expecting. "If you lose, their terms are you leave town immediately. No coming back. If you lose, they expect you to get gone."

I balked. "What?" Leave the city? That was impossible. Almost as impossible as fighting fairly against the small woman watching me with careful eyes. "I can't do that." There was no way I was leaving my mother here, and I wasn't willing to walk away from Orley and Noble so easily either. "I never agreed to those terms."

The man next to me sighed and narrowed his eyes at the older man openly mocking my surprise and refusal to fight. "You agreed when you said yes to the fight. You win, we get a stupid amount of money... lose... and you have to agree to go."

I looked at the woman, then back at the man who had brought a lamb to the slaughter. "Who is this guy?" And why did he have such a personal vendetta toward me?

"Channing Vincent. He's old money and deeply involved in local politics. He's a corporate raider. Buys up struggling business and devours them from the inside out. Makes his money on other people's misfortune." The lyrical voice sounded almost impressed.

I snorted. "Don't you do the same thing?"

Unsurprisingly, the man next to me nodded. "Yes, which is why you shouldn't take this gauntlet he threw down lightly. He clearly wants you out of the city. You need to know why. If you have to go through the girl to get that information, then do it." He turned and walked away without another word. He stopped next to a very large African American man and bent his head to speak softly. The bald, well-dressed man had been the head of the Devil's security for as long as the man had been running the underground. He was a misleadingly gentle giant, and I could tell by the way he was glaring at the rich men across the room that he wasn't any happier with the turn of events than I was. Sure, someone like the Devil could go through an innocent woman to get what he wanted. I wasn't wired that way. If I was forced to hurt the girl, I had no doubt my conscience would never get over it. Any wounds I left on her would be nothing compared to the ones I ripped into my own morality.

But what choice did I have?

I couldn't leave the city or my obligations.

A bet is a bet, even if the terms sucked. Nothing about any of it had to be fair. That was the risk you took when you banked on something illegal for a good portion of your income.

Growling a long list of swear words under my breath, I shoved the mouth guard back in and slowly stomped my way to the center of the roughly drawn circle. I kept my eyes on the girl as she followed suit. When she was standing directly in front of me, our size difference was even more acute. I towered over her and had to outweigh her by a solid hundred pounds, if not more. I wouldn't even fight a man if the difference were so obvious.

The girl lifted her eyebrows and very quietly muttered, "They know you don't want to hit a girl. This is a set up. That old rich guy wants you gone." She popped her mouth guard in so the conversation had to end and stuck out her taped-up hands for me to touch.

With little other options, I lightly bumped her fists with my own and tried desperately to figure out a way I could take her down without actually hurting her. I hoped the regular rules might bend in this particular situation. No one wanted a dead girl on their hands.... Did they? Sometimes, when dealing with these guys, it was hard to tell.

I was so caught up in my own shit I had no time or self-awareness to prepare for the flying roundhouse kick that immediately took me to my knees. I landed on the concrete with a thud, ears ringing, head thundering from the impact. The girl bounced lightly on her toes a few feet away, watching me warily. Shaking away the fog, I climbed to my feet and watched as the girl dropped into a low, professional martial arts pose. I wasn't sure if it was Taekwondo or karate since I only knew the basics of both, but this chick was trained and she could do some serious damage. My roaring head was proof of her abilities.

I had just found my balance when she started another attack. Her feet moved so fast it was almost impossible to keep track of them, and her tiny fists felt like hammers when they made contact with my chest and ribs. I played defense, blocking kicks and punches as she moved to the outer edge of the circle. With a roar of frustration, I finally managed to duck under one swinging leg and get close enough to wrap her in a submission hold. I took her to the ground with an arm around her throat and one of my legs keeping hers immobile so I didn't get kicked in a place guaranteed to bring me down. I tightened my hold until I could hear her breath struggling to escape.

I spit out the mouth guard and lowered my head closer to hers, hoping she could hear me over loud pants.

"Why does that guy want me gone? How does he even know who I am? Stop dropping your guard after you advance. You fall back a step after every kick. You need to move in closer to your opponent, not give them an opening to recover." I released her and used my core muscles to lift myself off the cold, hard ground.

The girl followed suit, rubbing at her neck as she also spit out her mouth piece. She shook her head and rubbed under her nose with the back of her hand. She made a low noise and rushed at me. I thought she was going to go for my head so I automatically lifted my hands to block my face, leaving my ribcage wide open. There was no way she didn't break bone when her kick connected. The pain was blinding and immediate. I lashed out before thinking. I heard the sound of my fist make contact and blinked in surprise. The girl's nose was gushing blood and sitting at an odd angle.

I gasped and immediately reached out. "Fuck! Sorry. I didn't mean to do that." I groaned when I tried to take a step toward her. My ribs screamed in protest and the sharp stab of pain made bile rise up toward the back of my throat.

The girl spit out a gross blob of blood and saliva. Her eyes narrowed and she threw a right hook that would've knocked my head around in one-hundred-and-eighty degrees if it connected. Instead, it glanced off my cheek and rattled my skull just a little.

"He wants you out of the way so he can get to his granddaughter."

I stopped moving, ice running cold through my blood. "His granddaughter?"

Since her target was still, it was really easy for the girl to execute a perfect leg sweep and take me down to the ground. Her weight on top of me was slight, but the elbow she pressed on my Adam's apple was sharp and pointy. It was my turn to struggle to breathe. I was changing my mind about her being a fair opponent. She was better than half the guys I usually went against in this circle. She thought about what she was doing, she was smart, and skilled, which made up for her lack of size. She was crushing my windpipe without any hesitation.

"Yeah. The old guy swears his granddaughter has been kidnapped and he can't go to the police. He's been shaking down every lowlife and junkie on the streets for weeks looking for information. I don't know how you fit into the equation, but he insisted that you need to get out of the picture." She was struggling to keep the upper hand. I used my greater weight and strength to shift her off my throat. Her gaze landed on mine and something dangerous flashed in them. "If I feel like I can't win this fight, he paid me an extra fifty-thousand dollars to take you out permanently. There's a switchblade in my boot."

She rolled to the side and moved the opposite way. Both of us were sweaty, bloody, and tired from making the fight look far more dramatic than it actually was. By now it was clear this girl could do as much damage as I could, but she was holding herself back the same way I was. That didn't mean she wasn't putting on a good show. I took a kick right in the center of my back, making my messed-up ribs howl in agony. I moved so I could catch that deadly leg and pin it to the ground. I lifted over her and grabbed a handful of her short, dark hair. Normally I would use the hold to smash my opponent's head on the unforgiving cement. With her I used it to pull her face closer to mine as I narrowed my eyes.

"I've got too many people counting on me to let you stick a knife in me. They're why I can't leave this city. I can't lose this fight." And when I was back on my feet and Channing Vincent was no longer a thorn in my side, I was going to track down whoever sold Orley out. My money was on Skinner. He was already pissed I beat his ass for harassing her, and there was no way he would turn down some quick cash in exchange for information.

The girl cackled and wrapped her hands around my wrist. I wasn't expecting her to get a knee in my gut or for her to use the momentum of my body when I folded over in pain to flip me neatly over her head in a somersault. Once again, I was on my back looking up at the pipes and heating ducts which crisscrossed the naked ceiling. This time she put her foot on my throat and steadily pushed down.

"If I let you win... I die. So, I can't lose this fight either." She shook her head and looked down at me with obvious remorse. "I've seen you fight. I've honestly always looked up to you and would have loved to have an honest shot at trying to take you on. I hate that it has to end like this. But it does have to end." The pressure on my neck grew until it felt like all of her weight was standing directly on my windpipe. I locked my hands around her booted ankle and tried to shove her away, but my busted-up ribs made getting the leverage I needed nearly impossible. Plus, I was starting to get lightheaded. Things were starting to fade in and out of my vision, and I could practically feel anger radiating from where the Devil stood. It had to kill him he couldn't intervene, and he was probably a little pissed that I was getting my ass handed to me by a girl.

Underneath the leather of her boot, I could feel the hard metal of the knife she warned me about. Of course I would never think to use it on her, but if I could get my hands on it, I was pretty sure I was past the point of reason and could use it on the lunatic who set all this in motion. I had a sinking feeling deep down in my gut that the next time I asked Orley to tell me her last name it would be the same as the bastard who set me up. The only granddaughter I could have possibly have come into contact with recently was Noble. If this asshole was the reason Orley had gone into hiding in the first place, I had first-hand proof she had good reason.

Wheezing and probably turning purple, I put more effort into freeing my throat, but the girl wasn't going to move. I was going to have to hurt her in order to get her off me. I could see strain and remorse written all over her ravaged face, but if it was her or me... well, it wasn't a choice I wanted to make, rather one that I had to.

I bent my knees so I could get the leverage I needed to push free. I also switched my grip from her ankle to her knee. It wouldn't take much to jerk the joint out of the socket if I moved the right way when I pushed to my feet. She clearly anticipated the move, because she immediately started to try and escape my new hold. She was slippery, but I was desperate. I refused to let go, even when I felt muscle and bone start to shift under my hands. A dislocated bone was no joke. I hoped it would be enough to get her to tap out, but if it wasn't... well, I would do what I had to do... just like the Devil.

She screamed. I swore. We were both red with exertion and miserable about the situation. I could feel her body resisting my movements, but it was close. In a second she wouldn't be able to use her lethal leg anymore.

"POLICE! Stop what you're doing. Everyone put your hands in the air."

The booming voice made me release my prey instantly and roll over onto my back so that I was staring at the ceiling. The girl dropped to her knees and put her hands behind her head with her fingers interlocked. Clearly, she was not a first-timer when it came to dealing with the law.

The man in the pinstripe suit calmly walked to the center of the circle where I was sprawled and watched as another man, one who was huge, bigger than me, even, sauntered into the mostly empty space. He was dressed casually in jeans and a long-sleeved t-shirt, but the gun on his belt and badge hanging around his neck were very formal and serious. I recognized him right away. He wasn't just a cop. He was my boss's older brother and one of the few people in law enforcement the guys on the wrong side of the law trusted.

I would bet my left nut the dark-haired Devil staged this little bust in order to keep me from having to do something I would regret down the road.

The big man pointed at me and the girl. "Get up. Go get cleaned up then come back here and explain what in the hell is going on." He shifted his gaze to the older man and narrowed his eyes. "And who are you? You're not a regular at the fights. Let me see your identification." The cop stuck his hand out and stared coolly at the rich guy.

The older man immediately stiffened. "I want my lawyer."

Typical. He had no idea how things worked here. Before the cop changed his mind, I grabbed the girl's wrist and practically dragged her toward the locker room. She protested all the way, insisting the fight had to end. Obviously, she was more scared of the rich guy than she was of me. Once I was in the locker room, I pulled open the locker where my wallet was stashed. I pulled out a couple hundred dollars and shoved it in the girl's hands even as she continued to protest.

"There's a back door no one knows about if you go through the showers. It's hidden in the third stall. Take the money and lay low for a while. I don't know what's going on with that rich dude, but you don't need to be in the middle of it. Make a run for it." I grabbed her shoulders and turned her around forcibly. "Go." I pushed her toward the showers, and after a minute she finally moved.

Swearing loudly, I kicked a bench, which did my seemingly forever busted ribs no favors. I took a minute to wash some of the blood from my face and to check out my bruising side.

Fuck me.

It looked like I was going to owe the Devil a favor after all.

Orley

When the call came in the middle of the night asking for a ride, there was no way I could say no. Not after all the ways Solo had stepped up to the plate when I needed something from him. I had to call Erica and wake her up since it was after midnight and ask her if I could bring Noble over for the rest of the night. Erica was groggy and confused with sleep, until I told her I was going to get Solo. The mention that the guy who takes care of everyone else needed help woke the other woman up instantly. She fired no less than twenty rapid-fire questions at me, none of which I could answer. Solo's call had been rushed and very brief. All I knew for certain was that he sounded like he was in pain, and there was a reason he couldn't drive himself home. It took every ounce of self-control I possessed to keep from launching into worst-case-scenario mode. But it was so hard to imagine Solo not being in control of any situation I could feel panic and fear trying to overshadow everything else.

None of my unease lessened when I finally found the warehouse, tucked in a part of the city that made my neighborhood look like Disneyland. The shadows were dark around these blocks; the feel of the abandoned buildings and deserted parking lots was twice as dangerous and desolate than where I lived. Even in the bad part of town, there were places that were worse than others, and it seemed I was collecting Solo from the worst corner on the scariest block.

He was easy enough to spot when I finally found the remote building. It was in better shape than the others around it. No graffiti decorated the outside, and the exterior looked new. Solo was standing under a burned-out street light. Head bent, the hood of his sweatshirt pulled up over his ball cap. He had his arms wrapped around his middle and it looked like the pole was the only thing holding him upright. There were two men standing nearby, deep in conversation. Both of them watched my approach with intent eyes. I hoped I didn't have to get out of the car because the one in the expensive suit made my skin crawl with nervousness, and the large, dark-skinned man hovering next to him looked like he could lift me over his bald head with one hand. I'd barely gotten used to how intimidating Solo could be without even trying; there was no way I was ready to jump in and play in the major leagues with the men currently keeping an eye on him.

I honked the horn and watched, holding my breath, as Solo painstakingly pushed himself off the pole. He was moving like a ninety-year-old man suffering from arthritis. Every step he took in my direction contorted his face into a grimace of pain. He waved off the large African American man when the giant took a step forward to offer a steadying hand. The man in the expensive suit said something that made Solo wince, but he nodded and stumbled into the passenger door. I leaned across the seat and shoved it open for him, watching with wide eyes as he practically collapsed into the old, worn leather seat. He flicked a sarcastic salute from the torn rim of his battered hat and leaned his head back. Even with his eyes closed, he looked incredibly pale in the low light.

I didn't bother to ask if he was okay, because the answer was obvious. Instead, I asked, "Do you need to go to the emergency room?" He didn't look like he was going to keel over, but he didn't look all that great either.

"No. Got a couple busted ribs. They can't do much but wrap them and give me painkillers. I can do without a thousand-dollar bill from the ER for shit I can take care of myself." His raspy voice was laced with aggravation and discomfort. He cracked a dark eye open and looked at me. "Thank you for coming to get me. Didn't think I was up to working the clutch and stick shift." He hooked his thumb in the direction of the empty car seat in the back. "Where's Noble?"

I tightened my hold on the steering wheel as a woman in an incredibly revealing outfit suddenly darted across the street in front of me. I gasped a little and slammed on the brakes, getting a middle finger flashed my way as she continued to run across the road.

Shaking my head in disbelief, it took me a minute to get my brain back to the question Solo asked. "She's having an impromptu slumber party with Riley. I wasn't sure where you were, so I didn't want to drag her out of bed and across town in case I got lost. Erica didn't mind watching her for the rest of the night."

He made a low noise and let his gaze drift shut once again. "Figures. Finally have you to myself and a free night without the possibility of an interruption and I can barely move." He grunted and winced as he shifted around in the passenger seat. "Hey, Orley... I wanna ask you a question. You don't have to answer right away because I think I already figured some things out. I want you to know, your answer won't change anything between us, whatever it is."

My shoulders locked and a shiver danced down my spine. I shot him a look out of the corner of my eye but didn't say anything, even when he muttered, "Is your last name Vincent, by any chance? And do you happen to be related to a man named Channing Vincent?"

I almost drove the car up onto the sidewalk I was so shocked. Solo let out a long string of swear words as the car swerved dramatically across the road and he was tossed toward the door. I was lucky it was the middle of the night, otherwise I would've taken out pedestrians and other cars.

Struggling to catch my breath, I looked at the man next to me who was staring at me with a patient, knowing gaze. He snorted and closed his eyes again. "I don't know the whole story. I hope you trust me enough to fill me in eventually. But even without hearing what you have to say, I can tell you I know why you left and why you don't want to be found. The guy is cunning and vicious. He set me up, even though I always thought I was too smart to fall for a ploy like his. I think it's twice as scary when the monsters are arrogant enough to hide in plain sight. I swear on my mother, I will die before I let that asshole get anywhere near you and Noble."

His warm hand reached out and caught mine, squeezing it tightly. I found the roughness comforting and the strength in his grip completely reassuring. I wanted to tell him that Channing Vincent wasn't above murder, that the man who I always called father was capable of outrageous acts of violence and brutality, but the words didn't come. Instead, I simply nodded and whispered, "He doesn't want me, but he will go through whoever gets in his way to get at my kid. It's late, and you need to take care of those ribs. The conversation about how messed up my family is can wait." I was secretly hoping it could wait forever, but now that Solo knew my last name, it was better I filled in the gaps for him rather than him wading through all the garbage information my father had paid through the nose to pump out through the media.

Solo sighed and squeezed my fingers again. "Are you offering to play nurse for me?" He wiggled his eyebrows under the brim of his hat. "I don't think anyone has patched me up after a fight since my mom put me back together whenever I got into fights after school."

It took me a little while to find a parking spot that wasn't too far from the apartment building. Solo was putting on a brave face, but I could tell he was hurting. I wanted to ask about the other guy, but it felt like if I had too much information about what he did in the middle of the night in the warehouse district, I was accepting this kind of thing as my new normal. I shouldn't be crushing on a guy who beat up other people for money. I shouldn't have a slippery, squishy feeling all around my heart when I thought about him getting hurt and the fact he *had* to hurt other people in order to take care of his mother.

When I finally found a spot, it took Solo several long, drawn-out minutes to haul himself out of the car; it took us a lot longer to walk to the front of the building than it should've. For once, I wasn't scanning every alley and jumping at every noise from the shadows. I wasn't terrified of the dark when I was next to Solo. But, I was scared for him, especially when he suddenly wrapped a heavy arm around my shoulders and leaned his weight against me. He was heavy, and his breathing didn't sound good. I instinctively wrapped my arm around his lean waist and tried my best to support him.

We both stopped briefly when we got to the front steps of the building. For the first time since I'd moved in, Lester's ragged, rumpled form wasn't sprawled out across the bottom step. The entire stairway was empty. Thinking back, I hadn't had to step over the homeless man when I rushed out to pick up Solo, either.

"Lester is always on the steps. I wonder where he got off to." I absently commented on the missing man and felt Solo stiffen where his strong, solid frame was pressed against mine. I was glad I was tall. He would've taken out a smaller woman when he suddenly jerked to a stop.

"Was he here earlier?" Solo's tone was sharp under the hitch of pain.

I shook my head and winced as he groaned after taking the first few steps to the front door. "No. I ran down the steps on the way to the car. He wasn't there."

Solo swore again and let me brace him with my hip as I pulled open the door. "Not good. Lester always finds his way back to the stoop. I hope nothing bad happened to him."

I silently agreed and shot dirty looks at the broken elevator as I helped Solo climb the agonizing five flights of stairs to his apartment. We were both sweating up a storm and grumpy as hell by the time I finally got him into his bathroom and helped him strip down so he could climb into the shower. I tried to keep my expression neutral and even, but there was a lot to take in once the man was standing naked in front of me.

I was a mom, so I should've been able to objectively check out his injuries without getting distracted by all the other goods, but it would be a total lie if I said I didn't check him out from head to toe as he practically fell into the shower. He was tattooed and built in a way that practically meant it was required I ogle him when he was naked. I checked him out thoroughly on behalf of all the women who would kill to be in my shoes.

It really was a shame we had the night to ourselves but he was too battered to do anything about it. Under the ink crawling up and down his ribcage, I could see ugly black and purple bruises spreading from his armpit all the way to the top of his waist. He also had a very distinct bruise in the center of his chest that looked like the perfect impression of the sole of a boot. In the light, I could see he had bright red marks all along his jaw and another bruise shadowing his high cheekbone. He looked like hell, but he was standing under his own power and managing to wash himself with one hand.

Collecting his clothes off the floor, I found a hamper to toss them in and went in search of an ACE bandage so I could help him wrap those nasty looking ribs. When I got back to the bathroom, Solo was awkwardly trying to pull up a pair of nylon track pants with one hand. The sight made my mouth go dry, and when I reached out to help him get situated, the feel of all that damp, tattooed skin under my fingertips was enough to make my brain temporarily short circuit. Our timing was always just a little bit off and it was really starting to suck.

He stood still as he instructed me on the best way to wrap the bandage around his torso. It made my heart hurt that he treated the entire ordeal like it was nothing new. He shouldn't know how to treat broken ribs like it was nothing, and I was slightly bitter about the fact that I now also had this knowledge.

Solo was slightly unsteady on his feet, so I helped him to his bed and found the mix of Tylenol and Ibuprofen he asked for in his tiny medicine cabinet. He popped the handful of pills without water and shuddered when they went down. He threw the arm on his less injured side over his eyes and sighed heavily. It was easy to see that today, and maybe all of his very busy, very hectic days, had finally caught up with him. He was ready to crash. It was like watching a very fast, expensive car run out of gas.

"Do you need anything before I leave?" I hated to take off when he was in such obvious pain, but he hadn't asked me to stay and I didn't want to overstep those tricky, invisible boundaries we were always tripping over. Plus, now that he knew my last name, there was a very small part of my paranoid brain worried he wouldn't want anything to do with me. It was one thing to be scared of monsters. It was an entirely different thing to know the woman you lived next to, the one you touched, and tasted, and cared for, came from those beasts you had battled.

Solo moved his arm and squinted up at me. Without his hat and his usual sardonic, remote expression, he looked so much more vulnerable... and human. At some point I'd started to see him as someone so much larger than life. Right now, he simply looked like a man. A tired, beaten, resigned man.

I let out a little gasp when his hand shot out and latched onto my wrist. All it took was a tiny tug for him to pull me down to the mattress next to him. He grunted a little when the bed shifted under my weight but curled his arm around me to hold me in place as he dropped a kiss on the top of my head.

"Not how I envisioned getting you into my bed for the first time. But it will have to do for now." His eyes closed and he gave me a little squeeze as I rested my head on his bare shoulder. "You're the only thing I need, Orley. I need to know you're safe. That you're okay. That you trust me enough to let me help you."

I sighed and carefully threw my arm around his toned stomach. I made sure to keep my touch light so I didn't hurt him any worse than he already was. "You're wrong. I think you need sleep more than you need me." Or the truth. But I didn't say that.

He yawned and nuzzled his nose against the top of my head. Between one breath and the next he was out. His breathing evened, his body loosened... except for where he held me next to him.

Even in his utterly exhausted state, and even though he knew my last name, it seemed like Solomon Sanders had no intention of letting me go.

Solo

Pain pulled me out of a fitful sleep, but it was the warm, soft body curled against mine that woke me up. All of me. A few hours ago, getting a hard-on was the furthest thing from my mind. Now, the rigid length between my legs was the only thing I could think about, even though my entire left side felt like it was on fire. Every single breath hurt, and the slightest movement made me blink away tears of agony. This was far from my first time dealing with busted ribs, but it never got any easier or less painful.

Orley was still wrapped around me. She didn't move throughout the night. Not once did she jostle or bump into any of my broken, bruised parts. Her arm stayed low around my waist and the long leg she had hitched across my thighs never moved close to anything it might damage. Her hair was a silky mess spread across my chest, with single strands catching on the scruff scattered across my chin. I rarely shared a bed with anyone overnight. I was typically too busy to stick around after the fun, and I didn't like my strictly planned schedule interrupted when I had someone else in my space. Orley wasn't like that at all. Somehow, without being aware of it, I'd made room just for her in my life. Having her in my space didn't feel like an imposition at all. It felt like it was meant to be.

I slid a hand across the curve of her hip and along the smooth line of her thigh. My eyebrows shot up when I got a handful of velvety soft, naked skin. I could've sworn when we went to bed she'd had on those black leggings she seemed to live in, but now all she had on was a long t-shirt, hiked up to her waist, and a pair of cute, pink panties that barely covered her. Those long ass legs of hers were free of both the covers and any pants. It was enough to remind me she was going to get up soon and go get her kid. We were also going to have to have a talk about the man who set me up and sent her on the run, but none of that felt like it mattered as much as taking advantage of the fact we had a few stolen moments together. I wasn't exactly up to acrobatics and stunts, but feeling her pressed against me the way she was, suddenly made the pain radiating along my side much more bearable.

Orley was still asleep when I dragged my hand up her side, knuckles brushing her ribcage. I took the fabric of her t-shirt with me and traced the subtle curves of her body. Her bright blue eyes popped open in alarm when I got the gathered material to her neck. She made a surprised little noise, but cooperated by ducking down when I tugged the cotton over her head. Her red hair floated around her face like a ring of fire, and she watched me with wide eyes as I caught the side of her face with my palm and tilted her head so I could drop my mouth over hers. The kiss was hesitant at first, tentative and soft. It was obvious she was worried about inadvertently hurting me; I could barely feel the touch of her palms on my shoulders when she shifted her hold on me as I started to thoroughly devour her.

We weren't going to be interrupted this time. Right now, she was still the girl next door who needed someone to look out for her, the only girl in years who'd interested me enough to make time for. There were no little eyes and ears to hide from. This was an opportunity I refused to let slip by, even if it meant my body felt like it was being turned inside out. Pain was just as sharp and prevalent under my skin as the pleasure.

Slowly, she started to kiss me back. I felt some of the rigid tension leave her shoulders, and her lips and tongue started to give under the insistent pressure of mine. One of her arms wrapped around my neck, and the other slid across my abs, careful of the bandage still tightly wrapped around my middle. She traced the outline of my belly button with the tip of her fingernail, and the little scratch against my skin caused my dick to throb against the nylon material of my pants. There was no hiding how deeply, and quickly, I reacted to her touch. My entire body felt like it was humming with anticipation. There was a buzz vibrating along all my nerve endings, making the acute pain firing along my entire left side a dull echo against everything else she was causing me to feel.

Orley pulled back slightly, eyes wide as she took in every feature on my face, obviously searching for signs of pain and discomfort. "What about your ribs?" One of her hands lightly drifted over the beige bandage strapped around my middle.

I lifted an eyebrow and dropped a haphazard kiss on the very tip of her nose and tugged her closer. I sighed in contentment when I felt the sweet drag of her breasts across my bare skin. "Well, you owe me one, remember? You're going to have to do all the work this time." I wiggled my eyebrows and smirked at her. "But that means I'll owe you one back." If we could keep going like that forever, I would have no complaints.

She studied me for a long, quiet moment. She was obviously weighing the likelihood of us getting another free moment like this against how badly I was injured. The small window of free, uninterrupted time apparently won out, because a moment later she was the one kissing me with delicate aggression, and her toned leg hitched across my thigh moved so it was rubbing against the erection straining to get free from my track pants. I hissed at the sensual contact and let my teeth sink into her lower lip. The kiss went from careful to consuming in under a second. Teeth clashed, tongues twisted, and every single place we touched felt like it was electrified.

I felt her hands shake a little as she helped me slide my pants down my waist. I couldn't heft my weight up off the bed like I normally would, so I got the pleasurable sensation of feeling her hands ghosting over my hips and down my legs. She was the only woman, other than the one who raised me, who had helped me dress and undress because I couldn't do it myself. That kind of care, the simple act of her being there when I needed someone, was enough for warmth to unfurl slow and steady in my gut. She wasn't a woman who was easy or convenient, but the more time I spent trying to figure her out, the more I realized I would fight anything in the world that tried to get between us... including the lack of time we had to be with one another.

Orley looked up at me from under her long lashes as she slowly crawled her way back up my body. The light brush of her fingertips against the inside of my thighs made my entire body shudder; the heat from her gaze made my cock kick in reaction as she zeroed in on the one part of me oblivious to the dull pain still curling around my insides. My dick didn't give two shits about broken ribs. All it could focus on was the way her lips were damp from her tongue darting out to wet them, and the kiss of her warm breath as her head lowered closer to the slippery, leaking tip.

I nearly bolted upright into a sitting position when her tongue suddenly danced across the rounded head, the tip skating across the weeping slit with a little flick that made me see stars. I wrapped my hands in her long hair and blew out a long breath, reminding myself if I moved wrong, this would all be over before it even got started. It took every ounce of self-control I possessed to stay mostly still as she tilted her head and opened her mouth so she could swallow almost the entire length of my throbbing erection. What she couldn't fit in the warm, wet cavern of her mouth, she wrapped her hands around, starting a torturous rhythm of stroking and sucking that turned my blood to lava and made every muscle in my body tense. My ribs protested... loudly. But, the rest of me felt so good and was so caught up in the way Orley was equal parts confident and hesitant as she took me apart, the complaint was easy enough to ignore.

I moaned in approval as she hummed around the unyielding flesh in her mouth. Her touch was remarkably gentle as she learned every inch, every pulse, every quiver of pleasure. Even as delicately as she was handling me, the sensation of her fingers learning my most vulnerable and sensitive spots was going to be forever branded in my memory. It felt so much better having a woman who cared touch me like I was special than it did to have a stranger's hands crawling all over me, desperate and impatient. Orley was mindful of my currently broken body, but she was still aware of the way I ached for intimacy and the connection we shared.

Her tongue licked and twirled with remarkable skill around the crown and down along the veiny length of the underside. When her lips touched the curl of her fingers, I gasped and pulled on her hair probably harder than I needed to. My hips lifted of their own volition, following the drag and pull of her mouth, but an instant later I regretted losing control. White hot agony blazed from my shoulder all the way down to my knee, and when I moaned this time, it wasn't in pleasure.

Orley popped off my cock with a narrow-eyed look and a mew of concern. I knew if I didn't distract her immediately, she was going to pull away because she was worried about how I was holding up. Using my hold on her hair, I tugged her away from my very eager erection. Once she was hovering over me, I wrapped a hand around the back of her naked thigh and urged her to straddle me. She still had on the barely there pink panties and I would never forget the way the wet spot in the center rubbed against the wet tip of my cock. So hot. So sexy. She was effortless when it came to seduction and temptation.

"If I have to choose between your mouth and that sweet spot my cock is trying to claim as its own, I'm taking the second option." I felt like our entire relationship had been weeks and weeks of foreplay, and while all of it had been a lot of fun, I really thought I might die if I didn't get a chance to have her at least once. I reached out and traced the elastic band of her underwear where it disappeared against the high curve of her inner thigh. "When I can bend over without feeling like my body is going to shatter, we can take turns learning each other's taste." I arched an eyebrow and made a promise I couldn't wait to keep. "I will lick every single inch of you. When I can move, I will fuck you so good, you'll forget you hate everything about this city."

I smoothed a hand over her porcelain cheek and watched as she took the words in. She must've decided the risk was going to be worth the reward in the long run, because she lifted up so she could strip off the rest of her clothing and settled back on my waist, her hands landing on the wall over my head since I didn't own a headboard.

"I don't know that I'm good enough to make you forget your name, or where you are, but I think I can make any discomfort you're going to be in for the next few minutes worth it." Both of her dark red eyebrows lifted, and a sassy grin tugged at her full lips. "Condom?"

I blinked in surprise since protection was usually the first order of business when I was with someone.

This girl really did turn my world and my priorities upside down. I was just so eager to be with her, to have her, I couldn't think of any of the practical things which typically governed my actions.

I shot an arm out and rummaged through the nightstand, finding a half-empty box and fishing out what I needed. When I handed it over, I expected Orley to blush or look away. I was never sure if I was getting the siren or the sweetheart. It seemed she was in full-on seductress mode because she ripped the foil packet with her teeth and rolled the latex down the straining length of my cock without blinking an eye.

I wanted to ask if she was ready. Sure, there had been a visible wet spot on her underwear, but I hadn't touched her, prepped her, tasted her the way I normally would. I was a lot of things in bed, but selfish was not one of them. I was ready to go off like a rocket thanks to the attention of her mouth, but that didn't mean she was turned on or excited enough for things to feel as good for her as they felt for me.

I shouldn't have worried. Orley wasn't someone who went with the flow. She was someone on her own path, used to calling her own shots, not afraid to take what she needed, but also strong enough to give back.

She bent down so she could kiss me, her lips teasing and light as they danced over mine. One of her hands cupped my jaw as she used the other to keep her weight braced above me. Even through the latex wrapped tightly around my dick, I could feel the heat and moisture emanating from her center. When the tip of my erection dragged slowly through her soft folds, I thought the top of my head was going to come off. Nothing had ever felt better. Her body fluttered around mine as the first few inches of my cock breached her snug opening. It was clear it'd been a while since she'd been with someone this way, and the thought of being the last person to know what it felt like when her body welcomed the invasion, the way it quivered and quaked as I slowly pushed into her, had me wanting to pound my chest like King Kong. It was an archaic, mostly unreasonable way of thinking, but now that I knew how well we fit together, how amazing her silky heat felt surrounding me, I wasn't sure I was going to ever be able to let her go. I sure as hell was never going to be able to walk away from her under my own steam. She brought me to my knees.

Orley made a strangled noise as gravity helped her sink all the way down the iron shaft she was rocking against. Once I bottomed out inside of her tight, wet channel, we both let out a gasp of surprise as our gazes locked. It was there in the blazing blue of her eyes. This thing between us was just as big, just as scary, just as consuming to her as it was to me. Neither one of us knew what to do with the emotions swirling between us; they were so much bigger and brighter than either of us had ever faced before.

Her thumb brushed across my lower lip and her eyes drifted closed as she started to slowly rock her hips up and down. Her expression was blissed out and there was a stain of hot pink across her cheeks. She looked amazing, and I totally got off on the way her body writhed and moved on mine. My abs constricted as pleasure started to coil tightly around my spine. She was right.

All I could focus on was the warmth between her legs and the way her inner muscles tugged at my cock with greedy, hungry little movements. She was careful with every lift and drop, so while the pain was still there, it was a faint memory compared to the new sensations she was giving me. For the first time, I was at someone else's mercy. Orley was the one calling all the shots, we were completely on her timetable, and I was totally under her command. It was different than what normally went on in my bed, but not in a bad way. It was a novelty to drown in the pleasure someone else gave; I was out of my head, not worrying about how what I was doing affected the other person.

I grunted as she rotated her hips in a little circle and let my hand rest on the sweet curve of her ass. "God, you feel good." She was so worth any pain I would suffer later.

She panted out a short breath and pushed her wild hair behind her shoulder. Her skin was starting to gleam with a fine layer of sweat, and all I wanted was to be able to lift up so I could put my mouth on those sweet, velvety nipples of hers. Next time. If I ever got the chance to devour her from head to toe, I was going to fulfill my promise and put my mouth all over her.

"You feel good, too." A faint smile pulled at her mouth and her head cocked to one side. "If I'd known boys from the city were so much better at sex than the boys who lived behind the gates, I would've been in big trouble."

I growled at her and pulled her down so I could get at her mouth. She moaned into the kiss as I sneered,

179

"Only this boy from the city can make you feel like this. Don't forget it."

She laughed against my lips and started to move more urgently against me. I could feel her body softening and getting slicker. She was having a hard time catching her breath and keeping her eyes open. The girl was stunning when she was on the edge of breaking apart and I wanted to be the one who took her to that precipice over and over again. I wanted to be the only boy from either side of the tracks who ever witnessed her when she got lost in satisfaction and surrender.

It took some finesse to get the hand from my uninjured side between her legs. As soon as my thumb touched the tight bud of her clit, Orley's eyes flew open and her back bowed. Her long hair slid across the top of my thighs and the way her pussy clamped down on my cock as if it was never going to release me pulled me into my own orgasm. Passion slithered up my spine and shot out in sparks along my nerves. My whole body tensed and pulsed in one long wave of release underneath her. My ribs screamed, but I ignored them and continued to toy with her sensitive bundle of nerves as she rode out her own spiral of pleasure. It was the closest I'd ever come to finding completion at the same time as my partner.

This girl and I were from completely different worlds. We ran on opposite frequencies and had very different final destinations in mind, but nevertheless, she was the one I was in sync with. She was the one who matched me step for step and kept up even when I didn't know if I was coming or going.

A moment later she grabbed my wrist and pulled my hand free from where it was still playing, still learning what made her eyes pop and her breath catch. She climbed off me with a grace that shouldn't be possible after how thoroughly we wrecked each other. She knelt on the bed next to me, collecting her hair in one hand as she blinked at me in a daze.

"As much as I would like to spend the day in bed with you trying to figure out all the ways we can do that without hurting your ribs, I have to go get Noble. And I want to check and see if Lester made it back yet." She tugged on her lower lip nervously. "I have a bad feeling about him being gone from his spot."

I groaned and raked my hands down my face. "You hop in the shower and worry about your kid. I'll go outside and check on Lester."

She made a face and reached out a hand to lightly trace my eyebrows. "You almost passed out coming up those stairs last night. I can stick my head outside. It'll be fine."

I grunted again, because she was right, but I refused to acknowledge my own limitations out loud. When you were an apex predator, you never showed your weakness. That's how you ended up as prey.

I held onto her hand as she moved to climb off the bed. Her blue eyes were shadowed when they met mine. She was something else to me now, someone important and precious, but I still barely knew her; having her last name and knowing her father was a world-class prick didn't change that. I needed her to give me everything, not just her body.

"We still need to talk, Orley. Don't run away from me."

For a split second, I could tell the thought had definitely crossed her mind. She cleared her throat and turned her hand over so she could squeeze mine. "I know. We'll talk."

I let her go, only because I believed she was going to come back to me, and because I could see that she knew even if she did run, I would come after her.

Orley

Lester wasn't on the stoop in the morning when I collected Noble from Erica's after calling off work for the day. He wasn't there when I went out to grab lunch because my fridge was empty and the only thing Solo had in his was bottled water and old pizza. The homeless man still hadn't made an appearance by dinner time, and Solo was doing a really bad job of hiding his growing concern every time I reported that the older man was still missing in action. On the plus side, Noble loved her mini-sleepover and was already rambling about the next time she was going to spend the night with Riley. I promised her I would make it happen, while selfishly enjoying my fake sick day. It felt like it'd been forever since I'd gotten a full day with my kid. Even if I had to pry Noble away from Solo's bedside every five minutes because she was so worried about him, it was nice to get my fill of childish chatter and sweet hugs and kisses. She missed me, too, but I came in second next to her favorite neighbor.

I left her with him while I ran to the store so I could grab enough stuff to stock both fridges. I felt like I needed to keep busy to keep my mind of the fact Channing had set Solo up. The details of the fight made my skin crawl, and I could barely make it through the gritty reply Solo insisted on laying out for me. As a result of Channing's dirty play, I was worried Solo was moving a little bit too slow to be a proper babysitter, but the instant my daughter curled up next to him on his bed, she crashed. I loved the way her black curls tangled in a chaotic mess around her face as she cuddled up to the big, tattooed fighter like he was her own personal teddy bear. Seeing her little body wrapped so trustingly around Solo's broken and battered one did something to my heart. It hurt, but in a good way. It was a sensation I'd never felt before, which was pretty much a daily occurrence now that Solo inserted himself into my life. Even when he told me to be careful because he couldn't go with me to the store, it sent shivers up my spine. No one worried about me or my safety like he did.

Every time I turned around, he was doing or saying something that made me feel things in a whole new way. I knew living in the city was going to change me, that I was going to be forced to grow up and adapt. I had no clue moving here in a panic was going to force me to learn how to love... not only myself and my child, but someone else, as well. Love wasn't for the weak and timid. It took leaving the gates of my old life to toughen me up enough to even consider risking something as fragile as my heart and my daughter's happiness.

After filling both fridges, I made dinner at Solo's apartment while he entertained Noble. I was slightly resentful all the man had to do was smile at my kid, and she was perfectly content in his company. I had to jump through hoops and run through a marathon of activities to keep her occupied. I pouted about it until I got a kiss from both Noble and Solo. One warmed my heart and made me smile. The other turned it inside out and made my breath catch.

We ate dinner together on Solo's leather couch, and for the first time in my entire life, I felt like I was part of a family. I wasn't worried about saying or doing the wrong thing. I wasn't struggling to find my place or willfully searching for approval and acceptance. I had a place where it was easy to feel like I belonged and no one else could possibly take my place.

Solo was a trooper and sat through two different Disney movies, chuckling occasionally as Noble belted out the wrong words to several of the songs. He promised her repeatedly he would take her back to his old school for a couple more classes and so she could run around the track once he was feeling better. She fell asleep with her head in my lap and her tiny legs across his. For the first time since leaving my old life, I let someone else put my daughter to bed. She was the only other girl who was allowed inside Solo's bedroom as far as I was concerned, and it made my heart squeeze, that the huge, tough guy went soft as melted butter for my kid. He didn't seem to mind giving his bed up to the almost four-year-old at all.

Before Solo made his way back to the couch, he stopped in the kitchen and made a couple drinks. He laughed at me when I told him I couldn't stop at a liquor store and get him a six-pack like he asked. I wasn't sure if he was amused by the fact I was still underage, or because I was probably the only human living in the city who didn't have a fake ID, or know how to get one. Either way, he made do with the vodka that lived in his freezer. I took the second drink from him and looked at him over the rim of the glass. He could've asked if I was ready to talk. He could demand the answers I really did owe him, but he didn't. He settled back on the couch, wincing a little with each movement, and silently waited until I was ready to put everything on the line for him. One of these days I was going to figure out how he read me so well when I was sure he'd never dealt with anyone who came from my world before.

I downed the vodka and OJ and pulled my legs up so I could wrap my arms around them and rest my chin on my knee. I watched Solo for a few silent minutes as he pretended to be engrossed in whatever was on ESPN. When he finally looked my way, I forced the first few words out, and was shocked at how easily the entire story poured out after I started.

"My last name is Vincent, but Channing Vincent isn't my father." It was the Vincent's biggest, most dirty little secret. I'd kept it for so long, the truth felt weird and wrong once it was spit out. "But he *is* Noble's grandfather." It was like a Shakespeare play. Rich people were bored and sad about their lives, so they went out and decided to play with the fates of others for pure entertainment.

Solo choked a little on his drink and blinked his long, dark lashes at me in surprise. "Say what?"

I needed the levity and his easy acceptance to settle into telling someone exactly how messed up my bloodline was. He always had exactly the right response, which made giving him what he asked for so much easier. I was used to being judged for the sins of my father, but all Solo could see was the scared woman baring her heart to him.

"Neither one of my parents was faithful throughout their marriage. My mom got knocked up with me on accident during one of her longer affairs, and in return, my father impregnated her best friend for revenge." I shook my head and closed my eyes briefly. "High society is actually a very small circle, so of course my mother's bastard, and my father's, ended up in all the same schools." No one warned me I was going to fall into my father's trap and into his son's arms when I was lost and hopelessly trying to find my way. I had no clue Noble's father had more right to the name Vincent than I did. I had no idea my father was silently waiting for me to find my way to the young man. He knew I would, because he was the absolute worst, which made him my best option for petty revenge. I was on a mission to bring home the most terrible boy I could find. He just happened to be Channing's son.

"Noble's dad is actually Vincent's son. I didn't know. My parents were horrible to each other, right up until the end. To each other, and often to me." My mom always made herself the buffer between me and my resentful father, but she didn't tell me the truth about my lineage until it was too late. I spent my entire teenage years chasing after love from a man who despised my very existence. Channing Vincent hated me because I wasn't his. But, to avoid a scandal and to appease my mother's side of the family, he had to pretend. It was simply how things were done behind those iron gates.

Solo's eyebrows shot up so high they almost disappeared into his hairline. "So, Channing knocked up your mom's best friend, and then years later that baby turned into the guy who knocked you up?" It really sounded like a bad soap opera when it was all laid out like that. I wouldn't believe a word if I were the one listening.

I nodded at him and sighed again. "Neither of us knew. Channing half-assed playing dad to me, and my mother's friend's husband did the same to Noble's dad. It's no wonder we were both so screwed up and attracted to each other. We knew each other our entire lives and had no clue we were both living a sham." I felt my hands clench and an angry flush start to race up my neck. I started to explain why Channing was so interested in Noble when he wanted nothing to do with me. "Since I wasn't his, Channing never had plans for me. No ambitions or aspirations. He never pushed for me to join his country club, or to follow in his footsteps and apply to his alma mater. He never brought me around his business or introduced me to the sons of his associates. He never did any of the things wealthy fathers do to ensure their daughters maintain the family fortune." I still remembered being heartbroken when I told him I wanted to intern with his company, only to be told there wasn't a suitable position for me. "If I was paying attention, I might have put it together sooner. Channing was furious when I told him I was pregnant with Noble. But his attitude totally changed when he found out who the father was. I wasn't his, but Noble is. She shares actual Vincent blood, so everything he denied me, he wanted to give to her." She was his heir… the only one he could claim without causing a scandal and upsetting the status quo. I'd been so blinded by relief that he actually seemed supportive, that I'd finally done something he approved of, before I realized no normal father would be celebrating an accidental teenage pregnancy.

I closed my eyes and swallowed hard. "I overheard Channing and my mother arguing one night after Noble's dad bailed. Channing wanted to use his bastard son to get custody of Noble. He was going to try and take her from me." I shuddered just thinking about it. "He was telling my mother that he knew someone in an institution who would have no qualms about locking me up for as long as he asked. He wanted me out of the picture so he could take my baby and turn her into the child he always wanted. "My mom wasn't having it. She let him run over her and dismiss me my whole life, but she finally stood up to Channing when he tried to get between me and her grandchild."

It was the only time in memory I could remember respecting my mother. She was screaming at Channing Vincent that she was going to expose all their dirty laundry and tell the world what kind of man he really was. She could ruin him with little effort and Channing must have realized he had finally pushed her too far.

I jolted when I felt the rough tip of Solo's fingertip trace the track of a tear I wasn't aware had fallen. "He hit her and told her he would kill her before she said anything to anyone." I rubbed at the wet streaks on my face and took a deep breath before plowing ahead.

"She must've lost her balance or something when she went down after he struck her. She was yelling at him, threatening to call the cops, and then everything went silent." I remembered leaving teeth marks in the back of my hand to muffle my scream. I remembered how quickly the metallic scent of blood filled the air. "She hit her head on the corner of his desk." At least that was the official story. The unofficial story was that Channing very well may have helped her connect with corner of his antique desk in just the right way. The only two people who knew what really happened in that room were my mother and the man who absolutely would kill to keep his secrets buried. "She died that night, and I knew if I didn't get out of Channing Vincent's house, I was next." I smuggled Noble out of the Vincent estate in the middle of the night and never looked back. Maybe I should've gone farther than the city just beyond those protective gates, but at the time, I was too scared to go too far from the only home I'd ever known. It'd taken the man sitting across from me, patiently listening to my living, breathing nightmare, to show me home could be found anywhere if you followed the right person inside. "Like I told you before, I knew Noble's dad was the weak link, so I paid him off and made him sign away his rights. Channing can't use him to get to my daughter." Well, he could, but not without bringing unwanted attention to himself and his past misdeeds. "If he finds me, he's going to get me out of the way so he can take Noble. If he does, there will be no fighting back. I honestly didn't think he would look for me in the city. As far as he knows, I can't survive without his American Express black card and weekly allowance." Channing had too much money and too many friends in high places. If Channing managed to remove me from the equation, who was left to fight for Noble? I was all she had.

Only, I wasn't the only one she could rely on anymore. There was someone else in her corner now. Someone who would never be intimidated by a man like Channing Vincent. A man who knew what it was like to fight for the people you loved. I firmly believed, without him saying a single word, that Solo would stand between Noble and anyone trying to hurt her or take her away.

I let out a surprised noise when I was suddenly yanked across the expanse of couch separating us. "Your ribs!" I didn't want to hurt him worse than he had to be hurting from the sudden movement, so I let him haul me into his lap. He tucked my head under his chin. For such a tough guy, he was one hell of a good cuddler. I leaned into the caress when he ran his hand down my spine and dropped a kiss on the crown of my head.

"No one is taking that little girl away from you. I don't care if I have to sell my soul to the men who run this city, I will do whatever it takes to keep you together."

I rested my forehead against the hollow of his throat and whispered my deepest, most profound desire. "I'd like it if we could all stay together for as long as possible. Our lives have been so much better with you in them." Even if there was only so much he had to give.

Solo was quiet for a long time, but eventually his arms tightened their hold. "You've both brought a lot to my life that I didn't know I was missing, as well. I'm not about to let anyone take that away."

I knew it was the kind of promise I couldn't expect him to keep, but just like I told Noble, I had to give him enough time to prove he could. I was going to have to be patient and believe he was always going to be able to be my hero.

"Am I hurting you?" I hated that he could barely move because Channing decided to play hardball.

A deep chuckle vibrated under my ear. "The ribs don't feel great, but I'll live. Just gotta give them time to heal. All the parts of us that break eventually mend with enough time."

Not only was he hot, great in bed, and wonderfully protective, he was also very smart. My heart had always been somewhat broken from the way it was mistreated in that opulent mansion on the hill. But time and distance from that life had indeed started to stitch it back together. Pretty soon the entire thing would be whole, just in time for me to hand it over to the man who not only stood between me and the rest of the world, but who also taught me how to stand on my own.

Solo

Orley was nervous.

Outwardly she was calm and composed, but her hand was clammy where it was clutched in mine and her fingers were twitching involuntarily. She kept telling Noble to behave and gently repeated the soft reminder that my mom wasn't like other moms. She told Noble over and over again how special my mother was, and the words did something to my heart. My mom was special. She always had been, even if I was the only one who recognized it before she got injured. It was cute the way Noble nodded so gravely every time Orley prompted her to be good so they would be invited to visit again. The adorable little girl took her assigned task very seriously. The look of determination on her cherubic features was almost an identical match to the one her mother wore when she was focused intently on something.

Since Orley had ripped open her past for me, I figured it was only fitting I take her to meet my mother. I knew so much more about her than her last name, and while most of it wasn't all that pretty, none of it was enough to scare me off. I was certain every ugly secret she shared seemed as dark and dirty as it could get, but the reality was, I'd witnessed far worse growing up in the city. I understood Channing Vincent was dangerous, especially since he knew Orley was hiding out in the slums right around the corner from his mansion. But he didn't frighten me a fraction as much as the man I worked for and the man I fought for. He was greedy, manipulative, and used to getting his own way, but he wasn't what I would consider a serious threat. At least, he wasn't now that I knew exactly what I was facing. Orley was terrified of him, regardless of how many times I promised to keep both her and Noble safe.

Getting out of the center of the city was a good break for all of us. My mom was having a good day, so it was time for a long overdue visit. I wanted Orley's mind off Vincent and the past, not that I planned on her tying herself in knots over meeting my mother.

I squeezed the hand practically vibrating in my grasp. "Stop worrying. Mom will love you. Both of you." I winked at Noble, who was holding Orley's other hand and the picture she drew for my Mom after her last bad day. "She's never met a stranger and makes friends with everyone. She's the staff's favorite long-term patient, even though she can be a handful."

Orley wrinkled her nose and huffed out a breath, which sent her dark red hair dancing away from her face. "I've never met 'the parents' before. I was never with anyone long enough to worry about having to make a good impression on someone who means everything to the person I care about." Her fingers flexed in mine again. "At the bare minimum, I used to be able to say I was from a good family, but that's not even the truth. Now all I have is the fact that I'm a single mom who is barely able to pay her bills, hiding from what remains of that not-so-good family. I sound like a real catch." She rolled her eyes toward the sky and I had to adjust my stride as her steps noticeably slowed. "You can do so much better, and your mom will see it."

I tugged at her hand and returned to a normal pace, practically dragging her and Noble behind me. "I've never brought anyone to meet my mom. This is a first for me, too. And it's not about being better, it's about doing what's right. You're right for me, and I have no doubt my mom will be able to see it right away."

She still didn't look convinced, but we were already at the entrance to the facility, so there was no more time to try and convince her everything was going to go smoothly. Once I pushed through the doors, I was immediately engulfed in warm welcomes and aggressive affection from several of the nursing staff. My mother's main caregiver was a woman in her fifties named Melody. She was a lifelong resident of the city, so she was as tough as nails, but she had also decided to take up where my mother left off and did her best to baby me every time I came to visit. She was one of the main reasons I didn't mind being used as a punching bag in order to keep my mother somewhere she got amazing care and was truly adored by the staff.

After greeting Orley with a brisk handshake and a speculative look, the nurse smiled at the little girl hovering close to her mother and stated, "You brought company with you this time. Who is this?" The older woman crouched down so she was at Noble's level, cocking her head with exaggerated amazement at Noble's drawing for my mother. "And what do you have there, you little cutie pie?"

Once again, the little girl proved to be braver than her mother. Noble proudly showed off the drawing to the collection of nurses who suddenly gathered. It had to be those wild black curls and innocent smile that stole every heart she encountered.

"It's for Solo's mommy. He told me she would like it a lot." Noble nodded definitively like my words were gospel. Melody looked up at me from under her lashes, doing a terrible job of hiding her smile.

"Yep, Solo's mommy will definitely like it very much. Are you ready to go and meet her?" Noble nodded enthusiastically while Orley turned white and looked like she was ready to bolt out the front door. Melody lifted herself back to her full height and gave me a critical once over. "Maybe Solo needs to have one of the nurses check him out before you leave. He looks like he lost another fight."

Noble's pouty bottom lip jutted out as her tiny eyebrows pulled together in a mini-frown when she looked up at me. "Fighting is bad. You get in trouble when you fight and get your privileges taken away." She stumbled over the word privileges, but the rest of the words in her quickly spoken sentence were clear enough for me to fill in the blanks.

Orley reached out and put her hand on Noble's head. She blushed a bright red and hurriedly uttered,

"Remember, we talked about how sometimes there is no choice but to fight. Like when you're protecting yourself or someone you love. It all depends on the circumstance."

Noble nodded as if she understood, but in a whisper loud enough to be heard in Alaska, she tilted her head in my direction and asked, "What's a sir-com-stance?" It was another big word she murdered with her limited vocabulary, but it was the cutest assassination possible.

I gave her another wink and told her, "The situation. Sometimes people end up in a bad situation and they have to fight, but generally fighting is bad and someone always gets hurt. It's a good idea to stay away from a fight if you can."

All the nurses laughed as she stuck out her small fist to bump against mine. I caught Orley's surprised look out of the corner of my eye. I'd been spending a lot of time with Noble lately, and it seemed like she was starting to pick up on some of my more common habits. The little girl turned to her mom and offered up the same fist for another bump. Orley complied with a small shake of her head as I got sly, delighted grins from the majority of the staff watching the interaction.

Catching Noble's hand and placing my free hand on Orley's lower back, I started to guide them away from the fascinated staff toward the little efficiency apartment my mother called home. Noble was practically bouncing up and down in excitement. This entire outing was a big adventure to her, and I hoped whatever her future held, be it here in the city or somewhere else, she never lost her sense of wonder and her infectious enthusiasm. Those things were definitely worth fighting for, no matter what was lost.

My mom opened the door after I knocked. For someone who'd been injured as gravely as she had, my mother somehow managed to look like any other suburban mom. She was around the same height as Orley and had the same dark hair and eyes as I did. Her face had settled into her age gracefully. The only sign of the violence that had forever changed her life was the obvious bald spot on the side of her head where the doctors had to literally piece her skull back together. Her eyes were as wide and innocent as the little girl's whose hand I held in mine. She blinked at me for a second, the same way she always did. Some days when I visited, it took her up to an hour to remember who I was. On good days it was usually quicker.

Today was a good day, because a wide grin broke out on her face, one Noble immediately matched. With zero shyness or hesitation, she stuck out the drawing and grinned up at my mom in all her gap-toothed glory. "Hi. I'm Noble. I drew this for you. It's me and Mommy and Solo."

My mother took the picture, eyes lighting up. "It's pretty. Thank you." She held the paper to her chest and gasped. "I'll draw you a picture, too!" She reached out and pushed my shoulder playfully. "You brought me a friend this time!"

Noble took my mother's exuberance in stride, and when I glanced over at Orley, she looked like she was caught somewhere between love and hate. It was a dichotomy I understood well. I loved my mother with all of my heart and soul, but there were moments when I hated what her life had become, what had been stolen from her, what I'd lost. Fortunately, the love always won out, and the same thing happened with Orley. A second later she had the same expression on her face she wore when Noble did something particularly adorable.

I cleared my throat and pulled the tall redhead by the hand so she was standing next to me. "Mom, this is my friend Orley. She's Noble's mom. They moved in next door to me not too long ago and I've been spending a lot of time with them lately. I talk about you all the time, so they were excited to come and meet you."

My mother stuck her hand out and Orley gave it a gentle shake. My mom repeated the motion in Noble's direction and the little girl shook her hand with a serious expression on her face as she practically yelled, "It's nice to meet you."

My mom's dark eyes drifted from Orley to where my hand was still resting on her lower back. Her eyebrows winged up and she tilted her head to the side a little bit. After a moment long enough to make the silence awkward, she stepped away from the door and waved us into the apartment.

"You're pretty." She stopped once we were inside the smallish space and looked over at Orley again. "Are you Solo's new girlfriend?"

Orley faltered a step, so I reached out to steady her. I smiled at my mom and nodded behind Orley's head as she stumbled over her answer.

"We... I ... Uh.... we're close. I think he's pretty great." I could hear her voice shake but she kept her eyes on my mother and the twitch in her hands was no longer obvious.

"He is great. I love it when he comes and sees me, and this time he brought a friend." She reached out a hand in Noble's direction, which the little girl immediately took. Together they practically skipped toward her living room. My mom was telling Noble all about her favorite colors and her favorite things to draw. She had the same careless delight in the little things as Noble. It made my heart feel like it'd been drop kicked by a hundred different emotions watching the two of them together.

I dropped a kiss on the top of Orley's head and asked if she was okay. She nodded briefly and exhaled audibly. "I'm good. You look so much like her. She's beautiful."

"She likes you." I reassured her as we slowly followed my mom and Noble.

Orley snorted and I got an elbow in the side. Luckily, it was the side without the broken ribs, but I still grunted at the impact and made a big deal of rubbing the spot dramatically for sympathy points.

"How do you know she likes me? Because she told me I'm pretty?" She sounded utterly skeptical.

I chuckled under my breath and smoothed my hand down the fiery fall of her hair. "Because she opened the door and let us in. Some days she won't even let Melody come in, and that woman has cared for her like she's family for years."

Orley blew out another long breath and turned her head so she could look up at me. "That's good, then. I want her to like me."

I lifted an eyebrow at her and wrapped my arm around her shoulders. "What about me? Shouldn't I be the one you're worried about liking you?"

She flushed and lowered her eyelashes to shield her gaze. The way the blue changed colors was always a giveaway to how she was feeling. I could read the truth in those different shades even when it was hard to trust what was coming out of her mouth.

"You like me."

I laughed again and gave her a hard side hug. "You're sure about that?"

She nodded, still refusing to meet my gaze. "I'm sure. This is the last place I would be if you didn't like me."

"True." No one else had ever mattered enough to bring them to meet my mom.

Two heads snapped up from whatever they were focused on when we entered the living room. My mother's eyes traveled over us, lingering on my healing face and the thickness around my middle from the bandage wrapped tightly around my ribs. Sometimes she lectured me for showing up looking like I played in the Super Bowl without pads. Other times she wasn't even fazed by the bruises and busted knuckles. I'd come home from school roughed up enough times, seeing me battered was nothing new, but today she focused her attention on Orley.

"If you're his girlfriend, you need to take care of him." It was stated so matter-of-factly both Orley and I were slightly taken aback.

"I will. Promise." She sounded so sincere it was impossible not to believe her.

My mother nodded and turned her surprisingly sharp gaze in my direction. "If you're her boyfriend, you need to take care of her. You can't be busy all the time anymore."

I coughed to clear my throat and hide my laughter. "Okay, Mom. I'll do my best to not be as busy anymore so I can take care of Orley."

She nodded and turned to put her hand on top of Noble's untamable curls. "And you both need to take care of my new friend. I like her a lot."

"That's the plan. I'm going to take care of both of them, and you." Or I would die trying.

Noble beamed up at my mother as if Orley and I weren't even in the room. It was obvious the two of them were enamored with each other. The little girl rested her tiny chin in her hand and mischievously replied with, "I like you, too. Do you like cake? We should have my mommy get us some cake!"

My mother clapped her hands excitedly and agreed wholeheartedly. "I love cake."

I sighed and let Orley go sit with the other two ladies who held different parts of my heart. I tugged the brim of my ball cap lower on my forehead, hiding the sudden rush of overwhelming emotions taking hold of me.

"I'll go talk to Melody and see if she can help us find some cake." I needed a second to get myself together.

I'd always worried about something happening to me leaving my mom confused and alone. Without having to ask, I knew Orley would never turn her back on my mother. If things went south, and if someone managed to take me out, I had no doubt the pretty redhead would be the bridge between my mother and the rest of the world. She guarded her past selfishly, but she gave her heart and compassion without a second thought. It was cute that she wanted my mom to like her, but it was even better that I knew instinctively she would care for my mother, simply because the older woman meant everything to me.

She wasn't just the right girl I happened to meet at the wrong time.

She was the *only* girl I was starting to think I couldn't live without *all* of the time.

Orley

It was a quiet ride back to the city, minus the occasional babble from Noble. She had a blast with Solo's mom and loved all the attention from the doting nurses. She got her cake and then some. I was pretty sure Melody went out and bought the closest grocery store out of sweets once Noble asked for them. It was obvious the staff cared immensely for their long-term patients, and the fact Noble immediately took a shine to one of their favorites made her even better in their eyes. It was hard to resist my kid and that smile of hers on any given day. When her pure, untainted heart and goodness glowed as bright as the sun, there was no way any functioning human could escape falling in love with her.

Solo seemed to be deep in thought. He'd joked around all afternoon, and I realized the way he treated Noble was very similar to the way he treated his mother. He was calm, patient, and managed to put a lid on all that simmering testosterone that usually swirled around him. He turned into a gentle teddy bear when he was around anyone who was obviously not a threat. It was another layer to the man that was fascinating to see. I had no idea how he separated the guy who was soft and sweet with his mother from the guy who was intense and intimidating enough to keep away the predators on the streets. Solomon Sanders wore a lot of different hats, and they all managed to look damn good on him.

I must have dozed off after getting lost in thought, because when I blinked my eyes open, the sun was setting, Noble was silent in the backseat, and Solo was pulling his car up to a familiar gate that was definitely not our apartment complex.

I yawned and stretched my arms as much as the small space in the front seat would let me. I pointed out the windshield and asked, "Did you leave something at work? Why are we at your garage?"

The place was scary as hell during the day. In the waning light of dusk, it looked like something out of a horror movie. A chill shot up my spine and I reflexively wrapped my arms around myself in a tight hug. For some reason, this garage reminded me of the place I now called home. It was full of surprises and nicer on the inside than anyone on the outside looking in would imagine. I shouldn't know what the city's biggest, most lucrative chop-shop looked like. In my previous life, I didn't even think things like chop-shops were real; they were simply something on TV shows and in movies before Solo came into my life.

After leaning out the lowered window to poke a code and scan his fingerprint into the fancy box on the outside of the gate, he turned to look at me with a serious expression. "Lester still hasn't shown up, which is suspicious as hell. I think something bad may have happened to him. No one goes in and out of the Skylark without the old guy making note of it. With him gone, anyone can walk in and out of the complex. Vincent obviously knows you and I are close, which is why he tried to take me out. The more I think about you and Noble in that apartment complex, the more it seems like a bad idea for you to be there alone. This building is a fortress. No one gets inside these gates, no matter how hard they try. The apartment where you waited when I fixed your car is still empty. I texted the Boss to see if I could use if for a couple days. I think you and Noble should hang out here until I can figure out how to get Vincent off your back."

The big, metal gates rolled open, and for some reason I was reminded of a jail cell. Solo said no one could come in through the gates, but the same thing was true for anyone trying to get out. I knew what it was like to be trapped behind sky-high walls that promised protection, but in reality, only prevented escape.

"You decided this without even talking to me about it?" I couldn't keep the bite out of my voice, even though I was speaking softly so as not to wake up Noble. My hands tightened into fists and I felt my face heat with silent anger. "And what about our stuff? You can't just haul a three-year-old around without preparing for it. Noble will be climbing the walls in an hour and she's going to have a million questions. Not to mention, I already pulled her away once this year from the only life and family she's known. Who knows how she'll react if I do it again? She might end up hating me." She was definitely going to throw a fit at being so far away from Erica and Riley. They filled the void left when Mrs. Sanchez ditched her. "I should have the final say in where my daughter and I end up."

Solo pulled his car through the gates and watched as they rolled closed in the rearview mirror. He turned his head slightly in my direction, but it was too dark so I couldn't really read his expression. However, there was a tick in the sharp cut of his jawline that indicated he wasn't exactly thrilled by my complaint. I understood he was a lone wolf, a man used to acting on his own without question, but that wasn't going to work for me and my daughter. My entire existence was a lie because I didn't ask enough questions and let someone else decide everything for me. I was done letting anyone else think they knew what was best for me and my kid.

"Make me a list of what you both need and I'll go get it. I promised to keep you safe no matter what it takes. This is me doing that." He sounded slightly disgruntled as he pulled the car to a stop in front of one of the massive garage doors that lined the front of the building. Once he turned the car off, he turned in his seat and looked at me through the shadows surrounding his face. "It should only be for a few days. What's the big deal?"

I huffed in aggravation and crossed my arms over my chest, turning my head so he wouldn't see me fighting back furious tears. "The big deal is it's my life. I have a job, bills, and most importantly, a kid to think about. I'm the one who should be in charge of making the decisions that affect us. You could've asked me what

I thought about coming to stay here for a few days and we could have discussed the pros and cons. Instead, you took control and made the decision for me. Haven't you ever seen a movie where the girl in danger is kept out of the loop for her own good by the hero, and then she ends up dead or captured because she wasn't prepared?"

He made a noise low in his throat and I could feel the waves of aggravation rolling off him. "I'm just trying to look out for you. For both of you."

Frustrated beyond belief, I sighed and leaned forward so my forehead thunked on the dashboard. "I know that, and I appreciate that your heart is in the right place. But, I have to think about what's best for Noble before I consider anything else, and you unilaterally making choices for the both of us means I don't have the opportunity to do that. You're forcing me to play follow the leader, and I can't do that. I can't follow anyone blindly when I have to protect my daughter. We have to talk about things like this and come to a solution that is suitable for everyone... not just you."

I jumped in my seat slightly when his hand shot out to pound on the steering wheel. Reflexively, I looked in the backseat to make sure Noble was still sleeping.

"I've been on my own a long time, and I haven't had to answer to anyone besides my boss since my mother got hurt. I'm used to reacting quickly and being on the offensive when it comes to making split-second choices. It never even occurred to me to ask you what you thought about staying here, because I assumed you would see it was the best course of action until the head is cut off the monster you're hiding from. You don't want Channing

Vincent to find Noble. Well, he would never think to look here, and if he did, he couldn't get in."

I sighed. Solo had proven time and time again he would go to the ends of the Earth to protect the ones he loved. Making this decision without including me in his thought process was just an extension of that. When your heart latched onto an alpha male, when you set your sights on the king of the urban jungle, it was important to remember he might not always be able to protect your tender feelings, but he would do his best to make sure you stayed alive. Solo's actions might not have been fully thought out, but how deeply he cared was evident in them.

I dropped my forehead on the dash again and groaned. "I understand where you're coming from, and if you explained all of that to me instead of simply deciding for me, I would have agreed. I need you to include me next time." God forbid there was a next time.

He made a growling sound and thumped the steering wheel again. "Only you know what's best for Noble, right?"

I slowly nodded. I might not always get being a mom right on my first try, but without any hesitation, I could honestly answer that I always put my kid first and always did what I considered best for Noble. She was my first priority in everything.

Solo flicked up the brim of his hat so I could finally see his eyes. They were as black as midnight and narrowed ever so slightly. I'd seen him angry before when he pulled the drug dealer off of me and when he saved me from the handsy landlord. But this was the first time his angry, dark gaze was because of me. I had to admit I didn't like it, and being in such a small, confined space when his big body was practically twitching with repressed aggravation was a little nerve wracking. It was a good reminder that, while Solo was nice to me and went out of his way to treat me well, he was still a dangerous man capable of great violence. Not that I was worried he was going to turn it on me, but it was always a good idea to be mindful of a predator's teeth.

"So if I tried to tell you how to take care of your kid, it would bother you, right? You would question who in the hell did I think I was trying to tell you how to raise your child when you've done it on your own for so long, wouldn't you?" He snapped out the questions and watched me unblinkingly as I slowly nodded. I would bite his head off if he tried to interject into how I cared for my kid. I would go mama bear on anyone who tried to interfere. "It's the same for me and how best to operate in the city. I grew up here. I know how this place works, and believe it or not, I know how guys like Channing Vincent operate. A criminal is a criminal no matter what side of the tracks they come from. I didn't mean to step on your independence or parenting. I was just trying to do what's right for the current situation. I'm not used to having my choices questioned any more than you're used to having someone try and tell you what's right for Noble."

I sat up in my seat and slowly reached out for his tattooed hand. "I want to be your teammate, Solo. I want to be in the game for once in my life. Not someone who sits on the bench. I did that already and realized I didn't know any of the rules."

It took him a second, but eventually he turned his hand over so our palms slid together. I was beginning to really like the rough feel of his skin against mine. It made touching him tangible and real. It proved he was more than a dream, more than a figment of my imagination. I was still having a hard time believing that someone like him existed, but when we touched, it made him seem more attainable and human.

"My name is Solo, and it's always been fitting. I've been a one-man show for a long time. I've never been much for teamwork, but I will try to do better in the future." He shook his head slightly and muttered, "But if I think something needs to be done for your own good, I may move without asking you first. I don't care if you end up hating me, or if it means we don't end up together. If you're safe, if nothing happens to you and Noble, I can live with the consequences of acting first and asking later."

I sighed again and briefly closed my eyes. He was a steamroller and I was a dandelion. "Like I said, I know your heart is in the right place and that makes forgiving your high-handedness fairly easy. I would like it if you took a second to put yourself in my shoes. A conversation is all I'm asking for and I don't think it's an unreasonable request." I didn't tell him there was no way I could hate him. I hadn't been able to from the start, even when all of my instincts told me I should.

"It's not unreasonable. I'll try to do better in the future, but for now, will you please stay here for a few days until we have a solid game plan on how to deal with Vincent?"

I nodded. "Yeah, we can stay for a few days, but I don't want to hear any complaining when you see how much stuff you need to get from my apartment to keep Noble entertained."

He finally chuckled under his breath. "Deal."

We both jumped and cranked our heads around toward the back seat when Noble ordered, "Stop fighting. Fighting is bad."

I guess we'd allowed our voices to get a little louder than we should have.

I gave my daughter a reassuring grin and reached out to pat her chubby little leg. "We weren't fighting. We were just talking about something important so it sounded very serious."

She gave me her three-year-old version of a scowl and kicked her legs. "I don't like it when you're mad at each other."

Solo chuckled again as he levered himself out of the driver's seat. "Me either, kiddo. It's pretty much the worst. Wanna have a sleepover for a few days? It'll be really fun."

Noble gave him a skeptical look as he poked his head in the backseat and started to unbuckle her from her seatbelt. "Can Riley come?"

Solo paused for a second and shot me a look. I shrugged, leaving him to deal with the pitfalls of a sleepy, grumpy toddler on his own. Noble was far better at putting him in his place than I would ever be.

"Uh, we'll see if she can come see you one day, but you aren't going to be here for very long, so you might have to wait to see her until you go back home."

I hid a smile behind my hand when Noble immediately went into tantrum mode. There were tears. There was kicking and screaming. There were tiny fists waving in the air. And there was a grown man looking like he wanted to run away and hide from the fussy toddler as she continued to wail at him. Solo wasn't afraid of anything, but he looked terrified as he handed Noble over to me once I finally got out of the car.

He looked at me with huge eyes as I rubbed a soothing hand up and down Noble's back. I lifted an eyebrow in his direction and told him, "If I could get away with it, I would act exactly the same way when you tell me what to do without asking my opinion first."

He sighed and dragged a hand down his face. "Point made. We're on the same team from here on out. Let's go upstairs and you can give me a list of what you need. I'll stop and bring some dinner when I come back."

Noble was still having a fit so I nodded at him and continued to whisper nonsense to my daughter. I told her everything was going to be okay and assured her we wouldn't be away from home for very long. What I didn't tell her was we were finally on a winning team for once, and eventually the game I'd unwittingly dragged her into was going to be over.

She was the trophy. One neither Solo nor I had any intention of letting the other side win.

Solo

Orley wasn't kidding when she said Noble was going to need a shit ton of stuff for a few days. I felt like I cleaned out the little girl's entire room by the time I was done collecting everything on the list. The other side of that coin was the very few things Orley listed for herself. She really did always put Noble first, and I should've known that squirreling her away without running the plan by her first was going to backfire. If Orley only had to consider herself, I had no doubt she would go with the flow and defer to whatever idea was best; she was too smart and too afraid not to. But when her child was involved, she turned into an immovable wall, impossible to get around and hard to break through. Noble was lucky to have someone so determined in her corner. Her mother was not only going to look out for her entire life, but more than that, she was going to teach her how to advocate for herself. I couldn't remember the last time someone who was so much smaller than I was physically stood their ground and refused to budge, even when I pushed them. Orley was so much stronger than she appeared to be. Tougher than she gave herself credit for.

On my way out of the building, I stopped by Carmen's across the hall and Erica's a few flights down so I could ask them to keep me updated if Lester showed up. Both women noticed he was missing and were worried about the older man. He might never come inside the building, but the homeless man was still considered a neighbor; he was as much a part of the Skylark as the broken elevator and the bad smells in the stairwell. For those of us who didn't step over the man like he was trash, he was part of our everyday lives... he was family. I still thought the timing around his sudden disappearance was too coincidental. There were two people Channing Vincent would have to go through to get to Orley... me and Lester. With us out of the way, snatching Noble away from her mother would be infinitely easier.

Erica asked a million questions about what was going on, and Riley chimed in that she wanted to make sure Noble was okay. I promised to have both of the Vincent ladies check in as soon as it was totally safe. Erica easily read between the lines and assured me she would let me know if anything seemed off in the neighborhood while I was gone.

I was in the drive-thru of a popular fast food joint, knowing Noble couldn't say no to chicken nuggets, when my phone rang. Seeing the Boss's info on the display, I touched the screen on the dash to connect the call, figuring he was calling to see if I was at the garage.

"What's up, Boss?" I crept forward as the minivan in front of me started to move slowly.

"Hey." His unmistakable baritone growl immediately made me sit up straighter, and my wandering attention sharpened to focus on his every word. "Where are you right now?"

I blinked as the car in front of me moved again. "At a drive-thru. Had to grab something to feed my girls." Whoa. I claimed them just like that to the person I looked up to the most in the world, and it didn't even freak me out... well... only a little.

"Need to tell you something serious, kid. Get somewhere you can talk for a minute."

The Boss sighed and I could practically see him running his hands over his face or rubbing that star tattoo near his eye. He only did those things when he was stressed out or thinking really hard about something. All hopes he was calling just to check in flew out the window. I told him to wait a minute when it was my turn to pay, then found a place to park in the lot so he could tell me why he called.

"Okay. I'm ready. Hit me." I took a deep breath and braced myself for what was inevitably bound to be bad news.

"You know my old lady used to live in your building, right?" He asked the question quietly, which immediately sent all my instincts on high alert. I grunted an affirmation and stared unseeingly out the window. "While she lived there, there was a homeless dude who kept his eye on her. He got roughed up a few times trying to keep her safe when her brother got her into some trouble. After she moved into my house, I tried to set him up in the apartment at the garage to say thanks, but he never wanted to take me up on the offer."

"Lester. His name is Lester, and he's been missing the last few days, which is why I wanted the girls in the apartment. Something doesn't feel right about him suddenly disappearing."

The Boss sighed again and I heard the sound of ice rattling around in a glass. The man wasn't much of a drinker, so the news had to be worse than bad. A sinking feeling took my guts all the way down to my toes.

"My brother called me a couple hours ago to head down to the coroner's office to identify a body. He had one of my old lady's business cards on him. The cops are calling it an accidental overdose. It looked like he got ahold of some bad stuff." The Boss sounded pissed.

I sucked in a breath and felt my lungs contract painfully. "More than likely, someone gave him a hotshot." There wasn't a scenario I could think of where Lester would turn down a hit. It would take very little effort to get him to shoot up something that was laced with a bad cocktail of drugs.

"That's what I told my brother. Lester came back from Vietnam an addict. He was a junkie, but he wasn't stupid. He knew his limits. The cops won't budge, but after you asked if you could stash your girls at my place, I got a bad feeling all of this might be connected." The ice rattled again and he swore. "Plus, my brother said he broke up that private fight you took on the other night. Got a call things were getting out of hand. He told me you looked like you were in over your head. Seems like someone wanted you and Lester out of the way."

I swore back at him and dropped my forehead to rest on the steering wheel. The thump didn't do a thing to distract me from the pain twisting around my heart. Hearing that Lester was gone felt like losing a favorite uncle. The guy was a mess, but he was always there to remind me to do the right thing when I got sidetracked. There were times when it felt like Lester was the only person checking in on me while I took care of everyone else.

Something wet hit my leg. I blinked in surprise when I realized I was crying a silent, steady stream of tears. They were landing on my track pants, making a small damp circle. I couldn't remember the last time I was moved to tears. Probably the last time I was with my mother on a really bad day and she couldn't remember who I was. Those days inevitably led to a tear or two, but I had no clue that losing Lester would affect me in the same way.

"I'll fill you in. I think all of this has moved beyond something I can handle on my own. I know how to fight with fists and the occasional weapon, but I have no clue how to fight back against money and privilege." I'd never had either of those things. "I might be in over my head and I can't risk drowning." Not with Orley counting on me, and not with Noble in the middle of the playing field.

I had to clear my throat and rub the back of my hand across my face before I could speak again. "If no one is going to claim Lester's body, tell your brother I will. He needs a proper burial." Not just because he served his country, but because he served our city. He deserved to be laid to rest with respect.

The Boss made a noise and I heard the sound of his chair scraping backward over the floor. "Don't worry about that. I called you before I broke the news to my girl. She's got a soft spot for the old guy. I'm gonna make sure he gets a proper send off. I do need the details of what you're dealing with, though. I don't know how to fight with cash either, but we both know a few people who do. Not gonna let anything happen to you and your girls, kid."

He hung up without a goodbye and I let the phone fall in my lap. The fast food made my car smell like French fries, and for some reason it reminded me of the night Orley came to pick Noble up smelling the same way. I wondered if I would ever smell the greasy, delicious scent without remembering how she felt underneath my hands for the first time.

Pushing out a deep breath, I shook my head and determinedly wrestled my emotions back under control. I was sad about Lester, but there were people depending on me; I couldn't let emotions get the better of me. Everyone who lived here long enough learned how to compartmentalize their feelings in order to keep their eye on the prize, which was normally escaping the city limits. If you allowed sadness, disappointment, and anger to consume you, the city would never let you go. Here, you had to be stronger than all the things trying to break your heart on a regular basis.

I drove back to the garage in a slight daze, and when I walked through the door of the hidden apartment, it took everything I had inside of me to plaster on a normal face and shove the worry and sadness aside. Orley picked up on the change in my mood right away. I could see the concern on her face and assured her nothing was wrong.

The worry didn't leave her gaze, and I realized she thought the reason I was being so distant was because of our little dust up earlier. It was the first time we'd really clashed, and now I couldn't look directly at her without picturing her bringing Lester something warm to eat when she came home from work. I didn't want to explain what happened to the older man in front of Noble. The little girl already had so much change thrust upon her, she didn't need to have the entire concept of death laid out in front of her before she turned four.

After a quiet, tense dinner, I showed Noble how she could FaceTime Riley and helped Orley make up the fold-out couch into a bed for the little girl. At some point, the apartment had been renovated from a spartan studio to a spacious one bedroom. Apparently, I was just one in a long line of people using the place to hide out, and the Boss decided to make it a more comfortable place to crash. It was actually nicer than either of our apartments at the Skylark.

I told Orley I could crash on the fold-out so she and Noble could take the king-size bed in the bedroom. She waved me off and told me Noble would be fine tucked in, surrounded with pillows. I got the sense she wanted me in the room so she could give me the third degree about my sullen mood. I collected my phone from a sleepy-looking Noble and made my escape into the bathroom. There was only one, and at the moment it looked like a sanctuary.

I tossed my clothes in a messy heap on the floor and turned on the water as hot as I could stand. I flinched when I climbed under the spray, and it opened the floodgates. Face hidden in the fall of the fast-moving water, the tears and emotions I'd kept on lock-down flowed freely. I pounded my fist on the slick tiles in front of me and breathed like I'd just finished running a marathon. It was impossible to think about going home and not seeing the unidentifiable lump of dirty clothes covering the bottom step. I was supposed to be immune to losing the people I cared about. That was the first lesson I learned living in this city, but I couldn't stop the pain of that loss from taking me to my knees.

I wasn't sure when or how I ended up on the tiled floor of the shower, but that was where Orley found me. I heard the door click open somewhere in the roar between my ears, but I couldn't bear to look up. I laced my fingers together and put them on the back of my head as I let the water wash away all evidence of my sorrow.

The glass door opened and the air shifted as Orley slid into the enclosure behind me. A moment later, her arms wrapped around me as her front pressed against my back. She was so close, there was no room for the water to run between the places where our skin touched. I felt her lips touch the back of my neck as her hold tightened when I started to shake.

She rested her cheek on my shoulder and made the same soothing noises I heard her make when Noble was upset. It was sweet. The last person who held me when I fell apart was a nurse whose name I never caught, the night my mother was shot.

"It's going to be okay. I don't know what happened after you left, but whatever is wrong, we can fix it." Her voice was a whisper that almost got lost under the water.

It was my job to tell her that. It was my job to make sure things really did end up okay. I doubted I would ever have the words to show Orley how important it was, how special it was to have someone in my life who helped carry the weight of my very heavy world for once.

This would be the moment I looked back and realized I was in love.

This would be the moment I would remember forever when things felt like they wouldn't be okay, because as long as she was there, as long as she took care of me and let me take care of her, things really would be okay no matter how bad they got.

Orley

I was relieved Solo hadn't locked me out of the bathroom when he disappeared, his heavy, dark mood lingering behind him. He was obviously trying to put on a happy face so Noble didn't pick up on whatever had thrown him off his game, but he was only slightly successful. She asked me no less than five times why Solo was sad when I got her settled into bed, knowing it was going to be a minute before she fell asleep in this new, industrial place. I read her a short story, hoping that would help the process along, but all she wanted to talk about was the odd way Solo had acted when he returned from our apartment complex. I answered her questions to the best of my ability, not knowing what was going on in that handsome head of his. Eventually, Noble's eyes got heavy and she seemed sleepy enough that I dared leaving her on the pull-out so I could go check on the man who had made it his personal mission in life to protect both me and the sleepy little girl.

I wasn't ready for the sight that greeted me when I walked through the bathroom door.

Solo had been in the shower for so long, I was sure he had to be simply hiding out to avoid my questions. Instead, the tiny space was filled with steam and fog so thick it was hard to breathe. Solo was on his knees in the glass enclosure and his wide shoulders were hunched over and shaking ever so slightly. I gasped in surprise and put my hands over my mouth to muffle the sound. I didn't want to interrupt his moment. He was clearly lost in his own feelings, and now was not the time to force him to deal with mine. When someone as strong as Solo was brought to his knees, it was going to take someone equally as strong to lift him back to his feet. I wasn't sure I was that person, but there was no way I wasn't going to try to be. It was the least I could do after he lent me his strength so many countless times.

I quickly stripped out of my clothes and tiptoed into the shower enclosure behind him. He didn't lift his head or move in the slightest aside from the tiny tremors working their way through his entire body. His breathing was ragged and his hands were curled into fists so tight his knuckles were as white as the tiles where he knelt. The stark environment made the mottled bruises covering his entire side seem even angrier and more severe than when I initially wrapped him. Seeing this leviathan of a man on his knees, clearly emotional over something monumental, was a vivid reminder that he wasn't invincible after all.

I wrapped my arms around him and hugged him as hard as I could. His skin was hot, and every muscle in his back was as tense as a tightly strung guitar string. He felt like he was going to shatter if I moved wrong. The water was still warm, which was a miracle considering how long he'd been holed up in here. I kissed the back of his neck and did my best to soothe away whatever hurt he was feeling.

He didn't say anything for a long time. He was quiet while I rocked him softly and whispered the same sounds in his ear that Noble liked when she was having a moment. It wasn't until the water started to chill that Solo finally seemed to shake off the shroud of sorrow he'd been wrapped in so tightly. His fists unclenched and one reached for my hand, while he used the other to pull us both to our feet. His face twisted in a small grimace of pain when he used his core strength in a way his ribs weren't entirely ready for yet. My knees protested at the sudden change in position, and I shivered as the droplets of cold water traveled down my skin.

With one hand braced at the base of my spine and the press of his body, Solo effortlessly backed me against the slick tile wall. His dark head dropped to the hollow where my neck and shoulder met, and I felt the brush of his lips against my collar bone.

"Is Noble asleep?" His voice was a husky rasp, which sent an entirely different kind of shiver through my naked body.

I wrapped my arms around his shoulders and nodded. I kissed his temple and pulled him closer, partly for comfort and partly for warmth. It was getting cold without the warm water surrounding us. Luckily, his big body emanated heat like a furnace.

"She was on her way when I came to check on you. Do you want to fill me in on what's going on with you tonight?" I ran my fingers along the nape of his neck and he leaned more fully into me.

We were pressed together so tightly there was no room between our bodies for anything to fit, including the water still clinging to our skin. My nipples beaded into tight, painful points against his chest, and my legs moved instinctively when he shifted one of his knees between mine. The wide palm resting on my low back slid downward until it was caressing the curve of my ass, and his breath was warm and damp against the pulse at the base of my neck. He roughly whispered, "Not right now. I feel so bad inside, but holding you, it feels so good. I'd rather focus on that."

The strong thigh shoved between mine moved and my hips shifted involuntarily in response. I used my thumb to trace little circles on the back of his neck and moved my lips to the curve of his ear. "But you will tell me?" Having Solo shut me out was almost as bad as having him make all my decisions for me. He promised we were going to be on the same team, and if that was the case, then he needed to let me play the game, win or lose. We would do either together or not at all.

He lifted his head and stared at me with those unreadable, midnight eyes. They were so fathomless, and so cold where the rest of him was like touching an open flame.

"Talk later. This now." I didn't argue when he lowered his head so he could touch his lips to mine.

Solo usually kissed with care and a touch of consideration. Not tonight. Tonight, he wasn't kissing me like the guy who lived next door. This wasn't the man who playfully raced around with Noble and watched out for an elderly veteran who slept on the steps. This wasn't the loving son who did everything he could to care for his mother, even when the odds were stacked against them.

No. The man kissing me right now was the one who ran through the city like he owned the streets. The one who grew up rough and ready to fight. This was the man who took no prisoners, who fought, who had others turn around and walk the other way when they saw him coming. This was the beast who lived inside Solomon Sanders' soft heart. This was the demon who kept the saint safe in the harsh world.

I couldn't catch my breath, wasn't sure I wanted to. He left me breathless and lightheaded as he used his grip on my backside to hoist me up the slippery wall. I heard the strangled sound of discomfort he made, but chose to ignore it. If he wanted to push past the pain, be it emotional or physical, I was here to support him, not scold him. I obediently wrapped my legs around his narrow waist, gasping into the carnal kiss as I felt his hardness immediately find that soft, yielding spot between my legs that now felt like it belonged to him as much as it belonged to me. My thighs quivered in anticipation and my core clenched as his tongue thrust in and out of my mouth. I felt the bite of his teeth on my lower lip and hissed when the tang of blood flitted across my tongue. I dug my fingernails into the inked skin across Solo's back and braced myself against the onslaught of all the emotions he was unleashing on me at once. I could taste desire and desperation. I felt the lingering sadness hiding behind the intensity of his passion. His anger was there in the rough hold of his hands and the impatient way his hips ground against mine. Pinned against the wall like a butterfly mounted in a display box, there was little I could do but ride out the swells of the storm.

Solo's head dropped to the side of my neck, and once again there was a drag of teeth and the slight sting of a bite. The arm he wasn't using to hold me worked its way between our bodies and a moment later calloused fingers were plucking at my pebbled nipples almost painfully. I let my head fall backward and made a noise when it hit the tiled wall harder than I intended. I'd never been the recipient of such aggressive, consuming affection before. Never had anyone handled me as if they might die if they couldn't get as close to me as quickly as possible. It was overwhelming, but it was also a total turn on. Solo admitted to never having anyone significant in his life for an extended period of time. Having him come at me like he was starving when I had no clue how to handle someone like him was almost too much. He treated me as if I was the *only* one who could deal with his relentless lust.

Hs teeth nipped their way across my exposed throat and I knew I was going to have the imprint of his fingertips on my ass for days because he was holding me so tightly. I closed my eyes and whispered his name, rolling my hips against the straining hardness throbbing between my splayed thighs. He always felt larger than life and bigger than average. Right now, he felt huge and close to impossible to take. I must've made a small sound of distress because Solo's demeanor immediately changed. He still held onto me like he had no plans of ever letting go, but his hands went from bruising to reverent and his lips went from punishing to pleasurable.

The fingers torturing my puckered nipples twisted and his knuckles dragged their way down my breastbone, across my belly, and down to the valley where his cock was taking up all the available space. Those same knuckles brushed lightly through wet folds until they knocked against my pulsing clit. My legs tightened around his lean waist and I curled a hand around the back of his head. His short hair felt like wet silk under my palm. His long fingers skated through damp flesh, outlining every tremor that followed. I felt the broad tip of his erection press against my fluttering opening as our eyes locked.

His looked like the night sky; they were so pretty when they glittered with arousal. The way he wanted me, the way he showed how much he cared, flashed like stars in the obsidian depths. I angled my hips closer, taking the first few inches of his rigid length inside my body. He was hot and hard, exactly like the wall at my back. I felt pliant and soft, letting my body mold around his. I took him in on a sigh, letting my head fall forward to rest on his tattooed shoulder.

Solo shifted his hold on my ass; I surrendered to the sensation of being taken as I let him have whatever he needed. He had a lot of negative feelings he needed to purge out of his system, and I was glad to be the martyr. If he was the pyre, I didn't mind burning on top of him all night long until whatever was haunting him had been chased away.

"Never thought I would have room in my life for anyone else. Didn't realize how much empty space I was rattling around in until you came along, Orley. I like how you filled my life up." I felt rather than saw the smile he flashed somewhere above my bent head. "Like the way I fill you up even more."

He wasn't wrong. It was almost hard to breathe with that impressive cock seated all the way inside of me. I was full of him in more ways than one.

The fingers delicately playing with my clit kept up their light strum and stroke as his hips started to kick in a smooth rhythm, driving my body up the wall and rocking upward into my clenching pussy with each fall. It was a brutal, quick pace which immediately had me panting into his damp skin and whispering his name through strangled breaths. I could feel warmth spreading outward from my belly, and all my muscles started to shake.

Solo groaned loud and low into my hair, and I sent up a silent prayer Noble had in fact fallen asleep. I already owed her an explanation as to why her favorite person had been sullen all night long; I couldn't think about explaining why mommy was moaning Solo's name over and over again. I hoped I had a few years left before we needed to have that kind of chat.

The scruff on Solo's chin scraped along my temple as his body hammered into mine. With every thrust and retreat I could feel his big body releasing some of the toxic tension that had made him nearly unapproachable all night. I much prefer him shaking this way than the way I found him when I first came into the bathroom. I tightened all my limbs around him and tried not to think about my moans echoing off the walls around us.

He growled into the space above my head, fingers losing dexterity and falling away from the tender spot hidden between my legs where he'd been drawing out every ounce of pleasure he could. His rhythm faltered, his hips crashed into mine hard enough to bruise, and his short fingernails dug into the curve of my ass hard enough to leave marks. I felt the firm flesh of his cock pulse and kick and heard his breath skip a few beats as a rush of warm wetness really did flood all the available space where we were joined. I lifted my head and watched Solo's eyes drift shut as he let himself get lost fully in his release. Finally, his features softened and the angry twist of his mouth relaxed.

When his eyes popped open, a tiny grin played around his mouth and his hands skimmed where I was still pinned between the wall and his muscular chest.

"Not gonna leave you hanging. Promise." I wasn't sure if he was talking about the conversation we still needed to have or the orgasm... either way, I would wait. I was still a little dazed from being captive to his emotional storm.

I didn't say anything when he leaned back, separating our bodies with a slick, sexy sound. Our eyes stayed locked as he found a discarded washcloth and cleaned us up. I stayed silent when he lifted me in his arms and started to carry me toward the unfamiliar bedroom. There wasn't any sound coming from the living room, but that could be misleading. Sometimes when it was quiet, it meant things were going to hell in a handbasket. Before we talked or continued what he started in the shower, I was going to have to check on Noble.

I didn't make any noise until an hour later when Solo finally told me about Lester. Then, it was my turn to cry and let grief sweep me away. Luckily, Solo knew exactly how to help me deal with the sadness that felt like it was going to swallow me whole.

Solo

It was a good thing I was used to making the most of the few free moments I had.

The longer I was with Orley, the more apparent it was that we were going to have to sneak stolen moments together between various interruptions for the foreseeable future. It seemed like we were always going to be interrupted by a phone ringing or Noble needing something. Yesterday morning, one of the Boss's guys showed up unannounced, just when things were getting good, to see if we needed anything. It was a nice gesture, but I almost ripped the dude's head off, which the Boss wouldn't have appreciated. I never considered myself a patient man, but I was learning I had an untapped well of tolerance and self-control. In all honesty, it made the occasions when I did get to be the sole focus of Orley's attention, and when she was the center of my entire world, all the sweeter and more intense. We tended to go at each other like we may never get another chance, which always proved to make the sex out of this world and impossible to forget, even if we were left hard up because something outside the bedroom door demanded our attention.

I was a young guy. I'd been sexually active longer than I would ever admit to my mother, and if anyone told me I would be okay with my girl dipping out in the middle of a spectacular blowjob because there was a toddler having a nightmare in the other room, I would have told them they were crazy. There were too many girls out there, and I already had my own shit to deal with on the regular. But, none of those girls were Orley, and none of those toddlers were Noble. I'd climbed out of bed almost as fast as the pretty redhead when I heard Noble shrieking from the other room. It might've taken a minute for my cock to calm down, but when Noble was secured in the big bed between me and her mother, I forgot all about my dick because it was my heart that felt like it was going to explode. I wasn't entirely sure how I ended up here, but I knew with every fiber of my being I wasn't going back to where I was before.

At this particular moment, the sun hadn't risen, and Noble was still dead to the world on the fold-out in the living room. After two nights, she'd finally adjusted to the apartment enough to sleep through the night. Not that she wasn't going to be up as soon as the sunlight hit the main window in the room, but until then, I had Orley all to myself. I was going to make the most of the time we had. My ribs felt a little bit better. It didn't feel like my insides were coated in burning acid every time I moved. I could even bend without grimacing as much.

That meant I could *finally* cover Orley with my body and fuck her into the mattress instead of her riding me like a professional rodeo queen. I liked having her on top of me, but I wanted to know what she felt like under me. I wanted those pretty blue eyes looking up at me, dazed with lust, while she bit her lip to muffle the sexy sounds she made when she was close to breaking apart. I fully planned on making all those fantasies a reality as soon as I was done mapping out every single part of her sweet, wet pussy with my tongue.

She'd been writhing under my mouth for a solid five minutes. She was pulling at my hair and squeezing my head between her thighs. I could feel her insides quiver, and every time she said my name under her breath, a rush of moisture followed. I was determined not to miss a single drop. She tasted as good as I imagined she would. I could feast on her forever, but knowing it was highly unlikely I was going to get more than one uninterrupted hour, I was going to have to save the savoring for another time when lives weren't on the line and her kid wasn't sleeping restlessly.

I slid my hands under Orley's very nice backside and pulled her closer to my mouth. I shifted tactics and used the edge of my teeth on her clit. Her entire body vibrated in my hands and her nails dug into my scalp hard enough to hurt. I grunted a little, and felt her hips roll, forcing her hips closer to my face. It was awesome to be with someone who couldn't get enough. Orley told me she was relatively inexperienced when it came to sex and intimacy, which reminded me she was still so young. But she rolled with everything I threw at her and came at me just as hard. It almost seemed like we were meant to be. We clicked when we were in bed together. We both blindly tried to navigate making a serious relationship work in a less-than-ideal situation.

"Close, Solo. So close." Her toned thighs clamped around my ears and her back bowed up off the bed. I could tell she was right on the edge, because she was soaking wet and her body was undulating wildly in my hands. Her breathless whisper was hot and so was the way her heels dug into the center of my back. I liked the trail of shiny, slick moisture I left along her inner thigh when I pulled my mouth off her flushed opening and dragged it down the soft line of skin.

She shoved a condom in my hand as I crawled my way up her body. Neither one of us mentioned the incident in the shower being less than well thought out, but I wasn't going anywhere—wasn't running like her piece-of-shit sperm donor—regardless of the consequences of needing her so badly I couldn't think straight. Once I had things wrapped up and good to go, I hitched one of her legs over my hip, braced a forearm above her head and let my body sink fully into hers. We both sucked in a sharp breath at the contact. I loved the way she engulfed me, greedy, and impatient. She used the heel resting on my ass to hurry me up, wanting the full length of my erection imbedded inside of her as deeply as possible. It was easy enough to tell when I hit her spot. Her entire body flushed and she made a keening, high sound that immediately made my dick harder than it already was.

I kissed her on the forehead and started to move. With each drag of my cock through the tight, wet clamp of her body, it felt like the top of my skull was going to blow off. Nobody felt as good as this woman. Being inside of her was my new favorite place and the only way I was going to give her up was if someone killed me. Being with Orley really did bring about feelings worth dying for. I never thought I would care about another person to that drastic of an extent, but here I was. I wasn't sure I was old and mature enough to call what we did making love, but I was certain it was a whole lot more than just sex.

"Love the way you feel under me." And I liked that I was the only thing she could see when her bright blue eyes opened; she was completely surrounded by my body and my need. The combination was absolutely euphoric.

"I love being under you. It feels safe here." Her hands cupped each side of my face and her forehead knocked clumsily against my chin as she started to nibble along the line of my throat. When her teeth grazed my Adam's apple, my hips kicked into hers involuntarily. Between all the interrupted sexy moments, and the fact I could still taste her all over my tongue, it wasn't going to take much to shove me over the edge into a thought-stealing orgasm.

Fortunately, Orley's control was stretched as thin as mine. I shifted my head so I could get my mouth on her pretty, pointed nipples. All it took was a little suction and a tiny bite on one, then the other, to have her bucking underneath me and coming apart around my cock. The pulse of her completion pulled my own from where it lingered in anticipation. Heat tap danced its way up and down my spine as my rhythm faltered and my hips rocked aimlessly into the cradle of hers, mindlessly seeking out every single last drop of pleasure. Now that I'd been inside her with nothing between us, I was going to have to move getting to the point where we could go bare up high on the priority list. If we were going to be forced to sneak in intimate moments amongst the chaos of our everyday lives, I wanted them to feel as bright and pure as possible.

I collapsed on top of her in a sweaty, satiated mess. Her legs locked around my waist and I could feel both of us softening and relaxing in a haze of utter bliss and satisfaction. We were good together, and each time seemed better than the time before.

Orley bit my shoulder playfully and kissed the small hurt. The tip of her tongue dragged along the tattoo that lived there and I remembered her telling me she wanted to trace them all. She wasn't even a third of the way there yet. She was still working on everything from my pecs up. I buried my nose in the hollow behind her ear and smiled against her skin. I'd never really experienced peace before she came along, but I understood the feeling now. When I was with Orley like this, there was nothing on my mind but how good I felt and pride at knowing I was the one who made her limp and languid. I always felt like I was carrying around so much responsibility, it was an honest-to-God treat to feel like the only thing required of me at the moment was making the woman beneath me feel good.

Of course, one of our phones chose that very moment to ring.

I didn't want to move; I never wanted to move, but I knew Orley wouldn't let me ignore the sound. It could be the Boss or someone from my mother's facility. If it was her phone, she would be worried it was her boss, or possibly Erica. I told her the girls were keeping an eye out for anything suspicious at the apartment complex. After what happened to Lester, Orley was terrified her father would send his henchmen after anyone who might know where she was stashing Noble. She didn't want her friends to get hurt in the line of fire trying to keep her safe.

I rolled to the side with a groan. Pushing myself up, I discarded the condom and looked at the phones on the metal nightstand which was too cool for this barely used room. The Boss had unique taste, that was for sure. Orley's phone lit up, but the number on the screen read *private*.

Normally, I'd just answer the call, but after making the promise to no longer make any unilateral decisions without her, I grabbed the ringing phone and waved it in her direction. "The caller ID doesn't recognize the number."

She pushed her tangled, sweat-dampened hair out of her face and squinted at the display. She waved a hand in the air dismissively. "Answer it. It's probably a telemarketer."

I swiped the screen and poked the speaker icon so we could both hear. "Yeah?" I failed to see the point in being polite if it was a robocaller.

"Who is this?" Surprisingly, the voice immediately brought Orley upright in the bed. She clutched the sheets to her chest and pushed hair out of her face. I noticed her hands started shaking and her eyes blew wide.

I cocked an eyebrow and looked at the phone in my hand. "I think that's my question. Who the fuck is this?"

The voice was disturbingly calm and cultured. I had a sinking feeling I knew exactly who was on the other end of the line.

"The thing about hiding amongst a bunch of destitute degenerates is that it only takes a little cash to find out the information one might need. A generous tip was all it took to get this number from one of those young girls who work at that disgusting excuse of a restaurant where my daughter works." He was so damn smug. I wanted to shove my fist down his throat and rip his heart out of his chest with my bare hands.

"She's not your daughter, Channing." The sarcasm in my tone was thick enough to cut with a knife.

A fake laugh echoed out of the tiny speaker. "No, but Noble is my granddaughter. She belongs with me."

Orley stifled a shriek and shoved a fist in her mouth to muffle the sound.

"I think I've made it pretty clear I'll do anything it takes to bring her home." The threat wasn't even implied, it was right there in my face.

"You're a murderer. No amount of money changes that. One day you'll have to answer for the things you've done." For Lester. For Orley's mother. Channing Vincent had a huge wake-up call headed his way.

"That is highly unlikely. I'm not surprised you're unfamiliar with how things work in my world. Have you ever had more than two cents to rub together, young man? Have you ever had anything handed to you?" He laughed that annoying, superior laugh again. "By the way, how is your mother? She likes that facility she's in, correct? Wouldn't it be such a shame if someone were to buy the place and shut it down?" I swore angrily under my breath and tightened my hold on the phone. I knew exactly what he was trying to do: bait Orley and cause me to do something rash and foolish so he could finally get me out of the way. "Don't delude yourself into thinking you and I are on the same level. You can't even see where I'm standing, you're so much lower than I am." He scoffed slightly and I could almost see him fixing his tie and looking down his nose in my direction. "Tell Orley I'm coming for Noble. I don't care who or what stands in my way. I want my granddaughter back. I don't care what happens to her mother, but the little girl is mine."

The call went dead and when I looked over at Orley, she was crying. When our eyes met, she lowered her head and tried to cover the sound of her sobbing into her folded arms.

I threw the phone on the floor and launched myself across the bed so I could pull her into my arms. I kissed the top of her head and rocked her back and forth. "Don't let him scare you. He wants you to do something stupid. He wants you to run so he can isolate you. He wants you alone and scared."

She sniffed and slowly reached out to wrap her arms around my waist. "What about your mom? What if he does something bad to her?"

"Not gonna happen. That's just what he wants you to think. He believes you'll take Noble and rabbit the way you did before in order to keep the people around you safe. If you disappear, if I'm not around to keep an eye on you, he's going to make his move and you won't have anyone to watch your back. You have to trust me, Orley. I've got people who make your old man look like a kindergarten teacher working on a way to neutralize the threat. I don't care if I have to sell my soul to the Devil, or if I'm chained to this city and the men who run it forever, I promise that asshole will never get his hands on you or Noble. You have to believe me."

She sighed and tightened her hold. "I want to, but it's hard. I watched him get away with murder, literally."

"The rules are different in the city. Money isn't the end all be all of things. Here, you have to be smart and ruthless to be at the top of the food chain. Channing asked if I'd ever had anything handed to me, and the answer is no. I've worked for every single thing I've got. He doesn't understand that I'm not the only one here who has the same story. The guys he's about to go up against aren't for sale, and neither am I."

She lifted her head and gave me a salty, wet kiss that tasted like tears. "There's one thing you didn't have to work for. One thing that was handed to you without any hesitation." Her voice had a rasp to it that was sexy even though she still looked devastated.

"What would that be?" I smoothed a hand down her hair and sighed when I heard Noble rustling around in the living room.

Orley leaned into the touch and whispered, "My heart. I handed it over without question what feels like forever ago. I'm pretty sure it was yours even before you became my own personal hero." She shook her head slightly. "And I'm starting to get used to the fact I have to share Noble's heart with you on a regular basis these days."

If that were the case, then she'd given me the most precious, treasured thing I was ever going to own. It would take an actual act of God for me to put that fragile, cherished gift at risk.

Living in this city prepared me for war, and not just the kind that was fought with violence and weapons. Sometimes battles had to be fought using strategy, not strength. Knowing what Channing was capable of, it was going to take more brains than I'd ever been forced to utilize and every single acquaintance I had.

Orley

"I told you, you can't leave. That's exactly what he wants you to do!" It was the first time Solo raised his voice at me, and it was scary. He was intimidating when he wasn't red-faced and angry. When his temper was unleashed, it was downright terrifying.

I held Noble, who was crying as if the world was ending, tightly to my chest and cast a worried glance over Solo's shoulder where a crowd was gathered on the steps in front of the Skylark. Erica was watching the dramatic scene between the two of us play out with worried eyes, and Riley was crying almost as hard as Noble because her friend was leaving and she had no idea when she would be back.

Carmen, the very pretty waitress who lived across the hall from Solo, was glaring at me and practically snarling. They all loved Solo and couldn't believe I packed up everything I could fit in my piece-of-crap car and was ready to hit the road. To them, I was breaking the neighborhood hero's heart, not doing what had to be done in order to protect my daughter. Everyone was already raw and on edge from Lester's death, watching me walk away from Solo in such a hurried, careless way wasn't going to make me any friends in this heated showdown.

I brushed my fingers through Noble's curls more for my comfort than hers. I met Solo's dark glare under the brim of his hat and chewed on my lower lip so hard I knew it was going to tear. He couldn't stop yelling and I couldn't get my voice above a shaky whisper. "I have to go. I told you, you aren't in charge of deciding what's best for me, and you won't ever be in charge of deciding what I should or shouldn't do for my daughter." The words burned on their way out and pushed Solo back a step.

"Stop yelling!" Noble's wail could probably be heard ten blocks away. "I don't want to go, Mommy. I don't want to leave Solo and Riley."

God, it was such an ugly scene. There was no way it could be missed. We were making a commotion that could be witnessed from miles away. I hated every single second of it, but it had to be done. Taking a steadying breath, I reached around Solo so I could pull open the back door of the beat-up sedan and deposit my daughter into her car seat. She cried and screamed Solo's name the entire time.

When we ran from Channing in the middle of the night, things had been so rushed and scary, there was no time to process what we were leaving behind. I was pretty sure Noble's three-year-old perception still didn't grasp the fact her grandma was gone for good and her grandpa was the reason why. However, now she fully grasped that we were about to leave her favorite person behind, and she was having none of it. The sound of her body-shaking sobs broke my heart, and it took everything I had inside of me to keep from breaking down into a worthless pile of goo right there on the sidewalk in front of the man watching me like he didn't even know who I was.

"I've got to go. One day you'll understand." The words felt like they were wrenched out of my chest. They felt clumsy and wrong on my tongue and I hated saying them. Hated everything about this situation.

Solo swore now that Noble was out of earshot. Walking away from him right now ranked right up there as one of the hardest things I've had to do, right next to becoming a single mom as a teenager and leaving behind a very affluent lifestyle to start over from scratch.

He must have seen me waver and the indecision in my eyes, because the next thing I knew my face was buried in the center of his chest and my silent tears were soaking into his t-shirt. I felt his hand on the back of my head, and a second later his beloved ballcap, the one which rarely left his head, was slapped down on top of my barely brushed hair. I was a mess, inside and out, and there was little the hat was going to do to cover it up.

Solo squeezed me so tight I couldn't breathe and I worried my ribs would crack. I hugged him back far more carefully since his side was still a galaxy of ugly bruises.

"Promise me you'll find a way to get in touch with me when you get where you're going." It was a command that was so Solo. Always looking out for me, even when he looked like he could happily murder me with his bare hands.

I nodded, wiped my eyes dry, and gently pushed him away so I could walk to the driver's door.

"Orley." I looked up when Erica called my name. Her eyes were kind but very worried behind the lenses of her glasses. "Maybe you should listen to Solo. If he thinks it's dangerous for you to go, maybe you need to stay here in the city for a little bit."

I let out a breath and slowly shook my head. "I can't. Not right now. I don't have time to explain all the reasons why, but it's better if I go. Better for all of you. Trust me when I say you don't need the added trouble of having me and Noble around." I almost whimpered out loud when I saw the other woman tear up a tiny bit. I choked on my next breath and jerked open the car door. "I'm going to try my best to come back... promise."

She must've understood there was deeper meaning to me leaving the perfect guy behind, because she lifted her own crying child into her arms and gave me a sharp nod.

Before I slipped into the car, Solo's hand shot out and he used his thumb to wipe away the last stray tears rolling down my cheeks. In a tone so soft and low only I could hear him, he growled, "Be careful. Don't do anything stupid." He tugged the brim of his hat down so our gazes could no longer meet and cleared his throat roughly. "Drive safe. Keep your eyes open. Take care of yourself and your kid."

I nodded mutely and got into the car, knowing if I waited any longer, I wouldn't be able to go.

Noble was still crying and kicking her feet. When I pulled away from the curb, it felt like I was leaving my heart on the sidewalk at Solo's feet. The shriek of "Mommy!" and the pleas to turn around and go back didn't stop no matter what I said or how much I reassured Noble everything would be okay. I suddenly realized what it was like when Solo begged me to trust him to take care of everything when I was a hysterical mess. It was hard to hear anything or process any emotion when your heart was breaking into a bunch of painful pieces.

Even though she was throwing the mother of all fits and making my head hurt, I still managed to keep an eye on the road behind me as I started to drive out of town. I was headed out of the city and far away from those gilded gates where the monsters lived. I was probably ten miles into the hasty trip when I caught sight of a black SUV following behind me. It took another five miles for a white SUV to join the black one. A loud rush whooshed between my ears and my palms started to sweat so badly it was hard to keep hold of the steering wheel. Noble must've realized I was about to break because she suddenly went quiet in the backseat.

"Mommy," her small voice was hoarse from screaming. "Look at the train."

I glanced in the rearview mirror and saw she was pointing in the direction of the train that was chugging down the tracks we were quickly approaching. The gates were already down, which meant both SUVs behind us were going to be on my bumper in no time.

"I see it, sweetheart. Can you count how many cars there are? And what colors do you see?" I wanted to keep her attention off the fact the gates suddenly lifted so I could zoom across them, dangerously close to the engine leading the long line of graffiti-colored cars. I would never normally take such a risk, but right now I had no choice. Luckily, Solo had spent some significant time working on my junker of a car while we were sequestered away in the garage. The old piece of crap was running like a sports car now and had no issue leaving the SUVs in the dust.

As soon as we were literally on the right side of the tracks, I picked up speed and raced up the street and around the corner to the very busy mini-mall where it would be easy for my car to get lost in the crowd.

It was easy enough to spot the expensive Range Rover standing out like a diamond in a collection of rocks. It'd been a good long while since I'd been around a luxury car, and the reminder of how messed up my life was at the moment because of the kind of people who could afford a car that cost as much as a condo made me hesitate momentarily, but there wasn't time to second guess. Those SUVs had to have made it across the tracks and were no doubt looking everywhere for me.

I shoved open the door, ignoring Noble's nine-hundred questions about where we were, why we were stopping, and about who the stunningly beautiful woman climbing out of the Range Rover was.

She was several years older than me, but approximately the same height. I wondered how it was possible for anyone to mistake the two of us for the same person. She appeared completely unbothered. The long red wig she was wearing was pretty close to my own auburn locks, but even though we were both dressed in black leggings and oversized hoodies, her pants looked like they were made of skin-tight leather, and there was no mistaking her body was about one-hundred times better than mine under the baggy shirt. Trying to keep my cool, I rushed to pull Noble out of the back seat and hefted the stuffed go-bag Solo had made me pack for the both of us onto my shoulder.

When I was situated, the other woman reached out and snatched Solo's hat off my head and snapped it on top of her own. She smiled a breathtaking grin at Noble and reached out to tap my daughter's chin in such a way that made me think she probably had kids of her own. It was a subtle, motherly gesture toward a curious child, and it also calmed some of my rampaging nerves.

The stunner lifted a dark eyebrow in my direction and held out a flawlessly manicured hand with the keys to the Range Rover. "The GPS is already loaded to take you up to the house. Don't be shocked when you get to the guard house at the base of the mountain. My husband is sort of a freak when it comes to security. The guards know you're coming, so when you get there, show them your ID and they'll let you up to the house." Her grin widened. "The house looks like something you would find in the Swiss Alps, so if you see a massive log cabin that makes you feel like you walked into a ski lodge on accident, you're in the right place."

I took the keys from her and gulped. "Thank you. I'm not sure why you're helping me, but thank you from the bottom of my heart."

She bopped Noble on the end of her nose and slid a pair of mirrored Tiffany sunglasses over her startlingly clear, gray eyes. I kind of wanted to be her when I grew up... whoever she was. She oozed confidence and control. She seemed like a badass and I could use a solid dose of that right about now.

"I was an exotic dancer when I was your age. I spent every single day trying to convince very wealthy men they were not entitled to every little thing they wanted." She reached out and tugged on one of Noble's curls. "I also have a baby girl I would die for, so it was a no-brainer when my husband told me Solo needed some help because he went and found himself a complicated little family."

I looked her over and gave my head a shake. "No one is going to believe you're me."

She laughed. "People see what they want to see. Just like that fight you and Solo staged in front of your building. People like drama, and a public break-up is kind of like an accident on the street. No one can look away, no one looks past the carnage. Get in the Rover and get your baby safe. If everything goes according to plan, everyone can sleep easy tonight. Don't worry too much about Solo tangling with Vincent. He couldn't have better backup than my old man. The worst thing you can do in this town is piss off my husband. Revenge is sort of his stock and trade." She pulled the brim of Solo's hat down lower and moved around me so she could get inside my crappy car. She told me to make sure I put on the dark wig and sunglasses she left on the front seat, then flicked her fingers toward the Range Rover in a get-going gesture.

It was official. Everyone in my new life was way better at subterfuge and deceit than I was. I felt like I stepped into a spy movie and everyone had the script but me.

As I was buckling Noble, who got her own tiny hat and sunglasses, into the expensive, high-end car seat in the back of the Rover, she asked again, "Who was that pretty lady?"

I sighed and bent forward to kiss her on the end of her nose. "A friend... I think."

In this upside-down world I called my own, friends were people I would've considered enemies, and my enemies were people who claimed to be my family. I wasn't sure I was ever going to adjust to it, but I was going to try my best, because just as Solo informed me when we first met, sometimes the best people could be found in the worst places.

Solo

Staying seated in the front seat of my boss's rare Plymouth GTX while the white SUV ran Orley's little car off the road just outside of the city limits might have been the hardest thing I'd ever done in my life. We parked in a clearing just off the side of the road, hidden by a roofing advertisement, but in clear view of the only part of the road wide enough for the collision to happen without both cars crashing. It was a strategic spot with a clear view of all the crazy events unfolding, yet allowing us our anonymity.

Logically, I knew the redhead behind the wheel wasn't her, and I knew Noble wasn't in the car. However, none of that stopped me from automatically reaching for the door handle when the car violently skidded off the road. A large hand with a bumblebee tattooed on it clamped down on my shoulder and held me in place. My boss was one of the few men who had the physical strength to keep me still when every instinct I had was screaming at me to bolt.

"Stop it. We have to wait until Channing shows up. Doesn't do any good to go after the hired muscle." He was right. I knew the plan inside and out. I had helped come up with the damn thing. But that didn't stop my heart from wanting to make rash decisions on my behalf. I'd had to fight tooth and nail to keep my shit together when Orley packed Noble up in the car and drove away. Sure, the fight was staged, but the fake break-up felt all too real and I was a little raw about it all.

"We sure Channing is gonna show?" That was the one outlier in the plan we couldn't one-hundred percent pin down. If Channing didn't show, then all of this was going to be for naught and there was a possibility Orley really would disappear on me.

"Yep. He'll show. As soon as his goons realize they have the wrong girl and there's no baby in the car, they'll call him for instructions. She'll say she'll tell them where Noble is, but only if Channing shows up and is willing to pay. He'll come. He thinks every problem can be solved with money, and he won't be surprised that someone from the city is trying to leverage this situation for fast cash." It was shockingly easy to use Vincent's own prejudice toward the poor against him.

"He won't come alone." I sighed. There was no way he was going to roll into an unknown situation without an armed guard.

The Boss waved away my concern with the same hand he'd used to keep my ass in the seat as the leggy redhead climbed out of the car when the goons approached. From this distance, she did bear a striking resemblance to Orley. Both were tall and willowy. She was even dressed almost identically to how Orley had been dressed when she left me standing on the sidewalk. Only, this chick wasn't wearing Converse. She had on some kind of spiked high heels with studs all over them and blood red soles. And my hat didn't look nearly as cute on her as it did on my girl.

The woman halted in front of one of the goons, not even flinching when he pointed a gun at her. Her head tilted to the side, and a moment later, she pulled the long red wig off and threw it on the ground along with my hat. Her actual hair was a rich sable color, cut in a weird, asymmetrical style that only someone with her sharp, elegant features could pull off. She looked far more expensive than Orley ever had.

The Boss rolled down his window and braced his arm in the opening so he could lean his head outside.

"You better be prepared to use that thing if you're going to point it at someone, hot shot. I told you already, if you want the kid, bring me your boss. If I don't see Channing in fifteen minutes, he'll never see his granddaughter again. I'm not scared of you, your gun, or your threats. If you make me repeat myself again, this is going to end so badly for you." The woman crossed her arms over her chest and tapped a high-heeled foot impatiently. "Tell your boss the Devil says 'hello.'"

He was the key to this entire plan working. Channing already knew the Devil was willing to set up an illegal fight where someone might lose their life. He would absolutely believe the man would be capable of kidnapping a three-year-old as long as he could profit off it. We were all betting that Channing Vincent wouldn't believe anyone who came from this brutal city could have any morals.

One of the goons lifted his hand holding the gun and made like he was going to slam his fist into the side of the woman's head while another made the call.

"Oh, fuck. If he hits her, we're all going to suffer the consequences." Hades wouldn't stand by and let his Persephone get hurt, not without bringing the entire Underworld to its knees.

The Boss snorted and tapped the dash with the side of his fist. "Don't worry about her. She can handle herself. You think a guy like him would put a ring on the finger of someone who wasn't almost as scary as he was? Sometimes I think she's worse since she willingly agreed to spend the rest of her life with him. She eats guys like that thug for breakfast."

I was about to retort that the goon had a gun and she didn't, but then the guy started convulsing on the ground like he was having a seizure. She calmly bent over and picked up his dropped weapon. A powerful taser gun was clasped in her other hand. The other goons watched with wide eyes as the stunning woman cocked a hip and pointed the weapon at them.

"Unlike your buddy, I only point a loaded gun at someone when I intend to pull the trigger. Get your boss down here, now!" The sharp bite in her tone even made me want to jump and obey her command.

One of the henchmen held up his hands in a gesture of surrender and showed her the cellphone clutched in his hand. "He's on his way. Take it easy."

She scoffed and pointed the gun at the front tire of the SUV next to him. He wasn't the only one who screamed at the top of his lungs in surprise as she fired off a perfect shot at the tire, then at the other SUV. She took out both the front and back tires so neither vehicle was drivable.

"You ran me off the road. Your buddy pointed a gun at my face and threatened to hit me. If your boss doesn't want to open his wallet, I guarantee your car isn't the only thing that will have bullet holes in it, so no, I don't think I'll take it easy." She tapped that expensive shoe again, and narrowed her eyes as another car made its way down the road.

The Boss shifted in his seat, reaching out to turn on the big, badass muscle car. The growl of the engine was sexy as fuck and I could freely admit to having car envy whenever he drove this particular beast.

He glanced at me, the tick in his cheek making the star tattooed near his eye jump. "Show time."

I nodded. "I just want to bring my girls home." Whatever it took. If I had to do the type of things I always swore I would never do, then so be it. I could live with disappointing my mother by becoming the kind of man she always warned me about. But I couldn't live without Orley and Noble. I couldn't leave my mom behind if she decided to run, so the only option was cutting the head off her monster so she felt safe enough to stay right by my side.

"You will." I wish I had his confidence. He was acting like all of this was no big deal, but to me, it felt like everything I loved was hanging precariously in the balance.

A dark blue Jaguar, followed by three more SUVs, suddenly pulled off the side of the road. Traffic was totally blocked, but the area was pretty desolate since this was the road leading right into the heart of the bad part of town. The bold woman actually looked bored. Making a big show of yawning wide and lifting the hand holding the gun to cover it even as she was surrounded by approximately twenty armed men. Vincent wasn't messing around. He brought a militia with him. It wasn't until Channing himself climbed out of the Jag and made his way to the woman that the Boss put his powerful car into motion.

We didn't have an army, but I guess we didn't need one, not when every single one of the thugs Channing Vincent had rounded up last minute owed the Devil a favor. By the time the GTX pulled to a stop next to the Jag, all of the men who had initially run Orley's car off the road were unarmed and secured with zip-ties. Channing was watching the scene, mouth agape, as a Rolls Royce Phantom joined the party; a familiar figure in a ridiculously expensive suit climbed out of the driver's side.

Channing Vincent turned in a slow circle watching the events unfold with wide eyes and mouth hanging open in disbelief. "I paid you. What are you doing? This is unacceptable."

All the new thugs chuckled under their breath. It was obvious Channing had been set up from the start. He went looking for bad guys in a rush, not knowing all the bad guys were already spoken for by the baddest guy in the entire town. They weren't loyal to anyone, but they were afraid for their lives and stuck in a city run by the Devil, which trumped any other allegiance out there.

One of the guys who'd driven to the site with him snorted and waved his weapon in the air. "You paid us... but he owns us." The gun was angled toward the Devil, who was standing next to the sexy brunette. The dark-haired, dapper man took the gun from her and tilted his head to make sure she was all right. His gaze then drifted to the man at her feet who was slowly coming out of the daze from being tazed.

"He the one who threatened to hit you?" The question was quiet and menacing in his slight accent.

The woman sighed and pushed her hair back from her forehead. "Yep." She held out her hand and made a gimme motion. "Give me the keys. I'll wait in the car until you're done with this." She cut a narrow-eyed look toward a shocked Channing Vincent. "You, sir, are an idiot. Trying to separate a mother and child. I hope you get every bit of what you deserve." She took the keys from her husband and, after planting a kiss on him, flounced away in a truly sassy way. I kind of agreed with the Boss; she might be even scarier than her husband.

The Devil in the perfectly tailored suit nudged the man on the ground with the toe of his wingtip and said, "This one goes back with us."

Holy fuck. I'd never heard him use that particular tone before, and I never wanted to hear him use it again.

The mob immediately jumped to do his bidding as he faced off with Channing. Over the other man's shoulder, the Devil's odd, gold eyes landed on me. "Your call, kid. How you want to handle him? It can be bloody, or it can be civilized. One guarantees he won't come after your girl ever again. The other..." He shook his head and shared an unreadable look with my boss. "I don't like loose ends, but that's just me."

I looked down at my hand when the Boss suddenly pressed something cold and hard into it.

A gun.

I'd never even held one before.

My heart leapt into my throat and my vision went slightly hazy.

"The safety is off, kid. Be careful with that thing." The lyrical, accented voice sounded amused, but the Boss looked anything but.

Channing was glaring at me, but I could see he was scared. He thought he was going to use his money and influence to get his way, but he had no idea what power plays were really all about. These guys didn't manipulate in the boardroom. They put them in the ground in unmarked graves and didn't blink twice. Shaking my head on a gulp, I very carefully handed the weapon back to my boss and scowled at Channing Vincent.

"I'm not a murderer. Not like him." I couldn't become everything I'd fought against my whole life. I couldn't let my circumstances control me. "I want him gone and I want him to suffer, but I can't kill him." Who would I be if I pulled the trigger? Would I still be someone Orley could love, someone Noble could look up to? I wouldn't risk everything I'd gained by taking Channing out.

I handed the gun back to my boss, and his heavy, tattooed palm landed on my shoulder and gave a squeeze. "Proud of you, kid. I knew you would make the right call. I always told you that you were better than me."

They were words I'd always wanted to hear from him but they were lost when he coolly and methodically pulled the trigger on the gun in his hand. "Holy fucking shit!" The exclamation burst out of me as I reflexively lifted my hands to cover my ears. Channing Vincent fell to the ground with a bloody, gory hole where his left knee cap should be.

I jumped about a foot in the air at the sound, and couldn't stop my mouth from falling open in shock. I always knew the Boss was a take-no-prisoners kind of guy. Witnessing just how ruthless and decisive he could be firsthand was something else altogether. I put a hand to my racing heart, and took a step back.

The Devil crouched down so he was eye level with Channing, writhing in agony on the side of the road. "He's a good kid. Your granddaughter is way better off with him than with you. And since the only reason you're desperate to get your hands on her is to hand over your fortune to someone in your bloodline, I went ahead and gave it to her already. All your accounts are now in the little girl's name. Even the ones you thought you hid so well offshore. Oh, and all the Swiss accounts you put under your wife's name. I have a couple of the best hackers in the world on my payroll, Vincent. The Boy Genius took every single asset you possess and passed them on to your granddaughter. No need for you to interfere in her life any longer."

"You can't do that!" The formerly rich businessman burst out, but the words were lost on a moan of pain as he clutched his destroyed leg.

"I can do whatever I want, and I just fucking did." He rose to his feet and reached out a foot so he could press down painfully on the wounded man's leg. "This hole in your knee hurts. Imagine how much worse it will be if we take out your other kneecap and then your elbows. I know ways to make you suffer for days, to never be the same again. And being poor on top of it will really suck. But I can also prolong the pain until you're begging me to kill you, Vincent. It's all up to you."

"I'll pay you!" It was the broken man's failsafe. He really thought he could buy his way out of anything.

The Boss snickered and the man in the expensive suit rolled his eyes. "I already told you, you're broke. Besides, I don't need your money. I have my own." He straightened his tie and glared down at the man who killed Orley's mother. I hated him for what he put her through, but I guess at the end of the day, I owed him. She never would have ventured into my city if he hadn't scared her to death.

"The kid doesn't want you dead, and I don't you want you bothering him and his girls ever again. So, these are your options, Vincent. You agree to turn yourself in for the murder of your wife and serve your sentence quietly, or you come with me and the guy who threatened to hit my wife, and you can find out exactly how I tie up loose ends."

The man on the ground sputtered as his eyes rolled back in his head. "There is no evidence I killed my wife. Even if I confessed, no one would convict me." Wasn't that exactly how all privileged, powerful men felt these days? Like they could do no wrong, even if they came out and admitted it. It was annoying, and I was going to enjoy Vincent getting every bit of what he deserved.

The dark-haired man chuckled and inclined his chin slightly. "I have a Boy Genius, remember? If I need evidence, he'll get me evidence in spades. Either way, you have nothing. Exactly what you left your daughter with when you decided to fuck up her life. I'm being generous, Vincent. It won't last long, so make up your mind." He crossed his arms over his chest and stared at the man while the Boss clicked his tongue next to me.

"Always so dramatic." He couldn't hide the dry humor in his tone.

The other man quirked a black eyebrow and scoffed, "You're the one who blew his leg in half. Touchy today, aren't you?" They were poking each other like kids on a playground, but both talked about killing the man on the ground as easily as others chatted about the weather. I was endlessly glad they were on my side. "Call your brother. Get the detective down here and have him take Mr. Vincent away. Make sure he knows he was behind the attempted kidnapping of a minor while you're at it." Those gold eyes shifted back to me and I had to suppress a shiver. "You really are a good kid, Solomon. For what it's worth, I think you made the right choice by not taking him out. You may live in a dark place, but there is no reason for your soul to end up tainted, or for it to go missing all together. Go get your girls and tell them it's safe to come home. I'll finish cleaning up this mess."

The Boss practically dragged me away as the Devil once again put his foot on the open wound on Vincent's leg and pressed down. The other man's screams of pain echoed loudly down the empty road.

"Do you think it makes me weak? The fact that I couldn't kill him." I was almost scared to hear his answer.

The hand clamped on my shoulder squeezed again and I was given a rough little shake. "No. I think you're stronger than anyone else on the roadside. It takes real strength to be the good guy in a bad place and still be respected and feared. When you're the only hero in a story full of villains, it takes so much more to come out on top. You were brave to ask for help not knowing what the outcome would be, and you were brave deciding to let him live. Who knows what will happen ten, fifteen years from now? Your choice might come back to haunt you, but you made the right one, which is usually the hardest. I'm always proud of you, kid. Today only made me prouder."

I didn't have a dad or an older brother. He was always the man I looked up to the most, so hearing those words made my hands shake a little. There were days, sometimes even months when I questioned what I was doing and if I would ever be able to reach my goals. Hearing him tell me he was proud of me was right there at the top of the list of things I'd always longed to accomplish.

Heaving a relieved, thankful sigh, I followed him toward the car. "Now all I have to do is convince Orley to stay in the city with me." Her options were wide open now that her biggest threat was gone giving her access to every cent of Channing's money for her daughter's future.

The Boss shook his head. "Oh, you know the Devil don't come to play. The money really is in a trust for the little girl, and if anything happens to her, it gets allocated to various different outreach programs that help children in need. Her mom can access small amounts as needed, but she'll have to go through him to get at it. It's his way of making sure the little girl is always safe and never used as a pawn. Your lady is going to have to figure out how to make it on her own, just like the rest of us. Luckily, she's got you to show her the way."

And that was exactly what I was going to do.

I could teach her how to live hard, and I would gladly learn all Orley and Noble had to teach me about loving hard.

Life was never easy in my city... and I wouldn't have it any other way.

Orley

The massive deck off the back of the house hidden away in the woods was beautiful and frightening. It literally hung out over open space, leaving the person standing on it feeling like they were floating in mid-air amongst the clouds and trees. I'd never seen anything like it. Noble was fascinated by it and by the densely wooded area where the house was tucked away. She spent over an hour pointing out every bird and squirrel while begging to get closer to the railing so she could look at the impressive drop. There was no way I was letting her anywhere near the edge, even if the slats in the railing were too narrow for her to fit her head through. I forced her to enjoy the view from the comfort of the patio furniture until she got bored.

The odd mansion came equipped with a playroom no child could resist, so when the outside lost its appeal, the playroom was where we ended up. This massive, palatial home was obviously worth several million dollars, but it was so very different from the cold, impersonal estate where I had grown up. Every room in this home felt like it was lived in and used by a family. Even though there was expensive artwork on the walls and what looked like priceless antiques scattered about amongst the toys and other typical messiness left behind by a child, there was nothing overly pretentious or showy about the house. It felt warm and comfortable. Even the silent, discreet staff greeted both me and Noble with warm smiles and friendly waves. They asked if we needed anything, making me feel like we were at a five-star resort, not a criminal mastermind's secret hideaway.

I was on the floor helping Noble build some kind of LEGO spaceship, assuring her if there were bears in the woods they couldn't get inside the house, when Solo appeared in the doorway of the playroom. He looked tired and resigned. His mouth was in a flat line that twitched just slightly when Noble caught sight of him and squealed in delight. The LEGOs were immediately forgotten as she rushed toward him, arms extended. He caught her mid-jump when she launched herself at him, lifting her high into the air.

My daughter sounded like she was going to have a heart attack of joy when Solo started smothering her face with smacking kisses. A deep, rumbling chuckle caught my attention and I felt my jaw unhinge slightly when my gaze landed on the tall man standing behind Solo. I always believed Solomon Sanders was going to be the most intimidating man I ever encountered, but I was wrong. The guy standing behind him had an aura of danger I could practically see. He was a giant. Taller and broader than Solo, but just as heavily tattooed. The fact he had a tattoo on his face and a wicked gleam in his pitch-black eyes didn't make me feel any better about having the guy so close to my daughter.

Solo squeezed Noble until she protested and inclined his head in the direction of the other man. "Orley, this is my boss. He helped me take care of our little problem. He's also offered to give us a ride back to the city, unless you want to stay here for a couple of days. Been awhile since you were in a house as nice as the one you left behind."

I leaned back on my hands and looked up at him as he continued to cuddle my daughter. When he explained the entire clandestine plan to me a few days ago, he wasn't sure how long I was going to have to hide out at this fairytale mansion in the woods, which is why I'd packed a bag. I'd never planned on staying any longer than necessary, even if that view off the back deck was to die for.

"It's safe to go home?" Because, even though I never intended for it to happen, the cold, hard city was now the place I wanted to be the most. Well, it was a close second next to Solo's arms. I appreciated the transparency of the city. The way I always knew exactly what I was dealing with and what kind of fight I was facing. I felt like a stronger, better person calling the city my home.

Solo nodded and bent to put Noble on her feet. She immediately skirted around him and ran to the other man. My eyes widened in horror when she pointed at his face and demanded to know, "What's that?"

The huge man chuckled again and crouched down so he was almost eye level with her. I could see now he was shockingly attractive in a rough and tumble kind of way. When he smiled, it turned his harsh features devastatingly handsome. The men in this town were simply a different breed. I doubted you would be able to find them anywhere else in the world.

"It's a star." His voice was a harsh rasp that would've made me shiver in trepidation if Solo hadn't been standing nearby.

"Does it wash off? Do you need some soap?" Noble cocked her head to the side and studied the man carefully. It would've been absolutely adorable if he didn't scare the crap out of me.

"Naw. It's there for good. I don't need soap, but I could use a glass of water. Want to show me where the kitchen is?" He shot a knowing look in Solo's direction as an immediate protest rose to my lips. Every cell in my body protested letting my kid wander off with the scary stranger. But Solo trusted him, and more than that, the man with the face tattoo had helped get Channing off my back somehow, so I owed him. Deep down, I knew there was no way Solo would let Noble wander off with someone who might cause her harm.

"My chick works with all the different foster kids in the city. She's always had a very soft spot for the little ones, so I'm around kids all the time. I swear, I won't break her. I'm just gonna grab a drink; you two figure out who's staying and who's going. We'll be right back." He stuck a wide, tattooed hand out for my daughter to grab and I gaped at his broad back as she happily flounced away babbling more about the tattoo on his face and her best friend, Solo. Apparently, she was really glad we weren't yelling at each other anymore. Our fake fight earlier in the day had broken her little heart, which meant mine was cracked open and bleeding freely hearing her tell him that.

Solo walked fully into the room, taking a seat on the floor across from me. He reached for a handful of LEGOs, absently clicking them together and popping them apart.

"He really is good with kids. Noble will be fine with him for a few minutes. I wouldn't have let him take her out of the room if I didn't trust him with every fiber of my being." His tone was quiet and almost shy.

"I know you wouldn't have. I'm still learning how to be a good judge of character. Channing Vincent is really no longer going to be a problem?" It was hard to believe. I'd been on the run and scared for so long, I wasn't sure how to function without fear behind every action I took.

Solo nodded. "The Boss, and another 'friend,'" he made air quotes around the words which made me laugh slightly, "made sure he's out of your hair for at least the next ten to fifteen years. He's going to have to answer for what he did to your mother. He doesn't have enough money left to pay for even the cheapest lawyer. So, he might even end up with a longer sentence than fifteen years relying on a public defender to try his case."

"What do you mean, he doesn't have any money? He's one of the richest men in the state." It was so easy to imagine him buying his way out of any conviction thrown his way. When Solo said they were going to get Channing out of the way, I pictured something much worse than what he was describing. I couldn't decide if I was happy he wasn't dead or not. It sort of felt like an anticlimactic ending after everything Channing Vincent had put me through my entire life. At least when I finally got a moment to process things, I could finally grieve for my mother properly, and I would rest easy knowing Channing couldn't hide behind his money anymore.

"All his assets have been transferred into Noble's name. She's got a trust fund bigger than this house waiting for her when she gets older. She is now a multi-millionaire. Everything they couldn't put in her name has been frozen by the government as they investigate all of Vincent's business dealings. He wasn't exactly a straight shooter. When the boss had people start digging deep into Channing's comings and goings, it became clear he's been doing some very dirty deals while no one was looking. He was doing some questionable stuff with investors' money. There's a whole lot of people really pissed off at him right now. He might not even make it to sentencing."

"All that money." I shook my head. It was hard to imagine all of it going to Noble. It was almost scary to think what she could accomplish with that kind of power at her disposal as she got older.

"Well, it's tricky." He cleared his throat and shifted his gaze away from mine; the LEGOs in his hands popped apart almost violently. "The money isn't in a normal trust. You're going to have to go through a very scary, very bad man to access any of it. It's kind of his way of making sure Noble is always safe and that the money can never be used against her." He blew out a breath and shoved his hands through his messy, dark hair. "If you want some of the money to move, to start over, to take

Noble someplace better, I can talk to him for you. I can set it up." His eyes lifted back up to mine and the frown was stamped back on his face. "I almost didn't tell you that part. The idea of you leaving the city tears me up inside. That fake fight sucked. It felt like you were really leaving, and parts of me felt like they were going to die watching you drive away. But, I can't make you stay, and I can't make that decision for you... even if I want to." His voice quivered ever so slightly, telling me he really was fighting against his natural instinct to push me in the direction he thought was best. He knew what was best for him in this instance might not be what was best for me and my daughter.

Without hesitation, I launched myself across the space separating us. He grunted painfully when he landed on his back on the discarded pile of LEGOs. I giggled as he cringed, not bothering to warn him he was going to have to be on the lookout for LEGO booby traps until Noble outgrew them.

I kissed him hard and long. Then pulled back to look at his shocked expression. Solo really thought I was going to go, even after everything he'd done for me. It was the first time in my whole life I felt wanted and needed in return.

"I've had money and was handed everything I ever wanted, and I was miserable. It wasn't until you came into our lives that I realized I could be happy, even if I had nothing but you and Noble. You made me realize I could make a life for my daughter without much help. Having you means more than having a fortune. You are worth so much more to me and Noble than any amount of money could ever be. I'm glad it's there for her, because I want her to have every opportunity possible as she grows up, and I know money can be a shield against a lot of bad things, but I want her to be strong and smart. She'll get that from you, not from a fistful of cash." I kissed him again and grabbed both his cheeks between my hands. "I can't tell you I'll always want to be exactly where we are now." I was going to be devastated for a long time every single time I stepped on the bottom stair and Lester wasn't there to greet me with his sage advice. "When Noble gets older, I have to think about things like being in a good school district and her having access to the best education possible, but I can tell you, I don't want to ever be too far from you or your mom. She needs you as much as I do." I understood that without him saying a word. And I loved him. There were things I would have to sacrifice for that love. Where I lived and where I raised my kid might have to be one of those things, so he could get what he needed from me, as well. I was serious about us being together, meaning we were on the same team. "You made me believe I could be strong, Solo. And you protected me."

He wrapped his arms around me, dark eyes serious as he gazed up at me. "There is no guarantee if you stay with me things won't get bumpy down the road. My life isn't a picnic, and things will never be easy if you choose to stay in the city. I can swear to you that I will always put you and Noble first in everything I do, and that I won't stop working toward being a better, more reliable man. But I'll always be a fighter, not a killer. I will always fight for you... for us... for this family you shared with me." He exhaled and I grinned as he blushed. It was the first time I'd seen him turn pink and it was damned adorable. He was always so sure of himself. Him being the uneasy, nervous one for once was a nice change of pace. "I love you. With my schedule and my obligations, I never thought I would have time to fall in love, but with you, it only took a second."

I kissed his chin and brushed my nose along his jawline. "I was your downfall."

It was amazing to me. All the dark, dirty, dangerous things that filled his life from the start, and I was the one who finally got him to slow down and breathe. I was the one who stopped him in his tracks. How could I not love him and want to stay with him?

"Loving two girls was my downfall. I couldn't be happier about that." He was right. It very easily could have been a bullet that brought him down. It was much nicer to know love was what eventually brought him to his knees.

"Mommy! Look what I learned." I looked up from where I was sprawled across Solo's chest, cocooned in his strong embrace.

A moment later, my kid ran into the messy playroom, the large man close behind her. I tried to keep my expression neutral when she dropped to her bottom, sat with her legs crossed, and the man followed suit. It took every ounce of self-control I possessed to not burst into hysterical laughter when Noble started clapping her hands against his in a really awkward, uncoordinated version of patty-cake. Solo didn't bother to hold back is laughter when the man sang the silly song and clapped right along with my daughter.

If this scene in front of me wasn't a perfect example of how weird, wild, and perfectly imperfect my world was now, I didn't know what would be.

I had to lose everything in order to learn how to appreciate the things that mattered most. I would never, ever forget how powerful and necessary that lesson was.

I wrapped my arms around Solo's neck and demanded between kisses, "Take us home, Hero."

I knew, with absolute certainty, regardless of what happened in our future, he would always be the one who not only saved me, but taught me the value in being able to save myself. He was always going to be a hero in my eyes.

EPILOGUE

Solo

"**B**ye, Daddy." Noble waved at me over her shoulder as she disappeared inside her classroom. Her teacher gave me a friendly nod, even though I was pretty sure the woman had to fight the urge to call the cops every single day when I dropped off the curly-headed troublemaker. Orley insisted it was all in my head, but I could always feel the eyes watching me whenever I was on the elite private school campus. The other parents and staff always looked at me like they weren't really sure what I was doing in their midst, but I had thick skin, so the judgment didn't bother me as long as they treated Noble well.

I was never going to get used to it.

No, not Noble calling me *daddy*. She'd been doing that since I convinced Orley to move in with me a couple of years ago. I started responding before the significance of the shift really hit me. Hearing her say it never failed to make me grin and to cause my heart to swell with inexplicable pride. Being Noble's daddy, and her mommy's man, was hands down the thing I was best at, and the one area of my life where I devoted most of my time. I'd learned balance, even if it'd taken more than one knock-down-drag-out fight with Orley to get there.

Hearing Noble call me daddy was nothing new, but I was still trying to adjust to her being in school half the day, and more than that, going to a private school where she had to wear a little uniform and shiny black shoes. I was used to her in Converse and jeans, running around the garage after me, dirty and greasy, as she asked me one-million questions about each and every car we crawled under. She had to fit me in her busy playdate schedule. It seemed like she was always running between Erica's to play with Riley and out into the woods to play with the Devil's daughter. She was already making powerful friends, even if she didn't know it.

My kid looked cute in her tiny plaid skirt, white shirt, and plaid bow-tie, but it was so far removed from how I'd dressed for school, she looked almost alien. Noble loved her teacher and the kids in her class, and this school was the best of the best near the new townhouse I bought just outside of the city. I was still close enough to my old stomping grounds to feel like I could keep my street-cred intact, but far enough away I could let Noble play in the front yard without worrying about her catching a stray bullet while she was outside. The townhouse was also closer to my mom, which made visiting her more often, and dashing off in the middle of the night if she had an episode, much easier.

When Orley told me she was going to talk to the Devil about paying for Noble's tuition to this fancy ass school, my first instinct was to argue. We lived a pretty modest life. I finally finished school and got certified as a mechanic, just in time for Orley to decide she wanted to go to college so she could get into the nursing field. She'd gotten very close with Melody and the rest of the staff who cared for my mother over the years and decided she wanted to help others the way they helped my mom. After everything he'd done for us, there wasn't really a way I could justify walking away from the Boss once I had my certification, so I agreed to go work for him in the legal part of his garage. Much to my surprise, he told me working as a regular mechanic would be a waste of my skills and talent, so instead, he set me up in a custom shop where all I did was rebuild and restore classics. It was all above board and clean as a whistle, but I was never going to be a millionaire. I made enough to keep us comfortable, and once Orley was working, we would be more than set, but right now, we were an average family on an average income, so private school shouldn't be in the cards. I didn't want Noble feeling like she had to keep up with the other kids in her class, or like she wasn't good enough because I wasn't a doctor or a lawyer. Orley and I were very careful to make sure she had everything she needed, but she most definitely wasn't spoiled.

It wasn't until he mentioned he was thinking about sending his daughter to the same school when she was old enough that I changed my mind about enrolling Noble. It wasn't about what I was comfortable with or what I could give her. It was about making sure she was set up for a bright, successful future. Just like my mother had wanted so much more for me, it was now my turn to want the world for the little girl whom I was going raise as my own. Regardless how uncomfortable the manicured lawns and majestic white building made me, this was where Noble belonged so she had the best options available at her fingertips.

I chuckled under my breath when a middle-aged man side stepped up to me, eyes cast downward like he was worried I might decide to mug him or something. I was planning on giving him a wide berth, but stopped when he stuttered, "Hey, you're Noble's dad, aren't you?"

I pushed the brim of my ball cap up with a finger.

"I am." And how fucking cool was that?

"Umm, Miranda is having a horseback riding party at the end of the month. She was insistent that Noble be invited. Did you know your daughter is the most popular girl in her class?"

I didn't know that, but I wasn't surprised. She was a social, smart, funny little thing, who made friends everywhere she went. She had the ability to put a smile on anyone's face.

"I'll have to run it by Noble's mom. She gets the final say on extracurricular activities." Knowing Orley, she was going to make sure Miranda's parents had zero ties to her old life before she agreed. Anyone with any connection to the Vincents or her previous life were automatically blackballed. Channing might've fallen from grace, but people still remembered his missing empire. There had been months and months of speculation as to where his money went after his arrest. Strangers came out of the woodwork trying to cozy up to Orley thinking she might know something about the vanished fortune. Little did they know, my girl was no longer gullible and naïve. She was harder to get close to than the Mona Lisa, and she'd gotten really good at telling the fake from the genuine.

"Great, that's great. Hey, is that your Coronet convertible parked out in the lot?" He sounded nervous but his wary gaze lit up when I nodded. "Is it the RT version? Weren't there only three or four of those made?" My car was guaranteed to give any car guy a boner.

"Yep. I built it from the frame up." I could sell the damn thing for hundreds of thousands, but I wouldn't. It was my dream car. The one I was keeping forever, or until I handed it down to Noble and found a new project.

"That's... unbelievable. I've always wanted a Ford Fairlane." He sighed and shook his head. "I'm probably not a cool enough dad to drive one of those, though."

I chuckled and fished a business card out of my wallet. "Driving a classic automatically makes you a cool dad. If you get serious about getting your hands on one, give me a call. I'll pass on the invite about the party to Orley." I was a cool dad with or without the car, and I doubted this guy had the balls to venture into the city where my shop was, but it never hurt to try and drum up new business.

I was getting into my car when my cell rang. Since Orley was in class until early afternoon I was surprised to see her name and pretty face on the display. Wondering if I forgot to do something she asked, I answered the call with a bit of trepidation. I thought I was busy before; I had no idea how busy I was going to be once Noble was old enough to start having her own social life.

"What did I forget?" I tried starting off with a joke in case she was pissed off. That was another thing I'd adjusted to slowly. Orley seemed so timid when she first showed up in the city. Now my girl had no problem letting that redheaded temper flare. Timid was the last thing I would call her now that she was a bonafide city girl.

"Uh, nothing. I'm actually home. I was wondering if you could meet me here and head into the shop a little later." There was something in her tone I couldn't identify and it immediately had me sitting up straight and wracking my brain to figure out why she was playing hooky. Normally, she was far too responsible to skip class.

"Sure. I can go in later." I made my own hours, so my schedule was often more flexible than hers, which is why I dropped Noble off in the morning. No one would miss me if I went in an hour or two later than usual. "I'll be home in like, twenty."

She mumbled a goodbye and a surge of panic hit me. Orley was very good about being upfront and honest with me about how she was feeling and what she needed from me. This whole situation was weird, and I didn't like the unease that slithered around in my belly.

I parked in front of the townhouse, not even slightly worried my car was going to get jacked or messed up in any way. That was another benefit to leaving the inner city behind. Guaranteed parking was always nice. I ran up the steps, pushed the door open and called Orley's name at the top of my lungs. I was too impatient to wait for her to answer me, so I prowled though the house looking for her.

I found her in our bedroom, sitting on the side of the bed, pale as a ghost, dressed only in a long purple robe. Her hair was piled in a mess on top of her head and her eyes were locked on something in her hand. Trying to get my worried, racing heart under control, I plopped down on the bed next to her and threw my arm around her shoulders.

"What's wrong? You sounded like a mess on the phone." I pulled her into a tight side hug and kissed the top of her head. I refused to believe there wasn't anything I couldn't make better for her.

She sniffed as if she'd been crying, and held out the object in her hand for inspection. I'd never seen an at-home pregnancy test before in real life, but I knew what it was without asking for clarification. Other than that one time in the shower at the apartment above the garage, we'd always been careful and never had even a close call, so I was stunned at the sight.

"Whoa. Is that what I think it is?" I leaned to the side a little so I could look at Orley's face. Her blue eyes were foggy with emotion and unshed tears.

"I haven't been feeling well. My stomach is upset all the time and I can't sleep through the night. I've been feeling off for a couple of days, and I remembered this was exactly how I felt when I was pregnant with Noble."

"But how? I mean, I know how... but we're always safe." Always.

She sniffed again and offered up a watery smile. "I'm not pregnant, Solo. I must be getting the flu or all the stress from finals coming up might be getting to me."

I huffed out a breath and reached out to smooth a few flyaway strands of hair away from her pale face. "Okay. You aren't knocked up, then why are you crying?" If she felt so bad it brought on tears, I was taking her to the emergency room. I would take care of her however she needed me to.

"I'm crying because when I saw the test was negative, I realized how much I wanted it to be positive. I love being a mom. We've never talked about having more kids in the future, but I want to. I want to have your baby, Solo."

I was stunned how passionate and sure she sounded. Expanding our family wasn't something that came up in conversation on the regular, but it seemed like she'd been giving it a lot of thought. Surprisingly, the idea wasn't at all terrifying. I never thought I would have time for kids, or to be an active and involved parent. She was the one who taught me to make time for the things in life that mattered most.

I hugged her harder and kissed her on the top of the head again. "I think I'd like that, you carrying my kid." Saying it out loud gave the idea roots to grow and sprout. "You want a ring on your finger and my last name before we make that happen?" Marriage was another thing we never really talked at length about. It didn't matter to me one way or another, and she said she was happy as long as we slept in the same bed each night. But having another kid might be a game changer.

"I don't need those things, but it might make it easier when you formally adopt Noble." That was something we definitely had talked about. No one was ever taking that dark-haired cutie away from me, and I wanted everything I could think of in place in order to ensure no one even tried.

Lifting off the bed, I moved so I could pick up Orley in my arms. I shifted around so I could lie her down and tuck her in under the down comforter. I kissed her forehead and realized she was indeed warm.

"Okay. I'll get you a ring, and then we'll make a baby. But first, you get some rest and I'm going to run to the store and grab you some Nyquil. Gotta make sure all of this baby talk isn't because you have a fever." I winked at her to let her know I was kidding.

She reached for my hand before I could move away from the side of the bed. There were tears in her eyes once again when she whispered, "Thank you for always taking such good care of me."

Deciding I cared more about her than her germs, I kissed her long and hard. "Always."

I would always take care of her, because it wasn't until she came along and set my world on fire that I realized I needed someone to take care of me, too. She called me her hero and told me I saved her all the time.

I often wondered if she realized she was the one who rescued me from myself and the joyless life that was doing its best to swallow me whole.

She joked that falling in love with her had been my downfall, but she was wrong. Falling in love with her was my salvation.

THE END

ACKNOWLEDGEMENTS

If you made it this far, thank you so much for reading *Downfall!* I would be so very grateful if you would leave a review on whatever platform you read, or listened, to this book. A review, good or bad, is the best gift a reader can pass along to an author. It's also a great way to see more of the books and characters you love!

If you have purchased, read, reviewed, promoted, pimped, blogged about, sold, talked about, preached about, or whined about any of my books... thank you.

If you are part of my very special reader group, The Crowd... thank you.

If you have helped me make this dream of mine a reality... thank you.

If you have helped make my words better and helped me share them with the world... thank you.

I also have a pretty special girl gang of professionals who help me turn my words into an actual book. If you are looking for an editor, I can't recommend Elaine York enough. I love getting to work with her. I adore her insights and her commitment to each project I send her way. She doesn't pull any punches, and she's not scared to tell me that I'm not quite there yet. She makes me work for it, and as a result, my readers get the best book possible. She is also the one responsible for making the guts as pretty as the heart of this book! Get you a girl who can do it all!

The same thing goes for Hang Le. She is my one and only choice to work with when it comes to my covers. She's brilliant. I love her style and her flare. She takes what I want and makes it better than I could imagine. Pretty sure her beautiful covers do more to sell my books than anything I put inside of them.

My friend, Beth Salminen, handled all my copy edits and proofreading this go around. Beth is wicked smart and super funny. The only thing better than writing books is getting to work on them with people who care about making your words the best they can be. It's a bonus when that person also wants the writer to be the best she can be. If you are looking for a pretty blonde to cross your t's and dot your i's, you need to give Beth all your money. She will also reluctantly go to see BTS at Citifield in NY with you... and dance the night away. She's a trooper.

I want to thank Pam, Sarah, Karla, Traci, and Meghan for giving up their valuable time and precious moments to go over the rough draft of this story. If you read it in my newsletter, you know my rough drafts are R-O-U-G-H. It takes an intrepid soul to take on all my run-on sentences, as well as my overuse of the word THAT. They don't get anything out of the deal other than my undying gratitude and unwavering thanks. There are some very special readers out there in Booklandia, and I feel like I've been so lucky to have most of them in my court since the very beginning. If you notice fewer errors and fewer typos in this book, it's all thanks to these lovely ladies.

Also, there is never a day that goes by where I am not eternally grateful for Mel, KP and Stacey. My book squad is aces and I know deep down to my bones, I couldn't do what I do without them.

Feel free to appease your inner stalker in all of these places. I love to connect with my readers:

This is the link to join my amazing fan group on Facebook: https://www.facebook.com/groups/crownoverscrowd ... I'm very active in the group, and it's often the best place to find all the happenings including: release dates, cover reveals, early teasers, and giveaways!

My website is: www.jaycrownover.com... there is a link on the site to reach me through email. I would also suggest signing up for my newsletter while you're there! It's monthly, contains a free book that is in progress so you'll be the first to read it, and is full of mega giveaways and goodies. I'm also in these places:

https://www.facebook.com/jay.crownover
https://www.facebook.com/AuthorJayCrownover
Follow me @jaycrownover on Twitter
Follow me @jay.crownover on Instagram
Follow me on Snapchat @jaycrownover
https://www.goodreads.com/Crownover
http://www.donaghyliterary.com/jay-crownover.html

Made in the USA
Middletown, DE
14 April 2019